Bruce was never sure whether it was the earth-shaking blast of the explosion or the flash that filled the sky, lighting up the whole glen, that woke him. Hamish claimed that a terrible thunderclap, loud enough to wake the dead, was his first inkling. Whatever it was, they met at the foot of the stairs, moments later, and raced for the door, pulling on clothes as they ran. Mary Jean, her long nightgown billowing out behind her, followed them quickly. All waited while Bruce located the direction and the source of the disturbance.

"It's the factory, of course, and there are more buildings waiting to go up! Hamish, you stay here with Mary Jean. I'll have to go. Help'll be needed, as well as comforting, I'm afraid."

Mary Jean screamed, "You're not to go and leave me!"

He turned to her, his tone unusually sharp. "Yes, I must. It's my place to go. Do not make things worse, Mary Jean."

The Isles of the Sea series:

Call of the Isles introduces Bruce MacAlister, a Scottish crofter's son who becomes a minister.

My Heart's in the Highlands The tragedy of a double loss shakes Bruce MacAlister's faith to its very foundation.

Fires in the Glen

Fires in the Glen

MOLLY GLASS

Power Books

Fleming H. Revell Company
Old Tappan, New Jersey

Scripture quotations in this volume are based on the King James Version of the Bible.

Library of Congress Cataloging-in-Publication Data

Glass, Molly.
    Fires in the glen / Molly Glass.
      p. cm.
    ISBN 0-8007-5340-2
    I. Title.
PR9199.3.G572F57   1990
813'.54—dc20   89-70072
                                                     CIP

Copyright © 1990 by Molly Glass
Published by the Fleming H. Revell Company
Old Tappan, New Jersey 07675
Printed in the United States of America

TO
the memory of Benny
a beloved father—not perfect but a
"guid man"

Appreciation is hereby expressed to the following: You know
who you are and why! Beth, Carolyn, Grace, John, Judith, and
Margaret

Fires in the Glen

—◦─⟨ **1** ⟩─◦—

"**I**t's not fair! Mary Jean MacAlister always gets to be the teacher, and I want a chance to be the teacher the day."

"But Stirling, Mary Jean's the oldest, and she kens mair than us."

"She's maybe older, but that doesna' mean she kens mair. . . . 'Sides, she's fae the highlands, and Nanny says—"

Mary Jean let the Blair twins argue. In a while they would get to the bit about her daddy being a minister and their daddy being a doctor, and then they would stop arguing, and she would be the teacher. If they didn't agree, she would just say she wasn't going to play at schools today. She glanced along the path leading from the summerhouse to Granny Mac's back door. She and her daddy were visiting Great-granny MacIntyre in her big house in Glasgow, the same as they did every year. The Blair family, who stayed in Glasgow all the time, always came to spend a day here with them.

Stirling was giving in. "Oh, all right. She can be the teacher if we can have history first."

Douglas held up his hand. Imperiously Miss MacAlister gave him permission to speak.

"Miss MacAlister, can we have a family history lesson the day?"

"Yes. We'll start with the MacIntyre family. You can ask me questions one at a time. Douglas Blair first."

Douglas beamed happily as he asked, "Is old Mistress Mac-Intyre older than Queen Victoria? And is she—"

The teacher interrupted, "One question each, Douglas Blair. Mistress MacIntyre is the same age as Queen Victoria. Now you, Stirling."

"You've got a funny mixed-up family, miss! Is she really our auntie? What for do you call her Granny Mac? And who's yer uncle Hamie, and who's this Jeremy Ward? Nanny says he's a floundering, and—"

Mary Jean's face creased in a frown. "First you should say 'why' and not 'what for' when you ask a question like that. Mistress MacIntyre is really my great-granny. She was my mammy's real granny, but she's not your real auntie at all. Next question, Douglas." Deliberately she ignored the questions about Uncle Hamie and Jeremy, partly because she wasn't too sure herself. Uncle was her daddy's stepbrother she did know; and Jeremy, at Mains Farm, he was just like a big brother to her, but at Strathcona House he was a servant.

Douglas, who always played the game the right way, was asking her something else, something she could answer. "Who's *your* real granny then, Mary—I mean, Miss Mac-Alister?"

In her story-telling enthusiasm the teacher forgot some of her dignity as she replied, "My real granny is away up in Aribaig, that's our highland farm, too. She's my Gran'speth, but her name is Elspeth Munro MacAlister Cormack and—"

This was too much for Stirling. Jumping to his feet he yelled, "We ken about her. It's the other granny I want to hear about. The one in India. Our Nanny says when a man dies there his wives are burnt in a bonfire along wi' him!"

The teacher's dignity vanished completely, but before she could speak, Douglas was yelling back at his brother, "Shut up, Stirling. Mummy says that's a lot of rubbish."

Miss MacAlister was tiring of this game. She smiled sweetly at Douglas. "It's not 'zactly rubbish, Douglas, but Colonel and Mistress Irvine, my mammy's parents, were in the British army in India. Scotchmen have only one wife, you know. Now that her man is dead, Mistress Irvine is coming home on a ship the now."

Silenced by this news, Stirling was impressed enough to be quiet while he digested it. But not for long. "Nanny says that—"

Mary Jean scrambled up, sending papers skittering across the wooden floorboards of the summerhouse.

"Your nanny's a big blether, and I'm not playing with you anymore, Stirling Blair. Away you go and be the teacher with Fessy."

As if the name were a signal, a scream rent the air at that moment. Douglas and Stirling catapulted together down the summerhouse steps, yelling as they went, "Fessy, we forgot Fessy!"

Mary Jean followed at a run. She, too, had forgotten about Felicity Blair, and she prayed as she ran that nothing bad had happened to the twins' wee sister. She was Uncle Peter's pet, and all three of the older children would be in for it if Fessy had gotten into trouble.

Betsy Degg, Mistress MacIntyre's maid, who had been serving at Strathcona House for many years now, heard the scream, too, as she opened the door to take the tray with lemonade and biscuits to the bairns in the summerhouse. Placing it carefully on the table, located just inside the kitchen door, Betsy hurried down the path in the direction of the commotion.

Although Glasgow was the place of his birth, it was Jeremy Ward's first visit to Strathcona House, and he was not enjoying it one bit. Completely content at the Mains Farm in Aribaig, engaged in what the maister described as the job of providing for Scotland's insides and outsides with mutton and wool—and even beef and hides, too, sometimes—he felt as out of place in the city as one of the farm's newborn lambs would have been. Only reluctantly had he agreed to accompany the Reverend Bruce and Mary Jean because Hamish, who normally went everywhere the reverend went, wasn't well.

At breakfast this morning, in the kitchen of this big, strange house, Jeremy had asked the maid for a job to do. "They don't need me the day, and I'm no' used to idlin' my time."

"Well, I suppose you could ask auld Jacko. He comes on Fridays to tidy the garden, and this is Friday. I heard him complainin' last week about the raspberry canes needin' sortin' and he's getting stiff in his auld age."

So Jeremy was happily "sortin' " the raspberry canes, exactly as instructed by Jacko. His thoughts strayed far away to Aribaig. They could ill spare him the now. The early tatties would be nearly ready, and although the harvest was later there than in some of the fields they had seen passing in the train, there was always a lot to do, getting ready.

The wee voice at his back startled him out of his dreaming, and he leaped up from his kneeling position. What he saw then shocked him to the core. At first he thought it was a fairy or a pisky, but Gran'pa Bruce had told him once—and he'd not forget it—that there were no such things. Concentrating on the small face gazing up at him now, he recognized it. Mary Jean called this wee one Fessy, and here she stood, naked as the day she was born! Strewn along the path behind her lay every stitch of clothing her nanny had so carefully dressed her in only an hour ago. He noted that she still wore her boots. If it weren't so pitiful, it would be comical.

"Go to yer mammy!" Jeremy's early life in the seamy back closes of Glasgow had taught him many things, among them that you could not argue with a shuttle-wit. This wee lass was surely one of them. He turned back to the raspberry canes, and his lips moved in prayer that she would go away. Instantly he felt the small body as it leaped onto his bent back. Shaking her off, not even trying to be gentle, he tried again: "Go in the hoose to your nanny, Fessy!"

"Fessy wants a sweetie!" This time she attached herself to his leg, wrapping herself around it like a monkey on a tree.

"Yer nanny'll gie ye a sweetie. Go away now." He grabbed her arms and pried her from his leg. Throwing herself violently on the ground, she started to scream blue murder. Tearing cruelly at her own face with her fingernails she let out screech after screech. Instinctively he knelt beside her and grasped the flailing hands.

Stirling reached them first and immediately added his own hysterical screams to his sister's. "My wee sister, what are you doin' to her?"

Jeremy had had enough. He jumped to his feet and ran. Reaching the hedge, he squeezed through it and leaped over the low wall, directly into the arms of the law, in the form of Constable Jenkins, walking his morning beat.

"What's all this, then? What have you been up to?" Screeches and yells had been reaching his ears for the last few minutes, but the constable knew better than to approach the gentry before they asked, so he had walked along slowly, waiting to see if more would happen. It looked as if he had been right. This rascal's guilt was written all over him. A burglar if ever he saw one. He caught the young ruffian by the collar and twisted it so that his captive couldn't struggle without cutting off his wind and marched up to the front door of Strathcona House.

"Peter, this is ridiculous. Take my word for it—Jeremy would not . . . and well, you must know that Felicity is, ah, different."

"I know no such thing. This Jeremy is a creature from the cesspools of society and has merely reverted the first chance he got. We both know what goes on in the closes such as the Gorbals. Why even to mention the name of my innocent wee lass in the same breath as that . . . that. . . . It's sacrilege, that's what it is." Bruce stared round wildly for someone to appeal to. Beulah MacIntyre, their hostess, avoided his eyes, and he knew that, although she did not oppose him, she could not support him either. Anyway, she didn't know Jeremy.

Agatha Rose Blair sat weeping on the couch in Beulah's drawing room. Her little girl, the one who had caused all the rumpus, was blissfully asleep across the mother's knees. Peter's fierce gaze touched his wife and child, gentling at the sight.

Having spent the afternoon vainly trying to have Jeremy released from the local jail, Bruce was becoming desperate. His long-time friend—that is until now—Dr. Peter Blair had charged

Jeremy with child baiting and interfering with a female under the age of consent. Realizing that might be the least of it, Bruce tried again, "But Peter, be reasonable!"

"Bruce, I've said my last word on the subject. If you consider this, er, vagabond above our friendship, then—" Walking to the couch, he tenderly picked up his daughter; then signaling to his wife to follow him, Dr. Peter Blair marched out of the room. His roar echoed through the halls: "Stirling! Douglas! Come along, we're going home." The boys, waiting with Mary Jean and a terrified nanny in the kitchen, rushed to their father. Douglas turned a tremulous smile on Mary Jean, but she did not respond. She was already on her way to join her daddy and Granny Mac in the drawing room.

Bruce paraded the floor. There was no one to reason with. Faye Felicity Gordon, Agatha's aunt and a sensible woman who would have understood, was far away in India, with the missionary society there, as was his own Indian friend Raju Singh. George Bennett, his philanthropic friend, who normally resided in his Duke Street house, was at present in America on a speaking tour and would not return for another fortnight. All these people would see this for what it really was: a frightened father's evasion of the truth. Everybody at the Mains would agree, too, but they were far away in Aribaig. He himself would never have thought Peter Blair capable of such blindness. His first blind spot was Felicity, his pitiful little retarded lass. Peter would not, could not, see anything wrong with her at all.

Pushing his hands through his hair in a gesture of utter helplessness, Bruce threw himself down on the couch. Mary Jean sat beside her great-grandmother. Both stared at him speechlessly.

What was he going to say to Mary Jean now? Felicity must have been about three years old when Bruce's daughter had asked him, "Is Felicity a gommeral, Daddy?"

The Reverend Bruce MacAlister had stopped writing at once, and after carefully wiping the ink from his pen nib, he had lifted his daughter to his knee. "No, darlin', and I never want you to use that word again."

"Is it a bad word then, Daddy?"

"Not exactly, but it's not a good word either." From an early age he had encouraged her to ask questions about anything, and they had an unspoken rule that one never answered a question with another question. However, he had answered her, and now he asked, "Where did you hear that, Mary Jean?"

"I heard Stirling say it to Douglas. They started to fight about it, but they're always fighting so. . . . If it's not a bad word then, Daddy, what does it mean?"

Caught this time, Bruce's forehead drew together in a frown of concentration. He badly wished to evade the question, nor could he tell her a lie, but somehow he wished she were a year or two older. "I'll tell you what it means, but I don't want you ever to say it about Felicity. Do you understand?" She focused the full value of her gray eyes on him, and immediately Bruce felt shamed. Of course she understood.

"The word means 'simpleminded.' It describes a person with a handicap. A *handicap* is something that hampers you or holds you back and is usually not the fault of the one with it."

She had given him one more expressive look before running off to play. The subject had not come up again, until today.

Suddenly his brow cleared. Prayer! He preached often enough that prayer was the only way to the answer, so he would again put it into practice. Friday-night prayer meeting at the Bennett residence! Even if George was away, Benny would be there, along with some other prayer warriors. Bruce MacAlister knew he would be welcomed with open arms.

After his first frantic struggle against what was happening to him, Jeremy became resigned. He should never have come to Glasgow with Reverend Bruce and Mary Jean, but, though he'd known that, he had not said anything to the folk at the Mains. Since the Cormacks had adopted him, when he was twelve, whatever that family decided for Jeremy Ward's life was good enough for him.

Even the times he had been on board their vessel, the *Revelation*, with Hamish and the reverend and Mary Jean, he had said nothing, although he had longed to be back at the Mains. Besides being seasick, he had felt homesick. Only when they preached the Gospel from the boat or the shore, just like the pictures in his Bible about Jesus doing that, did Jeremy enjoy it. Reverend Bruce, for all his kindness and understanding, didn't seem to notice that he, Jeremy, never wanted to be anywhere else but at the Mains, with Maister and Mistress Cormack and the dogs and the auld man who had told him to call him Gran'pa Bruce. They were all the family he ever wanted. Thoughts of them now brought a stifled sob, and his eyes misted over. He turned his head away to hide his emotions from the big fat bobby, who was watching him like a hawk.

"Aye, lad, an' ye should be greetin'. Ye're a disgrace, that's whit ye are. Strippin' a wee bit lassie. Could ye no' get somebody yer ain age? I ken there's plenty aboot."

Jeremy sighed. He had exhausted his ability to try to explain. The big man seemed to enjoy reminding him that this was Friday, so he would be here, in this smelly place, until Monday morning, when the magistrate—one, the bobby took further delight in telling him, famous for giving the extreme penalty to offenders such as he—arrived. Och, but no, Reverend Bruce would be here any minute to get him out, and he would beg to go home. He could go himself on the train, and it would be no bother to walk to the farm from the big railway station in Mallaig. Suddenly he, too, remembered to pray. He knew he was innocent, so he didn't have to be so worried. He also remembered a story from the Bible about Saint Paul. His time in prison had been spent praising the Lord. Jeremy was no singer, but he could speak the Shepherd Psalm. Yes, he would do that.

2

Being Mistress MacIntyre's servants brought certain privileges to Betsy Degg and Cook MacLaren, and they had changed their routine very little over the years. They still had their cocoa or tea along with a bit blether every night before retiring. One change that Betsy liked, though—she no longer needed to climb all the way to the attic at bedtime. She had been given Miss Jean Irvine's room a few years ago. The mistress's granddaughter—or she should say, Mistress Jean MacAlister, the reverend's departed wife—had been dead all those years, but the room would forever be "Miss Jean's."

The servants had exhausted the latest family news and had expressed their mutual shock at the outrage. Not knowing Jeremy, they had assumed he must be a bad lot, but Betsy had heard some of the arguments, and deep down inside, she didn't think Reverend MacAlister would have brought anybody here who was that bad.

Cook had replied, "Aye, but he's a big softy, that hielandman!" Still she wasn't sure either. She had listened for a while to the Blair's nursemaid and auld Jacko. . . .

Neither woman was surprised when Bruce appeared at the kitchen door. "Excuse me, ladies, but could I have a word with you?"

Cook, always the spokesperson, answered, "Certainly, Reverend, what can we get for you?"

"It's about my friend Jeremy and what happened in the gar-

den this morning. Did either of you see or hear anything that
might help me clear his name?"

They gaped at each other. *His friend!*

Cook began shaking her head. "I was busy making the noon
dinner, Reverend, and I knew nuthin' aboot it 'til Betsy here
came and tellt me."

"Betsy?"

". . . An' I was takin' the bairns their treats when I heard the
screeching, but I've tellt ye all this, Reverend." He seated himself at their table.

"Could you spare me a cup of tea? I've been doing much
talking, and it's thirsty work. I seem to have missed the meals
the day, with all this happening."

Betsy went to fetch a cup while the older woman looked
steadily at this man, whom she had watched from a distance
since the day he arrived at Strathcona House, a gangly country
boy, very serious and determined, a student of divinity as the
Mistress called such as he. That must have been about fifteen
years ago.

Finally, as he set down the empty cup, she made a decision.
"I saw nuthin' masel', but I ken somebody who did!"

Betsy and Bruce stared at her.

"Jacko, he came for his piece at dinnertime, and he tellt me."

Betsy was offended, "Och, Cook, and ye never said a word."

"Well, I wasna' sure. Jacko's hard to understand at times,
and Doctor Peter was in such a state aboot that wee gommeral
o' his—and the nanny, too, she was in a fair fettle, but she tellt
me after what she thought. I didna ken what to make of it."

"Say on, Cook, I need to hear this."

"Jacko didna' want to have anything to dae wi' it, and yon
Nanny is feart o' trouble wi' Mistress Agatha. She never stops
greetin', ye ken. I warned her years ago what that could do to
a body. But never mind that the now. Here's what I say, Reverend. I don't think this Jeremy did anything bad. At first I
wasna' too sure, but now, well the doctor'll no' have his sorrows to seek wi' his shuttle-wit, but his main sorrow is that he's
like Paddy McShane's auld horse when it has its blinders on."

She stopped for breath, and Bruce asked, "Where does Jacko live?"

"Naebody kens. He only comes on Fridays and—"

"Surely someone recommended him for the work here and would know his address."

Again the women looked at each other, and this time Betsy spoke, "Paddy. Aye, Paddy McShane might ken."

"Where can we find Paddy?"

"He'll be at his hoose. He doesna' go out at nights now. I ken where he bides, and it's not far. When mistress needs him, I go to fetch him. After breakfast the morn I'll take ye—"

"Betsy!"

"Aye, Reverend."

"Do you recall the very first time I ever saw this place?"

"I do that, Reverend. Why Miss Jean was that daft aboot ye, she—" She stopped, appalled at what she had nearly said.

"It's all right, Betsy. I know about it. She and I had many a laugh, because it was the same with me after—I mean before—"

The three sat silent for some time, then Betsy broke it again, "You want me to go to Paddy's the now and no' wait 'til mornin', don't you, Reverend?" He turned to her, and she was dazzled anew by the brilliance of his glance.

"I do that, Betsy. I'd be much obliged, but we'll go together. Paddy can drive us home or—"

"Och, no, Reverend, it's just round the corner on the other side of the square."

Paddy's amazement when he saw the couple standing on his doorstep could not be hidden. "Come away in. It's yersel', Reverend, and Betsy fae Strathcona House. I hope nuthin's wrong wi' the auld lady."

"Thank you, Paddy. Nothing's wrong with Mistress MacIntyre, I'm glad to say." Quickly he outlined their reason for visiting at so late an hour, and Paddy listened gravely.

"Aye, I do ken where Jacko bides."

He was silent for so long that Bruce had to prod him. "Can you take me there?"

"Aye, I could. But he'll not be pleased."

"A man's reputation could be at stake and maybe his very life in danger."

"I ken ye say Jacko saw the rights o' what happened. Will they take his word? Could yon nanny no' tell the truth?"

"She didn't see it and can only surmise, like the rest of us here. Besides Doctor Peter feels . . . ," Bruce's voice trailed off. Even in this dire situation his ingrained loyalty to Peter surfaced. Betsy broke the silence.

"Jacko'll do it for me."

The jaunt through the midnight streets with the mists closing in on them, along with the seemingly endless wait as Paddy rapped on the narrow doorway, had the feeling of nightmare to Bruce. When the Irishman finally reappeared with the reluctant Jacko in tow, the feeling increased.

Back at George Square Police Station the sleepy sergeant in charge was less than sympathetic at first. "I couldna' let this miscreant go on the say-so of the likes of him. This charge report says a Dr. Peter Blair made it, and it's very serious indeed. Interfering with a young female. The magistrate's awful strict on that."

Bruce's patience suddenly snapped. "This man saw the whole thing and is willing to testify how the charge is ridiculous. Why, he just made a statement that the child—she's not quite—well, she's retarded, and she attacked Jeremy."

The policeman laughed grimly. "All the worse if the victim's a shuttle-wit, and she attacked him? I believe that one, like I'd believe. I'd believe—" He glanced round for an example, and his eye caught sight of Paddy's rig, just outside in the archway. "That your auld nag can fly." He softened slightly as he saw the stricken look on the minister's face and the serious expressions on the others'. The old "tally" appeared terrified, and well he might, with all the trouble they were causing at the moment, with riots breaking out wherever they opened their chip shops. The toff with the minister's collar seemed to be either praying or getting ready to greet. The maid was whispering to Paddy McShane. Everybody on the beat knew Paddy. "The reformed tatty howker" they called him. It was said respectfully though, and after thirty years of serving the area and never a speck of trouble, so it should be.

Soberly the sergeant said in a gentler tone, "If it was up to me, Reverend, I'd let ye take him the now and bring him back on Monday mornin', when he's to go before the magistrate, but I canna. These are serious charges, and until we have evidence to prove otherwise or the one layin' the charge withdraws it, the miscreant must remain in custody here."

"I do understand, Sergeant, and thank you. Could I just see him to have a word of prayer and comfort?"

The man considered carefully before replying, "Only yersel', then, and I'll need to lock ye in." Besty gasped and would have protested, but Paddy shook his head at her. Bruce disappeared along the corridor.

Jeremy heard footsteps on the stone floor, and he raised his head from his hands. He, too, had been praying and reciting the Psalms, but no help had come until now. Much confused as to why he should be here, his confidence that Reverend Bruce would get him out was childlike in its simplicity. Imploringly he gazed at him through the small square opening.

Bruce was speaking, "I know you are completely innocent of this charge, Jeremy, but the law is hard to convince. I'm sure by morning I'll—" Unable to pronounce the words that would condemn Jeremy to even one night in this stinking place, let alone three, he stopped. The iron grating showed him enough of the jail cell to prove it was more of a six-foot square with a row of shelves. Other cells along the passageway held loud snorers, tiered in rows, but thankfully Jeremy had this place to himself. Terrible as the conditions undoubtedly were, at least he wasn't locked in with a hardened criminal.

"I've been in worse places, Reverend. I just thought I was done wi' all that. When can we go home to the Mains?"

Bruce could hardly answer. "We'll be going the minute I can get you out. I'll not even bother with any more kirk meetings, and now that Peter—"

"Ye've fell oot wi' the doctor, and it's my fault."

"Maybe we've had a temporary misunderstanding, but it is

not your fault, Jeremy. That poor wee lass of Peter's—and he, well, he can't see it!"

A hand touched Bruce's shoulder. "You'll need to leave, Reverend. My relief'll be here in five minutes, and I'll be in trouble if ye're still here."

"Yes, Sergeant. Don't worry, Jeremy. I'll get you out. Well, I'll be back first thing in the morning."

But many mornings would pass before they saw each other again.

The bare shelf that served as chair, table, and bed gave small comfort to Jeremy's short, wiry frame. Falling into a restless sleep at last, after tossing and turning for hours, he awoke again with a start when he rolled too close to the edge and crashed to the stone floor. Feeling his way back onto the narrow wooden bench, he banged his head on the one above. His cry of pain changed to a moan as he remembered his surroundings. Telling Reverend Bruce earlier he had been in worse places was the truth right enough, but these past eight years had been a lot different for him. At the Mains he had his own attic room. Mistress Cormack let him paint the walls how he liked, and last spring they had let him pick some of that newfangled wallpaper, which he had pasted up with great pride, matching the pattern exactly. Gran'pa Bruce had told him the design reminded him of pictures of what he called Corinthian columns, and Jeremy liked that. His whole being cried out now with longing for his own place there: his chest of drawers and the wardrobe Reverend Bruce had told him they sawed in half before they could get it up the narrow stairs and then had to join it together again; the wee table beside his bed, with the lamp maister had brought him from Inverness one time. Jeremy wasn't one for reading a lot, but he did like the *Illustrated* papers Taylor the Postie brought every Friday. His big Bible, too, was illustrated with lots of pictures of the folk like Moses and King David and Jesus marching along the sands that reminded him of the beach at Maren.

Jeremy was close to twenty years old by his own rough reckoning, but at the thought of his adopted family and his home, a lump came in his throat. Outside in the street he heard a dog barking, and suddenly that was the last of his brave coverup. He pulled a big hankie from his pocket. Mary Jean had presented it to him on his last birthday; they had made it up that his birthday should be the day he was saved, and they always had a celebration on it. Mary Jean had worked for weeks to sew his initials on the corner of the hankie. Jeremy sobbed his heart out into the fine white linen. Nobody would hear him in this scunner of a place.

But somebody did hear. "Hey, lad?"

Jeremy ignored the voice at first but then decided to at least answer. "Whit dae ye want?"

The sound came from through the thin wall and not from the passageway outside. "It's no what I want but what do you want?"

Jeremy crouched as far from the wall as he could get. The question needed no answer.

"I see! Ye don't want oot o' this hole then?"

"I do, but they'll come for me the morn."

The laughing noise reminded Jeremy of one his mother's friend used to make when he chased Jeremy out onto the streets. "They'll nut come for you at all! Once yer left in a place like this, ye can rot for all the gentry care."

"My friend Reverend Bruce MacAlister isny like that. He said he'll come, and he will."

The laugh was even more pronounced this time. "Aye, an' Queen Victoria will invite me to tea this week an' a'."

Jeremy crouched down further. More was to come, though.

"Be that as it may, lad, if ye want oot the now, and no' wait til mornin', I can help you."

It was Jeremy's turn to laugh. "If you can get me out, what aboot yersel'?"

"Och, but I'm not locked in. I'm just here to help the likes of you that's been jailed by the gentry for nowt. Do you want help or no'?"

Some of the cunning learned in his younger years returned to Jeremy. "What will that get for you then?"

"Oh, it's a wise one is it? All the better. One good turn deserves another, and if I help ye oot o' here, ye'll only have to run some messages for me, and then ye're your ain man again. Not bowing to the gentry, eether."

Jeremy knew all about "running messages." "Naw, I'll wait my chance here. I ken the reverend'll come for me the morn."

"I heard them talkin', ye know. If yon doctor charged ye, an' they think ye done what they say, ye'll not get away wi' less than five year, and yer 'reverend,' as ye call him, much as he might want to, will no' be able to help ye at all!"

Jeremy absorbed this. Except for the part about Bruce, he could believe it.

The unseen voice continued, and now it echoed Jeremy's own thoughts. "If you're such a smart chiel, and I think ye are, ye can easy get away by yersel', efter ye've done some messages for me."

"How can I get oot then?"

"That's more like it. I'll be wi' ye in a jiffy!"

3

Before returning Jacko to his "hole in the wall," as Paddy McShane called the place where the gardener lived, they had delivered Betsy safely to Strathcona House.

Asking Paddy to wait, Bruce had escorted the maid to the door and was turning away when she asked, "You're not comin' in then, Reverend?"

"No, Betsy, and in case I'm not back at breakfast time, ye'll help Mistress MacIntyre with Mary Jean? Just tell my daughter I'm away to see about Jeremy. She'll understand."

"It's mair than I do, Reverend, but I'll make sure they're baith all right."

"Thank you, Betsy."

She nodded as she closed the door.

"Paddy, are you in need of sleep?"

"If ye're meanin' whit I think ye are, then I need no sleep this night. Whiles I sit readin' or communin' all night long. Where are we bound then, Reverend?"

"A fair distance, Paddy. What about the horse?"

"I take it ye're not in a big hurry? If that's the case, the horse'll be right enough. She's not auld, and she's had an easy day. How far are we goin'?"

"About forty-five miles, I'd say. As long as we arrive by breakfast time, we'll be fine."

"Right ye are, we can stop for a rest aboot half roads then.

I've maps under yer seat cushion, should ye want them. But if
ye tell me where we're bound, I'll maybe ken the road. I mind
once Mistress MacIntyre hirin' me to bring Miss Jean back fae
yon lassies' school in Stirling she didna' like. Beg pardon, Reverend."

"Don't worry, Paddy, Jean told me all about it. We're going
to a place in Fife called Burntisland."

Paddy absorbed this information before stating, " 'Tis glad I
am yon John MacAdam has made dacent roads to run on, and
we'll just go round by Stirling 'til they've finished the bridge
ower the Forth."

"Paddy, when you need a rest I can take the reins. I am a
farm boy at heart, you know."

"I've aye kent that, Reverend, the way ye conseeder the
beasts. Aye, I'll no' be feart to let ye take the reins."

"Beggin' your pardon, Bruce, lad, but am I hearin' right?
Ye've come all the way from Glasgow in this jauntin' car, and
ye've been travelin' all night, and it's not to tell me there's
something the matter with my Peter or his family?"

"Up to a point, sir, all is well enough with your Peter and
Agatha, the twins and the wee lass."

A cloud seemed to pass over the elderly man's face and he
turned away. They had just finished a sumptuous breakfast,
served by the young woman now hovering in the background
and introduced to Bruce as Deborah. He had paid her scant
attention, after a perfunctory bow, his business being with Dr.
Peter Blair, Senior, who still wore a puzzled frown as he peered
through half-closed eyes at Bruce.

"Up to a point ye say. What point?" Then to the woman who
had moved in closer, he bit off the words, "Deb, sit doon, will
ye? Ye're jerkin' aboot like a hen wi' its heid cut off." Obediently the woman whom Bruce now recalled as being Peter's
youngest sister sat down opposite her father and at Bruce's left
hand.

"The point is wee Felicity."

The old physician groaned, while his daughter gave a startled gasp. "Felicity? Reverend Bruce, what of her?"

Bruce glanced from one to the other. This was a delicate subject, and he recalled how even Granny Mac would not get into discussing it, while the child's mother merely wept.

"You can say on, Reverend. I do know about such matters. After all, my father and one of my brothers are physicians."

The doctor nodded. "She'd be one herself, if they'd let her. What of the wee lass, then?"

Bruce proceeded to give the details of the happenings of the day before, trying to be fair to all parties and not really sure, judging by how Peter felt about the child, how these other relations would react. He need not have feared.

Peter's father rose quickly from the table, knocking his cup over as he did, and shouting, "I knew something of this nature was bound to happen sooner or later. Did I not tell that thick-skinned son of mine—"

"Quietly, Father, you'll only upset yourself." He calmed down at once, pushing a hand through his still-abundant head of gray hair.

"What's to do? What's to do? Deb, can you think of something?"

"With your permission, Father, I could go to Glasgow and talk to Agatha Rose. Between us we could try again with Peter, but remember that last time."

"I do remember—that's what's bothering me. You've a wise enough plan, Deb, but too many ifs. I think I'll have to take more serious measures. As a doctor myself, and still practicing a bit, I would have some influence with the magistrate. If I tell him the child is a simple and has done the likes of this before, maybe we widna' need to bother our Peter. He just willna' see!" Placing a hand gently on Bruce's shoulder, he continued, "You're bleary-eyed wi' want o' sleep. The fellow—what's his name?—Jeremy'll be none the better off if you make yersel' ill. The Irishman is sleepin' already, I hear. Get to a bed for an hour or two whilest we make our arrangements."

Truth to tell, Bruce needed no second bidding, as he realized

the logic of his friend's father's statement. Without demur he
followed the young woman to a room. The big, sprawling bun-
galow he remembered from the visits made during his student
years and the room she showed him to were both familiar.
Catching a glimpse of the glorious ocean view, just before Deborah drew the curtains across the window, he knew this to be
the very room—Peter's room.

The woman withdrew, saying, "If you need anything more,
Reverend, ring the bell beside the bed."

"Please call me Bruce, Miss, eh, ah, Deborah." But the
woman had quietly closed the door as she slipped away.

He fell asleep immediately.

Beulah MacIntyre sat across from her great-granddaughter
and wondered, as she had many times before, how such a
young girl could be so quiet and still. Certainly Jean, the child's
mother, had never been rambunctious, but she could never stay
as quiet as this for long, either.

"Mary Jean, I thought you liked your porridge?"

"So I do, Granny Mac, but I'm not hungry, thank you."

"Don't worry about your daddy. He'll likely be home by
teatime."

"I know, Granny Mac. I'm not worried about my daddy!"

Beulah studied the child again. In some ways she did resem-
ble her mother, but mostly she favored Bruce—not in coloring
so much as in mannerisms. But those eyes—asked to describe
their color, you could say the blue sky or the green sea or the
purple pansies in the garden outside. They reflected their surroundings or, like now, the mood the child was in. Beulah
knew both she and Mary Jean were just putting in time until
they heard from Bruce. She prayed now he would have the man
Jeremy with him and that peace would have been declared with
the Blair family. She could not understand what was happening, and she felt too old for all this cafuffle.

"Gran'pa Bruce says that word sometimes."

Beulah started. For Mary Jean to say something without be-

ing asked and for the girl to read her very thoughts was dis-
comfiting to say the least.

"What was that you just said, Mary Jean?"

"The word you spoke, *cafuffle*, Gran'pa Bruce says that word,
too, sometimes. Granny Mac, this is a bad one. You can have
good ones and bad ones."

"Your daddy will sort it."

The eyes, dark with this unnamed sorrow, turned on her
again. "Aye, he will, but not the day!"

But it was not for want of trying.

Dr. Blair, Senior, routed out his magistrate friend, who in
turn did the same to the one responsible for the district that
included George Square. Between them they prepared a writ of
release for one Jeremy Ward, of Mains Farm, Aribaig, in the
county of Inverness.

A jubilant Bruce arrived breathless at the jail, exactly twenty-
four hours after leaving it, but all to no avail.

"What did you say?"

"I said we've no person of that name or description here."

"But I saw him here just last night. I even visited him in the
cell. I'll show you—"

"You canna go through there, Reverend. It's for authorized
persons only—"

But Bruce was already through. He rushed headlong down
the corridor. Reaching number twelve, he peered through the
grating.

"Ye want a wummen?" Drunken laughter followed him as he
made his way slowly back to the desk.

"I don't understand. The sergeant told me last night that
Jeremy would be in that cell until Monday morning's hearings."

"That sergeant is not here. He's been transferred to another
beat!"

"Why? Can you tell me why?"

"That I cannot, and I must ask you to leave the premises
now. You've already caused a disturbance." Shouts and catcalls

echoed down the hall, to confirm this, and Bruce sadly turned
away.

"What I fail to understand is, if they had released Jeremy,
why is he not here? I know if he was free and uninjured, he
would find his way straight here." Dr. Blair had tried to answer
this and other similar questions many times in the past hour.
Now he was becoming concerned about the hieland laddie, as
his son used to jokingly call Bruce. Yes, his son. That one was
going to answer to him for this. He sighed again. Young Peter
had enough troubles, and he himself was too old for such emotional upheaval.

Mistress MacIntyre came to his rescue. "Bruce, we can do no
more today. We're all most sorry about your Jeremy. I'm sure
we had no idea he. . . . I mean, how he meant so much to you
and your family."

Bruce turned his icy blue gaze on her for an instant, and she
flushed.

"I'm sorry!" Then, "Dr. Blair!"

It was an appeal, and the doctor responded, "You are correct,
mistress, we all need rest. I suggest a good night's sleep, and
we'll start the search again in the morning. Nothing will be
gained by roaming the streets of Glasgow at this hour on a
Saturday." He pulled his watch from the waistcoat pocket above
his corpulent stomach. "Beg pardon, Sunday, and two o'clock
in the morning, so it is!"

Bruce began to protest, but Blair kept his advantage. "Let me
remind you of your responsibility to your own motherless
child."

Bruce gave in, and went first to peep at Mary Jean. She lay
awake, waiting for him.

"Daddy!"

"Yes, darlin'?"

"We can't go home to Mains without Jeremy."

"We'll find him, my pet. Now go back to sleep."

"Now that you're in, I'll go to sleep, Daddy."

"Good night, my wee love!"

*   *   *

Jeremy had vanished without trace. They searched everywhere. After three days and most of the three nights as well,
Bruce was almost ready to admit defeat. Then, as a last resort,
when he and Dr. Blair found themselves standing gazing up at
the clock high above the arched Trongate, he remembered the
very strange place and stranger people, where Raju Singh had
taken him on that never-to-be-forgotten day just before his and
Jean's elopement.

"Will you wait here for me, Doctor? I'll not be long."

From the outside everything seemed the same as before. At
his knock the door opened the merest crack and a hoarse voice
said, "Nuthin the day!"

Just as Bruce turned sadly away, a different voice called out,
"You're thon minister. Whit dae ye want wi' us?" Bruce
wheeled round, but the door still showed only a crack. The
disembodied voice asked, "Are ye just yersel'?"

"Is that Ony?" His own voice an echoing whisper, Bruce
waited.

"Nae names. Whit is it ye want?"

"I'm looking for someone. That last time I was here with my
friend from India, Raju. Oh, sorry, I forgot—no names! Anyway with your help I had my watch returned!"

The door opened a few more inches, and the voice said,
"Come in then."

Seated on the cushioned floor, a few minutes later, with no
one else in sight, Bruce was aware of many eyes watching from
the shadows. He directed his gaze to the man he knew to be
Ony. Detecting the very faintest of smiles, almost hidden in the
deep creases of the face of the other man, he followed the
fellow's glance—the watch in his waistcoat pocket.

"I never had the chance to thank you, Ony, for finding my
watch."

"I said nae names. Ye talk too much, and I dinna ken what
ye're talkin' aboot. What is it ye want the now?"

Haltingly Bruce proceeded to explain.

Rejoining Dr. Blair ten minutes later, Bruce merely said, "The search is already under way. We can do no more!" Wisely the older man left his many questions unasked.

Baffled at the intensity of the search and exhausted by the emotional turmoil being transmitted from Bruce and his daughter, Mary Jean, the doctor sighed his thankfulness. Only once in the three days had he gone to see his son. He had returned to Strathcona House, admitting to Beulah, as he requested a place to sleep under her spacious roof, that the atmosphere in his son's home was impossible to tolerate.

Later on, as Bruce was putting Mary Jean to bed the two elders talked in Beulah's drawing room.

"I'm right bamboozled, mistress, I must confess. Such a fuss that could have been prevented from the start."

"I agree, Doctor, but I'm afraid I'm losing patience with Bruce. I'll admit it's all most unfortunate, but can he not see that the young man mustn't want to go back with him, or he would be here by now? Anyway he's just a serving man."

The other scratched his head. "Did it never occur to our dear minister that the fellow might be wiser than we think and is already on his way to Aribaig?"

"He's absolutely sure this Jeremy would have let him know somehow if he was at all able. He thinks he's been pressed or worse."

The doctor's laugh was sardonic. "There's no wars the now. Who would press him?"

"Doctor, there's *always* fighting!"

Bruce reentered the room, and the conversation lapsed.

The older man yawned. "Bed for me, then. See you in the mornin'."

"Granny Mac, I hate to give in, but I don't know what else to do. He's just disappeared off the face of the earth." Bruce's shoulders shook as he turned away.

"Bruce, I have to risk your anger, but could he not just be hiding until, I mean in case Dr. Peter—?"

"If he was at all able, he would have let me know somehow; and it's all right, I'm not angry with you. More with myself and not even with Peter. Who knows what one would do if faced with the heartbreak of a wee lass like that?

"Peter can't face it, that's the trouble. I hate what he's done to somebody we consider a member of the family at the Mains, but I don't hate Peter. He cannot help the state he's in the now. He's protecting himself from the truth about Felicity.

"Meanwhile I have the sad errand of going back to the Mains without Jeremy. Add to that the fact that my best friend is estranged. . . . Och, Granny Mac, I'm fair desolate."

The old lady made no attempt to deny his words, but instead she whispered, "I'm so sorry, Bruce!"

At last he rose. Dropping a kiss on her snow-white head, he asked, "Shall I fetch you anything?"

"Thank you, no, Bruce, Betsy will be waiting to help me to bed. Good night!"

"Good night."

4

"**M**ary Jean. What more could I have done? You understand, pet, don't you?"

But his daughter would not meet his eyes. Instead she sat and stared out of the carriage window without saying a word. Though not chatterers by any standards, the two usually did carry on some kind of conversation, either about the country they were traveling through, the people left behind, or about those being visited. Today, as their train clickety-clacked its way across another of the many viaducts between Glasgow and their destination, no conversation was in progress. Down below them the Caledonian Canal teamed with barges and small boats waiting at the sluice gates, but even that brought no utterance from her.

"Darlin', it's not like yourself to sulk, and I don't think you're truly sulking, but could you tell me what you're thinking the now?"

Finally her voice came, a faint whisper at first, but gaining strength with each word: "I hate Fessy! She's a wee besom, and I could just murder her."

The shock of her venomous words brought Bruce to his feet.

Except for them, the carriage was empty, and for once he was truly grateful that his own grandmother, Margaret Munro, who resided in Edinburgh and whom Mary Jean had christened Granny Munny when she was a two-year-old bairn, insisted they always travel first class. As he resisted accepting monetary gifts from this extremely rich arm of his immediate family, he somehow could not refuse the tickets without appearing churlish. The Munros were large stockholders in the London Midland Scottish Railway, so it was not really taking her money when he used the privilege tickets she sent him. Thankful again that he did not have to consider other passengers, he forced his thoughts back to a side of his daughter he had never before seen. Had she just spoken a mouthful of obscenities, he could not have been more horrified.

"Mary Jean!" At a total loss of what to do or say, he watched her.

Face turned toward the magnificent view rushing past the window, she spoke again: "Well, so I do, and I hate Uncle Peter, too. I used to like him, even when he roared at me, but not since Fessy came."

Still she did not look at him or speak his name. Sending a quick prayer for wisdom, he waited. "My pet, we mustn't blame Fessy or judge Uncle Peter," he finally answered. "Circumstances change people and—"

She cut him short. "I *do* blame her, and I'm not calling him Uncle Peter again. He's not my uncle. Fessy might be a daftie, but she knows more than they think. She torments Douglas, too, and she's took off her clothes before. Granny Mac's milkman says she's full of 'Auld Nick,' and I believe him."

"Wait now! Wait just a minute. Say all that again slowly and one thing at a time. First, what do you mean she's done that before and she torments Douglas? Och, I'm sorry, pet, here I tell you one thing at a time, and then I throw two questions at you at once. Just tell me slowly now."

"Uncle Hamie knows, and he can tell you. I don't want to, Daddy."

He stifled a sigh of relief. Her tone had softened a mite, and she had called him Daddy.

"All right. You don't need to tell me all the details. It seems I've been blind myself, but I think I'm beginning to see now. Aye, I see some things now, and you're right, Hamish can tell me more. It's you I'm concerned about the day. Mary Jean, I have never heard you speak in that manner before. You've shocked me. Will you not say—"

"No, I'll not say I'm sorry. Don't ask me to, Daddy. I'm *not* sorry. I can't help it. Jeremy's lost in Glasgow town, and he'll not be liking it." These were indisputable facts, and Reverend Bruce MacAlister ignored his daughter's actual words. It was her manner and her attitude he deplored. The taint of venom cut him to the heart. If she would only weep and allow him to comfort her or ask him what they were going to do now. For the first time since her birth, he felt a widening chasm yawn between them, and a feeling of devastating helplessness swept over him.

The panorama unfolding from the train windows passed unheeded as Bruce pondered this side of his child. She certainly had reason to be upset but not to this extent. King David's prayer for his son Absalom came to his mind, but immediately he rejected the thought. She could not be holding this against him, her father, who would give his very life for her. Surely she would be herself by the time they reached Aribaig and his mother and the rest of the family talked to her. If not then, when they got back to their manse in Cairnglen parish, she would have started to get over it. Then there was Hamish. Hamish must see it Bruce's way.

But Hamish agreed with Mary Jean.

Bruce had made one more reference to their problem before the train chugged into the station, and he reached up to the rack for their luggage. "You're not blaming me, are you, Mary Jean?"

"Not 'zactly, but he didn't want to go to Glasgow, you know."

"Did he tell you that?"

"He didn't say it, but I knew."

During the short journey by public omnibus to Aribaig, where he would hire the ancient hansom cab to take them to the farm, he thought: *I only wanted to offer Jeremy a chance to compare life on the farm crofts to that of the city. After all he was little more than a child when he lived there.* He followed that by, *Yes, but I should have known better.*

Regrets were futile he knew, and he had been taught so all his life, but he also knew human nature still harbored them, and Bruce MacAlister was a very human being. The senior Doctor Blair's parting words at the station in Glasgow had been somewhat less than reassuring: "Well, Reverend, it's no' as if he's a laddie, and if they've pressed him into the army, he'll be on the road to the Egyptian fightin' by now. If he's all ye say, he'll be back—and maybe even the better for it—in a year or two."

It had been his idea to introduce the positive part of this message to his daughter on the journey, but he knew Mary Jean would not take that as comfort any more than he did.

Helping her from one ancient vehicle to another, he chuckled as he remembered the doctor's faintly hidden attempts at matchmaking. The information that his Deborah was a bonnie cook, and that Mary Jean needed a mother's hand, as she was too much surrounded by men, was only some of the ammunition aimed at him by Peter's father. At the time Bruce's mind had been too taken up with Jeremy, but here and now, for some reason beyond his understanding, the words echoed. "She'll be a fine wife for some lucky man, and she's fond o' bairns."

He had not had the heart to tell the father how, without words, both he and Deborah had known Bruce MacAlister was not that "lucky" man.

If anyone had asked Bruce's mother, Elspeth Cormack, during the early summer of 1889, if she needed anything more to make her happy, she would have said no. Nothing in her own life could add to the happiness she knew. She had Andrew, the best and kindest of husbands. Their farm provided a comfortable living. Other men of her household were all good-natured, God-fearing people, who cared for and respected her as the woman of the house. Bruce MacAlister—or Gran'pa Bruce, as everyone except his friend Dugald called her first husband's father—must be approaching his eightieth year but was as spry and bright as he had been when she first met him all those years ago. Although nowadays, on cold or wet mornings, she found him easy to coax to stay indoors by the fire. Never a day passed that she did not thank God for Jeremy, too—a Glasgow waif, picked up in the extremes of an epileptic fit at the fairgrounds in Aribaig that summer when Bruce, her minister son, first started out in his caravan ministry. Jeremy, although no kin at all, was like a second son to Elspeth, and he never wanted to be anywhere else but with them at the Mains. Elspeth's thoughts switched to the one time she had asked Jeremy if he would like to live anywhere else, and he had given her such a look of hurt dismay that she never mentioned it again.

In her prayers, too, after Bruce and Mary Jean MacAlister, she always put in a petition for Hamish Cormack, her husband's son by his first marriage. Hamish was a living miracle, a new creature since his adventure in the sea with Bruce. Hamish described all that best himself when he gave testimony about being "saved fae the watter and fae masel'." Since then, he would add, "Ma life's no ma ain but belangs tae Jesus and then tae Bruce MacAlister, ma brither!" The lads, as Andrew still called them, although not sharing blood kinship, had a closer bond.

Mary Jean, her darling granddaughter, was a blithe spirit, and although a daddy's girl, she still had a special place for her Gran'speth. A rare wee one for giving folks a made-up name.

Singing as she worked, Elspeth had spent this morning preparing for the wanderers' return from the annual visit to Glasgow. Usually the three meant Bruce, Mary Jean, and Hamish, but this time Bruce had asked Jeremy to go in Hamish's place. They had come to the farm earlier this year so that Hamish could rest awhile. He had been struck by one of those terrible headaches he got occasionally since the time he had been hit on the head defending Jeremy a few years ago. Oh, it would be good to have them all home again, even for a little while.

Her dreaming thoughts were interrupted by her husband's voice: "You'll be rubbing that table away to nothing if you polish it anymore!"

She laughed joyfully. "Och, you, you're just jealous because the tea's not made yet. I'll go and put it on the now."

"The tea can wait a wee while. Just you sit here and have a bit blether with your ain man. It's not often we have the chance to be by oorsel's." Surprised but obedient, she sat down where he indicated on the sofa beside him. He reached for her hand.

"Ye're gie happy, are ye not, lass?"

"I am that, Andrew. I have all a woman could ask for."

"Ye never hanker after being a grand lawyer in Edinburgh town then?"

Shocked, she gave him the benefit of her brilliant blue eyes, and he got a glimpse of where Bruce and Mary Jean got theirs from.

Before she could protest, he went on, "Aye, yes, 'tis a grand feelin' that we have all things here, and Bruce has his living so near now. No watter to cross when we go to see them, but just an hour or so on the train."

"He was blessed indeed to have got that parish in Cairnglen after—"

" 'Tis not so bonny as Skye, and yon factory, wi' its smells and all. Still he seems content enough."

"In a place where they manufacture gunpowder, it has to be less than paradise, but the smell is prosperity, according to Hamish."

A frown creased Andrew's brow for a moment but cleared quickly enough.

His wife talked on. "A dangerous prosperity, but with all the roads and railway beds being blasted out of the rocks and places, somebody has to produce the explosive stuff."

"It's used for other purposes not so noble, Elspeth. We ken that."

"Yes, we do, but there's been no wars since the Crimea, in fifty-eight."

"There was the Indian mutiny, too, and some of that lingers on."

"Why do we speak of such matters, Andrew? Have you some purpose?"

"A bit of a rumor from Taylor the Postie this mornin', when

ye were so busy ben here. Then there was the story in last
Friday's *Illustrated*."

"What story was that, Andrew?"

"I'm talkin' ower much."

"What story, Andrew? I know you too well, and you must be
saying all this for a reason."

"Aye, you're right. The story has it that the recruitin' ser-
geants are at it again. They're after good, healthy young fellows
for the Egyptian affair."

Elspeth turned white. "You're never meaning Bruce?"

"Not Bruce, no. They seldom bother wi' the clergy. I'm
makin' ower much o' this, and yon press gangin' is illegal now.
Come on, it's time for that tea. I hear Gran'pa and Hamish."

Gran'pa Bruce was telling Hamish, "They'll be leaving Glasgow on Friday mornin' an' be hame by teatime. I've a notion to
go wi' ye in the cairt to meet them, but no, if Elspeth and you
and Andrew go, that would be one too many comin' back."

"Not at all, Gran'pa, you come on, and Jeremy and me can
walk beside the horse on the way home. Mary Jean likes to sit
on Samson's back, and he doesna' care."

"I will then, lad. My, they've only been away a bit mair than
a week, an' it seems like half a year. 'Tis glad I am you're all not
so far away now. Tell me this, when his mother canna hear you:
Does he like that place, Cairnglen? My idea is that it's gie dirty!"

"That's the factory. It's bonny enough if ye take a walk on the
braes. The heather moors are no' so high, but they're no' so far
away either. He likes it fine. Ye ken weel he hardly sees the
place; it's the folk—

"What's ailin' that dog? She never yelps like that for onybody
else but Bruce or Jeremy. It canna be? But wait, I do hear a
horse!" he rushed to the window. "It is, they're in the hansom
fae Aribaig! They're hame! Elspeth, Faither!" The sudden silence in the next room told him the recent occupants were already on their way.

He hurried to join them in time to hear Elspeth shriek, "Jeremy, where's Jeremy?"

                    *   *   *

"I'm not a great believer in the saying, 'No news is good news,' yet it does have some value in that I'm sure if he was dead we would somehow ken."

The others seated round Elspeth's kitchen table only nodded in reply to Gran'pa Bruce's statement. The whole matter of Jeremy's disappearance from the jail cell had been deliberated upon for the past two hours, and nothing better than this had been offered. Andrew Cormack, the stoic, had been through a similar situation with his own son. At the age of seventeen, Hamish had run away from the farm. Circumstances then had been very different, to be sure, but the sharp memory of not knowing stabbed Andrew's sensitive heart afresh as he glanced at this same son, a prodigal, now restored and made new in every sense of the word. Aware of his father's glance, Hamish looked across and smiled forlornly. His thoughts ran along similar lines, but unlike Andrew, Hamish knew about the possible fate that lurked in wait for one such as Jeremy. They had opposite backgrounds, as he, Hamish, had been reared in this good Christian home, surrounded by a caring, loving family, while Jeremy had originally come from a home where no one cared if he lived or died, so long as he contributed in some way to the habits of the woman he called Mother. He had escaped that environment, but knowing nothing else, had soon slipped into the life of the Glasgow streets—picking pockets, procuring, following fairs and cattle shows round the country, doing anything and everything for the money.

Gran'pa was speaking again. "Maybe old Dr. Blair has the rights of it then, although I thought the days of the press gangs a thing of the past. What would you say to that, Hamish?"

"Aye, but 'tis not in the past altogether. They still offer the queen's shilling, and if you're fly, ye can get away wi' it. Jeremy's no' that fly ony mair."

He looked at the three men, then glanced at the door leading to the stairs, as Andrew reassured him, "The women'll no' be back the nicht. Mary Jean was sleepin' on her feet, and Elspeth, well, she'll stay wi' her for a while."

"I was goin' to say then that the ane time I was nearly cor-

nered by the pressmen I got oot o' it by lettin' on I was daft.
When they told me to make my mark on yon paper, they didna'
ken I could write my name an' read a few words as well. I tore
it up and made as if I would eat it. They threw me oot, and I still
had the shillin'!"

A bitter laugh came from Bruce. "Maybe we've done Jeremy
a poor turn by teaching him that all things work together for
good."

"Nay, lad, hard as it may seem to us the now, we ken that
word is true. Whatever becomes of young Jeremy, we ken he'll
not revert. As soon as he's able to, he'll be hame here. The hard
thing for us to thole is that he's not able, and we're imaginin'
the worst things that are keepin' him." His listeners absorbed
this and then waited for Gran'pa's summation, which they
knew would soon be forthcoming.

"Although he was not born to it, God's Word has since been
planted in Jeremy. It has sprouted and will bear blossom, then
fruit. Of all the books in the Bible, he liked to hear the Psalms
best, but he liked to read Luke's Gospel. He told me once that
in Luke's Gospel the Lord was aye doin' something—either
stilling the tempest or casting out devils, healing the sick or
feeding the hungry. For us now we have to go about our own
work and leave it be. We've done all we can, and now we stand.
The word of the Lord says: 'Heaven and Earth shall pass away,
but my words shall not pass away!' "

The four-fold "Amen!" was joined at that moment by Elspeth's contralto as she came into the kitchen. They all knew
she had been communing, and even if her face was begrutten,
she had made her peace with God.

Mary Jean's attitude proved to be a different matter. Each of
the men had tried, Elspeth had tried, but the child would not be
comforted.

"I told you, Gran'speth, I hate Fessy, and I'll not be playing
with the twins again. I'm going to ask Jesus to help me forget
them and Uncle . . . I mean Dr. Peter Blair and his wife, too."

"But my love, should you not be asking Jesus to help you

forgive them all? I love Jeremy, too, and I was angry with them all at first, but I knew I had to forgive them, with God's help."

"I'll not! I'll not! Our Jeremy could be dead, and I heard Gran'drew telling Uncle Hamie that he could have been sold as a white slave. I'll not forgive them, and I don't care, and I'm not going to talk about it anymore." Her listeners knew she meant that, and as she had not wept or asked any of the grownups for help, they left her alone after that.

On the day they were leaving for Cairnglen, Gran'pa Bruce told his grandson, "She's gie young to hold a grudge long. She'll soon forget, when she's goin' to school and has all her other interests. We'll all be prayin' for Jeremy and for Mary Jean as well. Don't try to coax her any mair. She'll come to you when she's ready!"

Bruce had to be content with that for the present.

5

At first sighting, the small town in the Trossachs, known as Cairnglen, where Bruce MacAlister had been called to minister, seemed to have everything—it retained a distinct highland flavor without many of the disadvantages of the true highlands, further north. Until the wind changed, that was, carrying a certain aroma miles up the glen, almost to the Tay Valley. Not that the natives used the term *aroma!* Close to 2,000 souls called Cairnglen home, although more than half that number were incomers, having arrived thirty years ago, with the same breeze that wafted the smell that spelled prosperity.

When they had first come to Cairnglen, the manse, located a good fifteen minutes walk from the church, had held the biggest surprise for Bruce and his little family. They felt delight, too, at the providence that had used a lady (some said a lady-in-waiting to the queen, a woman who wished to remain incognito) to bequeath the coach house to the kirk on condition that it be used only for a manse on into perpetuity. The only other condition attached to the bequest read that under no circumstances could it be sold.

Arriving there after the painful time in Aribaig and Glasgow, Bruce, Hamish, and Mary Jean were in no mood to appreciate either the gentle beauty of their surroundings or the convenience and comfort of their home. The journey had consisted of a bone-racking half hour in the horse-drawn bus, two hours in the train, and a walk in which Hamish took the lead as he pushed the wheelbarrow carrying their luggage.

Upon reaching the house—really two carriage houses joined together above an archway leading to an empty stable—each of the occupants went silently to his or her own corner.

Determined to end this controversy, Bruce decided he would first go to his study to read the bundle of letters that had accumulated during his absence.

He had scarcely opened the first one when Hamish appeared at the door. "Reverend!"

Bruce sighed. When his stepbrother addressed him as *reverend*, it meant someone of whom Hamish disapproved was close by. He waited.

"A liddy to see ye!"

Talking broad Scots into the bargain, Bruce noted.

"I tellt her ye were busy but—"

"I do beg your pardon, Reverend MacAlister, but your man here didn't quite interpret my message properly."

Hastily Bruce rose from his desk, scattering the letters and papers onto the carpet.

"Madam?" A smile transformed the otherwise serious face, and suddenly Bruce was recalling the brief, happy days following Mary Jean's birth, days he had pushed to the back of his mind, because they usually also brought memories of days and black nights he preferred to forget.

He moved quickly to the other side of his desk. "Miss Faye Felicity Gordon?"

"The very same. May I sit down? It's quite a walk from the town."

"Of course. Of course. Excuse our ill manners. You've fairly flummoxed me. Hamish, this is Miss Gordon, a dear friend of Granny Mac's and, of course, of Jean's. You've heard me speak of her often enough, I'm sure. Miss Gordon, this is my brother, Hamish."

Faye Felicity stepped up to Hamish, hand extended. "How do you do, Hamish? You must forgive me. I should have known who you were from Jean's letters and from, well—"

Hamish barely touched the fingertips before turning to pick up the fallen papers. "I'll bring the tea."

"Well, when did you—?"

"I didn't know you—" Faye Felicity laughed, and Bruce gave a mock bow.

"Ladies first with the questions."

"I can answer yours then. Auntie Mac didn't know that we— I mean that I—was coming to Scotland so soon, and she may not have mentioned I had gone on furlough straight to York-shire. After ten years in the swarming streets of Calcutta, the Yorkshire dales, heavenly enough for about two days, began to pall. Now, you!"

"I haven't been through all my letters yet. Although I was in Glasgow a week ago, Granny Mac and I scarcely had time for a word together." Rifling through his letters as he spoke, now Bruce brought one out from the bundle. "Aye, here's one from her, right enough. But is that all you have to tell? Ten years on the mission field in Calcutta, a journey home, a week in York-shire, and a few short sentences to bring me up-to-date?"

Faye glanced round the comfortable room, and her eyes stopped on the ivory writing tools before she answered, "I'm sure you don't need all the details about Calcutta at this mo-ment. I was hoping to stay for a day or so and—" Bruce was gazing at her, his brows furrowed in their familiar pattern. Questions toppled over one another, but he kept them in. There had to be much more. Something was strange about all this! Jean had described this woman, who had been such a vital part of her life, as outright and straightforward. Though Bruce had never paid much attention to Faye Felicity until now, today he examined her carefully. His searching gaze discerned much, delving beyond the facade of pebbled spectacles and tightly rolled brown hair, liberally sprinkled with gray. He found him-self calculating her age. She must be over forty. Her complexion held a dusky tinge from the climate of India.

"Do I present such a dilemma to you then, Reverend?"

He felt the blood rush to neck and cheek, something that had not happened for a long time. "Forgive me, I shouldn't stare so. It's just—"

"I haven't meant to impose on you and should certainly have sent some warning, but formalities fade in the environment from which I have just come."

Hamish entered with the tray and would have left again, but Bruce called, "Stay a while, Hamish."

"I've a lot to do, and the bairn'll be waiting."

Ignoring the first part, Bruce said, "Tell her to join us here as well."

Shaking his head, Hamish walked out, and Faye raised expressive eyebrows.

Bruce tried to explain: "Our manners are terrible, but we've been having a wee bit of an upset." She busied herself with the tea things.

"I believe I've some inkling of why, and that is one of my reasons for coming so, well, without invitation, or—"

Bruce waved that aside.

"As they say in the best of society, cream or lemon, Reverend?"

"All right, we should settle something at once. If you're to stay here, even for a short visit, oblige me by calling me Bruce."

"I will, if you call me Faye."

"Agreed. Now I'll have three spoons of sugar and a dottle of cream, if you please. No lemon. I didn't know we had such creatures!"

"You don't. I was being facetious, and I'm sorry." Smiles crossed both faces as the two began to sip their tea and nibble on the pancakes lavished with butter and jelly that Hamish must have scrambled together in a hurry. Faye placed her cup carefully on its saucer. She had already noted the china, a MacIntyre heirloom and part of Jean's dowry.

"Before your Hamish returns with the child, I must tell you that I made a quick visit to my niece Agatha Rose's house." Bruce raised his brows but said nothing as she continued, "The moment I realized what had happened I decided to come at once to Cairnglen rather than wait. Ah, Agatha Rose is behaving like the spoiled little girl she sometimes is, and Peter, I'm amazed at one whom I considered a most enlightened individual as well as a modern physician having such a single-track mind."

Bruce held up his hand, and she stopped speaking, "I'm sorry Miss—er, ah—Faye, but please don't be laying judgment on Peter. None of us know what we might do if faced with a similar situation."

"I think I know what *you* would do. Auntie Mac has told me all about the happenings in Inverechny, when Jean died and you were thrown to the lions of the kirk session and subsequently out of your pulpit."

Bruce's laugh held no humor. "Did she not mention my temporary insanity then? How I managed to malign every person who offered to help me, including your Auntie Mac and my own mother? Even Agatha Rose, an innocent bystander, came in for some of my wrath when she accompanied Jean's granny to Skye for the funeral."

"Yes, I've heard all of that. I also know you came out of it and immediately resumed your ministry. It's been *five years* since Peter and Agatha—"

Bruce raised a protesting hand. "Please, stop. I see no edification in this comparison. The matters you speak of are not even similar."

They sat in silence for a short time, then Faye spoke again. "I can leave as soon as Hamish comes back. I've taken a room at the inn. A few days' holiday in your glorious Trossachs may help me reach your level of calmness and recover from this attack of anger at my relatives. I have some other private concerns I had hoped—"

For a moment Bruce thought she would crumple into tears, but she rallied as he said, "Forgive me, Faye. I have no business to criticize you. Of course you must stay here at the manse and not the inn. You must have noted how spacious it is?"

"Yes, I did notice, and I sense quite a story. Maybe you can tell me about it before I travel back. However, I must decline your kind offer. The proprieties must be followed, and I couldn't stay here."

"There *is* quite a story about our coach-house manse. As far as the proprieties, they bother me not a whit, but you must do as you think best. Now at least join us for meals. Hamish is a wonder with tatties and herring and other Scottish delicacies."

"Thank you, Bruce. I will, on one condition, that I'm forgiven for my earlier ill-chosen words."

"Say no more on the subject for the time being. I hear Hamish and Mary Jean. She has taken the incident of Jeremy hard, and I must ask you to—"

"Yes, I understand, please trust my discretion and compassion."

"Hush, now. They're here." The door opened, and Hamish entered the study, but he was alone and seemed flustered.

"She'll no' come in. She says she has to make up for lost time with her music lessons."

Faye and Bruce looked at each other. Bruce rose. "She's got no need for lessons the now. This nonsense has gone too far. 'Tis bad enough she's ill-mannered to you and me, Hamish, but did you not tell her who our guest is?"

"I did so, but—" He addressed a disappearing back as Bruce swept from the room and ran up the stairs.

Hamish started to follow, then stopped to glance at the visitor. "You'll excuse us, mistress?"

"No, Hamish, I'll not excuse you. I believe your reverend brother should handle this himself. Besides, I have something I want to ask you."

Hamish glanced doubtfully from her innocently inquiring face to the open door. What should he do?

"Now, let them be, and tell me about this wonderful coach house and how it became a manse."

Hamish turned back in to the study. Yes, he had been told the story of the house and how it became a manse. He would tell this nosy body, who was stubborn into the bargain, all he knew.

"I'll show it to ye fae the ootside first then, if you please."

Following him obediently through the door and down the three huge boulders that formed the steps, she immediately found herself in the garden. Similar boulders marked a pathway to the corner, and Faye guessed, all round the building. But the arched opening, wide enough for a stagecoach to pass through, intrigued Faye. A trellis, promising a profusion of climbing roses, decorated both sides of the arch and joined at the top. Similar trellises adorned either side of the doors. Beyond these ran a herbacious border, a multitude of buds just showing beneath its verdant leaves. Years in India had made Faye most appreciative of this lushness in her native land.

A sigh, a mixture of wonder and exasperation, did not escape her guide's notice. "The flooers'll be oot in a week or twa. They're bonny!"

"I'm sure they are, Hamish. Did you plant all these?"

"No' me. I make sure the weeds ar no' takin' possession and that the ivy stays inside its boundaries, as Bruce would say. The liddy that built the place had gardeners an' aw thing."

"It must keep you busy?"

He glanced at her under lowered brows. That question, or ones like it, were asked him quite regularly by the women of the parish. Those who knew better left it now, but at first his life had been plagued by them. He changed his usual answer. "It does that, I'm glad to say."

"Bruce tells me you're a good cook, too."

If he noticed she said *Bruce* and not *reverend*, he let it pass. "Och, he's easy pleased, and hunger makes good kitchen."

"Humble as well, I see. Hamish, tell me more about the lady who built the house."

"Well, it's only aboot fifty year ago, and she was ane o' them that wait on the queen, ye ken?"

Faye smiled as she murmured, "Lady-in-waiting."

"Aye, that's it. She was to get marriet and stay here, but he deid."

Faye sighed again at this understatement. Such a weight of true-life drama contained in one short sentence.

Hamish kept talking: "Efter that, it was empty for a while,

and she deid hersel'. She had nae kith nor kin, and she left this hoose to the kirk for a manse. They canna' sell it for the siller, Bruce tells me." They had reached the back porch, and Faye noted the neat rows of sprouting vegetables and some fruit bushes. A clothesline fluttered with the usual array of garments, and Hamish hastily tried to lead her back under the arch.

"As I said, Hamish, you must be busy with this big house, and already you've done a washing since returning from Aribaig."

" 'Tis a big hoose, but we keep the one side shut, except when Elspeth comes—or Mistress MacIntyre."

"Elspeth?"

"Aye, she's the Reverend Bruce's mither and me faither's wife."

"Oh, yes, I see. I should have known that. Does Mistress MacIntyre come often?"

"Och, no. She's only been the once, when Mary Jean got the prize at school. I'll need to get in noo. I've the dinner to make, and he'll be needin' me."

"Let me help with dinner. I'm not used to idling my time either."

"It's a' ready." He disappeared through the porch doors, and she was left to gaze at the uncluttered landscape.

A longing to tramp over the moors swept her. Would the stern hielandman, as Auntie Mac used to call him, offer to be her guide, if she asked him? Maybe that would offer a better opportunity for her to reveal the true reason for her visit. Earlier, hesitation to mention it had overcome her, because she wished to find out for herself if Bruce MacAlister could be all others said he was. She still had to confront and be confronted by his daughter, Mary Jean MacAlister.

--·◦◦⦃ **6** ⦄◦◦·--

"**H**ow do you do?" The tiny voice greeting her was barely audible, and Faye had to lean close to hear.

"I'm very well, thank you, and I'm pleased to meet you, Mary Jean. I was your mother's friend, you know."

"Yes." A nudge from Bruce brought a few more words from his daughter. "Aye, I know, Miss Gordon." Wisely Faye did not press further.

As Bruce spoke the simple grace Faye Felicity recalled those times when she had been living at Strathcona House and he had been a divinity student. *What a fine person he was—and still is. No wonder Auntie Mac gave him preference above the others,* she thought. In her work as a missionary nurse, Faye had met a great variety of ministers. She knew well the leaning toward conceit some of them had, but it seemed entirely absent in Bruce.

Coming back to earth with a jolt, she found Bruce gazing at her expectantly. "Would you like that Miss—er—Faye?"

She laughed. "I'm sorry, Bruce, I was in a brown study. Could you also please stop calling me Miss-er?"

His guarded answering laugh still caused Mary Jean to sit up and to show a reluctant interest. What was this? Uncle Hamie didn't call her daddy Bruce, and everyone else except Gran'-speth and Gran'drew, and of course the greats, called him Reverend. Maybe this ugly old woman would need to be watched.

Faye was answering Daddy's question. "Yes, indeed, Bruce,

I would like to see more of your town. From what I've seen, I already have some understanding of why Sir Walter used the area as background for *Lady of the Lake*, but why call it the Trossachs? It seems such a dull name."

"The name might sound dull, but the scenery is far from that. The word means 'bristling country,' and you can see why with the trees and the bonny glens. Not so majestic as Skye or the rugged mountains round about Aribaig, my old home, but it's more gentle, designed for people."

"Do I detect a poet hidden inside Bruce MacAlister then?" This time his laugh rang out hearty and strong, and Faye's heart skipped a beat as she caught a glimpse of what Jean had adored in this man. What a tragedy!

"Poet indeed, not at all! Jean was the one inclined that way, and she never got to finish anything." The others at the table watched with growing alarm as one after another unspoken rule crumbled. Never had they heard him be this expansive about Mary Jean's mammy.

The child forgot herself enough to remark, "You never told me my mammy was a poet, Daddy!"

Bruce gazed at his precocious daughter for a long moment before responding, "Likely because she wasn't one in the real sense of the word, Mary Jean. She used to write pages and pages about her life in India and Strathcona House. She also wrote a lot about Skye."

Mary Jean wanted to hear more: "That's what's in all the notebooks then?"

Faye had picked up some of the undercurrents. The child was not so deeply in Bruce's confidence as she had first supposed, not concerning Jean anyway. Thinking it time to change the subject, she said, "Maybe I'll take a long walk up on the moors tomorrow. If they're as gentle as you say, I shall be able to manage the climbs. Can I coax anyone to come as my guide?" All three spoke at once.

"I could spare an hour in the morning, right enough."

"The hoosework can wait a while."

"I know a short cut to the Dochart Falls."

Faye Felicity understood at once. The other two responses had nothing to do with her charm or anyone's desire for her company. She was simply not to be alone with Bruce MacAlister. She would just have to wait and watch for her chance.

By the end of the week, she had been told the unpronounce-able names of so many lochs and bens, seen an endless number of ancient bridges and landmarks, some from before Roman times, and of course, had viewed the truly impressive castle, that she began to feel like a walking encyclopedia. Not once had she been alone with Bruce. She had expected to leave for Glasgow on Monday morning, and if she was ever to discuss the true reason for her unheralded visit, she would have to act quickly. She simply must talk to Bruce alone, and it would have to be Sunday.

While Faye hatched her plan, the lady of the manor unwittingly came to her aid.

Her stay at the Cairnglen Arms, the only establishment in the town worthy to be termed as a hotel by Cook's Tours, had not gone unnoticed by the local gentry. On Friday, when she had returned from her day's outing, which always ended in a feast provided by Hamish, she had been amazed to find a note addressed to her. Bursting with curiosity she ripped open the rich vellum envelope.

> Dear Miss Gordon: Forgive the familiarity, but it is difficult to avoid in a town this size. We are *at home* on Sunday at three of the clock. Could we beg the honor of your presence to partake of afternoon tea. Cordially yours, Grace Mannering (Hon.) . . . RSVP.

Faye's first impulse had been to ignore the invitation. Any unchaperoned woman such as she would surely be in for some form of criticism or even ostracism. The woman knew her name, so she must also know she was a missionary nurse but would not know how her work took her out tramping the streets of Calcutta without escort or chaperone.

On Saturday morning she had second thoughts and scribbled a brief note of acceptance.

The inn was very close to the kirk, and she had good reason to be glad of that when she awoke on Sunday morning to the pounding of rain on the roof. Faye had asked for a room on the top floor, so that she could view the rolling hills from the window, but today the street below was scarcely visible, let alone the view.

Guessing correctly that the "at-home tea" on Sundays would include the manse family among its guests, yesterday she had casually mentioned the invitation while the four of them sat at the dinner table. Bruce had chuckled. "You'll enjoy it, fine. She's a grand old lady, if a bit gossipy."

"You've been to her teas then?"

"Aye, the manse is free to go any Sunday, without invitation. As a matter of fact, I go about once a month, and tomorrow would be a good day to get it over with for this month." Faye watched the two guardians carefully, for so she had begun to call them in her mind.

"Does everyone go?" Heads were shaken vigorously. Apparently not even the fear of whatever they thought she was after could make them endure this tea party, unless Bruce demanded. He didn't, and she had said no more.

Cairnglen, situated en route to Ben Nevis, was listed as a one-night stop with Cook's Tour, so a good few extra worshipers filled the kirk. The lovely pink sandstone and the stained-glass windows were exquisite. Faye would have delighted in discovering more of its history, but her time could not be wasted further.

Joining the brave little band of people splashing their way to morning service to the ringing of the bell, Faye had felt thankful she had brought her mackintosh, much worn in India during the rainy season, and the giant 'brolly provided by the hotel. How would the manse manage to arrive dryshod?

Bruce had insisted Faye sit in their pew, and the two watchdogs had made room for her. While Hamish had handed her a psalter, the man she had heard called Willie the Beadle had pumped the organ bellows, and the congregation had shuffled into silence.

That service was behind them now, and all Faye's questions about the manor house and its occupants had been asked and answered. *Plush* would be her description of the room where they sat, but then, for the past ten years, her living quarters had been of the sparest. She pushed all other thoughts to the background as she sat beside Bruce. He was not a bit awkward, handling the dainty cup and saucer or the tiny cubes of bread-and-butter sandwiches. At last she seized her chance. It was now or never. "Bruce, I must speak to you, and without your—er—um—family in attendance!" She had almost said *guardians*.

His brow furrowed in the peculiar way she had noted a few times during the past days. Then it cleared. "All right. The church in ten minutes. It's never locked, and Willie the Beadle'll not bother you."

Putting on her best company manners, she thanked her hostess and slipped away. She had made a vague promise to speak to the ladies' group about India on some future visit. Vowing privately that indeed she would, if they asked her again after . . . , she glanced at the sky. The rain had stopped, and she politely declined waiting for a ride in the carriage that called for the minister and his family every Sunday, regardless of the weather. Trying to dodge the puddles, she made her way quickly along the roughly paved street, until she reached the church and entered the porch door, just as Bruce had instructed. A few minutes later he followed her in.

Without preliminaries she began. "It's about Raju."

Bruce's amazement registered in the raised eyebrows and a startled, "Raju?"

"Yes, Raju and me. Raju and I to be grammatically correct. We love each other and wish to marry."

Bruce's thoughts raced, and recollections tumbled over each other during the following three seconds. This woman had meant much to his Jean: friend, confidante, teacher. Her presence in his home this past week had stirred many memories, and the words she spoke now brought them rushing back in full force, until her full meaning broke through, then seemed so incredible that he had to stop the rush of words. "Whoa! Wait a minute! Raju Singh and you? This is impossible, I mean—"

Her laugh held a bitter note. "Not you, too? What is so impossible about two people who love each other? Nothing else should be important in the situation." She bit her lips to keep them from trembling. "Raju said that whatever your reaction should be would settle the question for him—for us." Here her stoicism broke down, and the tears came in a torrent.

Perplexed, Bruce rose to pace the floor. They were in the diminutive vestry, and he had automatically seated himself behind the solid oak table he used as a desk, where so many life-changing happenings took place. "Faye, I apologize for my hasty remarks. I'm just surprised, not shocked." He bent to pat her head as he would have done to comfort Mary Jean. Faye leapt to her feet and threw her arms round him. He had little choice but to place his own arms round her as she leaned her head against his chest.

Presently the sobbing eased and she lifted tear-drenched eyes to his. Without the round, pebbled glasses, he saw their true color and depths. Irrelevantly he thought of the chestnuts that would fall from the tree in the lane later this year. Something besides the extraordinary intelligence in her eyes drew his attention. It was a deeply ingrained awareness of the human condition. As Faye drew away from him his thoughts came back to the situation here and now. He produced his ever-ready hankie, she took it and blew her nose. Then like a trusting child, she allowed him to wipe her face.

He waited until she seemed more composed before saying, "Tell me all about it, Faye Felicity."

"I first met him when I met you. Remember Auntie Mac's annual reception? I mean the one for Jean—who had just completed her teachers training—and for the student boarders. Peter Blair had just become a licensed physician, and you—"

"I still had my finals to sit, but it was almost done."

"Yes, well I don't need to remind you of your own actions on that particular night."

"Maybe not, I remember it all. Colonel and Mistress Cameron Irvine, Jean's parents, were on furlough from India. They had their two Indian servants with them. I remember the girl's name, too, *Larissa*. And of course Raju. I understood from Jean and others that those two would be—"

She shook her head. "No, although Jessica Irvine always wanted that to happen. Raju knew why, and the rest of us could guess. Anyway, when Raju and I first met, we felt that spark between us. At first I ignored it, thinking, among other things, it to be an old maid's fancy. Then we fought it separately for years, until at last we admitted it to each other. Still we only felt hopeless futility. When Cameron Irvine succumbed to India and the Punjab and what it can do to a man with his weaknesses, and Jessica returned to Scotland, dragging a heartbroken Larissa, we finally faced up to it. We were working so close together at the mission, I in the clinic and he in the school, where we always had many matters to discuss. No one suspected us for the simple reason that no one would have believed it. If such a thought had ever been voiced, the person voicing it would have been lynched, socially. Something like that would have been, as you said yourself, impossible. A brown wallah and a white angel of mercy?"

She stopped to gulp in a breath, and Bruce asked, "Where is Raju now?"

"At the London mission offices. He awaits my word about your reaction."

"What then?"

"Let me tell it. Raju is the one who opposed me. I had almost to, well, kidnap him to make him see we might have a slim chance of happiness, and then he said if you—if you could approve, we should go on with plans."

"This is incredible. I always thought Peter, I mean that you cared for Peter, who never knew, and that's why you stayed in India so long."

"Auntie Mac has that impression, too, and I did not enlighten

her. Once, when they thought I was jealous of Agatha Rose
having Peter, it was not as they thought at all. I felt jealous of
how smoothly that romance would go, as yours and Jean's did,
and oh, Bruce, forgive me!"

"Nothing to forgive. You're speaking the truth, although it
didn't seem that smooth at the time. Go on."

"We want your blessing. Without it, Raju will go back to
Calcutta alone, and I. . . . No one will understand at all. Auntie
Mac would be horrified, although she would try not to show it
too much, as she likes to think of herself as an enlightened
woman. My parents, especially my father, would die of shock
and cut me off. The money would matter not at all, but he
literally might die of it. I couldn't do that to Mother. My brothers, well, some of them might not care, but the others. . . . And
Peter Blair and Agatha Rose—at one time he might have had
some understanding, but he's changed terribly in his trouble
and changed my niece along with him. They're almost unrec-
ognizable as the couple we knew. His sense of fairness, and
that humor—all gone!"

"Not gone, just buried for a while. I believe Peter will eventually come out of it a better man before God."

"I pray you're right, but in the meantime, you are our only
hope."

"Faye, what can I do or say that will help you? You have just
described in detail the difficulties. I can only speak for Bruce
MacAlister. I cannot change society."

"That's all we ask. Speak, then, for Bruce MacAlister, that I
may take your message to my love."

"You have my blessing. For what little good it may do!"

A light appeared in Faye's face as she walked toward him,
and she fell on her knees at his feet. This woman was beautiful
in her joy. "That's all I need to hear. Raju can do the rest. I'll
take this good news to him. We plan to apply for missionary
service in America, the western states. We can work there together."

"But Faye, that will be almost as difficult as India. Remember
the States have only recently finished their own war about col-

ored skin and different races." He had pulled her to her feet at once, and she now moved across the room to gaze out of the small, stained-glass window set in the granite wall. Only minute portions of the outdoors were visible, but she was seeing nothing.

"I know. Together we can face anything except hurting others. This would hurt my loved ones. They must never know!"

"*Never*'s a long time, and the Lord is good. He still answers prayer."

She turned to face him again. "I remember Jean Irvine MacAlister coming home from an eloped honeymoon and saying to her Granny and me, 'It's our lives, Bruce's and mine. Even if you love us, you cannot live for us.' For one so young she was very wise, and I discern the same kind of wisdom in her child. Oh, I know what you're going to say, Bruce, that this is a different situation. But think, please, is it so terribly different?"

"Actually I was not going to say that at all, but rather, when would you like me to perform this so-secret marriage ceremony? Please Faye, no more tears, and we'd better be getting home to the manse, or they two will be thinking it's *us* that's eloped!"

"What should we tell them?"

"Just the bare facts for the now. We'll tell Mary Jean it's a secret, never to be spoken of unless you yourself give her permission."

"And Hamish?"

"He'll be so relieved it's Raju and not me you've set your cap at. Out you go now, or my reputation in Cairnglen'll not be worth a docken leaf."

7

The atmosphere in the Cairnglen manse lightened considerably. Mary Jean forgot her bad feelings about Jeremy and her fears about Faye long enough to ask countless questions about India and the mission in Calcutta. Did a widow truly throw herself on her dead husband's funeral pyre, as one schoolteacher had said? Did they really worship cows, and did they have the caste system she read about in a book on India? Finally her father broke in with a laugh, as Hamish, too, was listening avidly for the answers Faye Felicity had not yet had time to give.

Bruce protested. "If I can get a word in, I'd like a chance to ask Faye a few questions myself. Not about her past life in India or her future in America, but about the immediate present. Some practical details, for instance."

"Raju is the practical one. He has already changed his name to Ralph Smith. He will wear only his English suits, and with his Oxford accent, he'll easily pass as British. You may have noticed that his skin is fairly light, and his eyes are blue, not black. His genealogy is Aryan Brahmin, you know."

Wondering how he should tell her not to be so defensive, Bruce's brow furrowed. "Enough said! But by *practical* I meant marriage plans, the license and such."

"When we return all that will have been taken care of."

"Good! Enough questions for tonight. It's very late, so Hamish will walk with you to the inn. No doubt you have your own arrangements made to get to the railway station in the morning. May we expect you back in, say a fortnight?"

"Yes, we will write you from London. I cannot tell you how much this means to both of us."

"Then don't try, my dear. I owe much to Raju, or should I begin saying Ralph, and I trust him implicitly. Until then, *au revoir*. Mary Jean!"

"*Au revoir*, Miss Gordon!" Faye opened her mouth to object to the title but Bruce signaled with his eyes to let it be for now as Hamish ushered her out the door. Armed with an enormous umbrella, similar to the one Faye had used earlier, they ventured out into the rain.

Mary Jean, sure that her questions had not been answered, had some for her father. "Daddy?"

"What is it, darlin'?"

"These two people were special to Mammy, were they not?"

"Yes."

"Should I call him Mr. Smith? I mind your telling me how he found your watch for you. How could he do that?"

"I've wondered myself, but I was told not to ask. M'love, your mammy wrote many notebooks about her life in India as a child and her subsequent life at Strathcona House. Someday I'll give them to you to read, but not yet. Maybe we can ask Mr. and Mrs. Smith, when they become that, to stay with us for a wee while before they go to America. Would you like that?"

"I would, Daddy. If Raju Mr. Smith could find your wee watch in all of Glasgow, maybe he could find Jeremy, too."

Bruce gazed at the liquid eyes for a long moment. Was this an olive branch? "We'll ask him when we see him."

Lying on his bed, thinking of those faraway days at the end of his student years in Glasgow and in Strathcona House, Bruce was far from sleep. Some memories were still too painful, and his thoughts veered to the next few weeks. It would be good to see Raju and hear his own version of this courtship with Miss Faye Felicity Gordon. That faraway time when Raju had left to return to India, sailing on the same ship as Faye Felicity, no one had dreamed that the two would wed. Recalling the strange place in the Trongate where he had been so intrigued with the motley brotherhood of Raju's friends, Bruce's hand automatically reached out to the nightstand. Yes, Gran'pa's watch was there all right. Warned not to ask questions about the night when he'd lost it, Bruce never had found out how Raju had recovered it for him. Bruce considered Raju a very special friend—and not only because of Jean. Yes indeed, he would be pleased and indeed honored to perform this marriage ceremony.

"You will marry us then?" Raju Singh, the inscrutable Indian, almost sang the words.

"Of course I will, my friend."

"I wanted that all the time, but I did not dare hope."

Bruce looked offended. "You grieve me, Raju. Why did you not feel you could hope for such a foregone conclusion?"

"Too much time back in the Punjab with Sahib Cameron, I suppose."

"What happened to him, Raju?"

Their talk was taking place in Bruce's study situated above the coach arches. Faye and Mary Jean were closeted with the village seamstress, and Hamish was baking a very special cake. Mary Jean had been duly admired and made much of by this— to her anyway—exotic creature. Sad thoughts of Jeremy seemed to have been left aside for the moment.

Glancing at the door, to ensure they could speak freely, Raju answered Bruce, "The man killed himself with selfishness. He loved the life of a colonel in the army, having the troopers and the servants fulfilling his every whim. Sometimes he would call for the same thing ten times in the course of one hour. He burned out his stomach with too much rich living. The club was his life, but it brought about his death!" Bruce gazed long at Raju, an as yet unspoken question in his eyes. This drama was only too real.

"No, Bruce, I know what you're thinking. Your punch that day had no bearing on his early death. It was exactly as I told you, and Mistress Irvine, Jean's mother, is not too heartbroken. In fact I hear she is to marry an American millionaire."

"What of the colonel's soul, Raju?"

"He would not listen. At the end, when he was unconscious, I prayed and asked the Lord, for Jean's sake, if I could pray in proxy for her father. I did it anyway, but there is nothing to tell us—"

"Nothing! I know. I've had this situation with others, and it is difficult to know how to comfort the family."

"In his case very few cared. It is our Christian duty to love unconditionally, but Cameron Irvine, as a person, was most difficult to love. Once, a very long while ago, he could have had Jean to care, but after she found out about him and Larissa, she despised him."

"Raju, what did Jean find out about Larissa?" Raju gazed for so long at the floor that Bruce got up and walked over to stand behind him. He placed his hand on the other's shoulder. "I'm very sorry, my brother. You should all have hated him."

"His wife did hate him; his daughter despised him; his mother-in-law tolerated him but disliked him strongly—by the way she knows nothing of this. Some of it may be in Jean's journals, but considering everything else, we do have some things to thank the late colonel for. In any case Jean was sent home to Scotland after she made the dreaded discovery. Need I say more? Mistress Irvine never indicated she knew, although I'm sure she did. Her plan to have Larissa and me married was thwarted by Larissa. Strangely enough, that abused girl did love the colonel. He could have tossed her out into the gutter, but he did not. What a tangled web life can be, my friend!"

"Jean knew of all her father's weaknesses?"

"Not the complete story, but of course she had her suspicions, and it finally came out between them when, I mean, after you hit him that day."

"I believe I've heard enough, except that I'm still puzzled Jean told me nothing of this."

Raju was silent for some time, then: "Would you have listened? Cameron's name was anathema to you."

"Well they're both gone now. We know Jean is safe with Jesus. We don't know that about her father."

Raju nodded sadly as Bruce went on, "And you, Raju, all this time you have been so faithful to that family! Now there's Faye Felicity. Who would have dreamed, that day you and I strode through the Glasgow streets on our way to the tryst with Jean, that any of this would be possible?"

Raju laughed softly. "I never dreamed it possible, and I still think we're mad!" Bruce joined in the laugh. "These determined, wonderful women."

"My Gran'pa would say at this point, let it rest there and be thankful. Leave go and let God have His way."

"Ah, your Gran'pa, the wise man from the north!" The laugh turned to a chuckle of delight.

Sobering, Raju had one more request to make: "Wear your kilt, please, for my camera."

A look of concentrated pain crossed Bruce's face. The last time he had worn the kilt had been at his own wedding, and the memories could still pain him. He picked up on the camera before answering, "*Camera?* You're interested in the art of photography then?"

"Yes. It's fascinating. I may make a career out of it in the land of freedom and opportunity. Will you?"

"I will."

The ceremony, with only Bruce's immediate family circle in attendance, took place in the parish church of Cairnglen that Faye admired so much. Love and joy had transformed the bride. As Bruce pronounced them man and wife his thoughts flew to his own wedding once again and what might have been, but his heart was at peace.

Awaiting the arrival of the one-horse closed brougham, hired for the day to take them on the first stage of their short honeymoon, the bride and groom stood before the manse. Raju and Bruce were close together—one so darkly handsome, the other fair as Adonis. For moments neither spoke, and then in a rush they enfolded each other in an embrace. *Men don't cry*, might be what boys are taught, but these two were frankly crying and frankly real men.

Mary Jean, still all dressed up in her blue bridesmaid's costume, ran up to them as the vehicle clattered through the arch. "Come back and tell me more about my mammy, Mister and Mistress Smith!"

Clasping his daughter's hand tightly, Bruce watched the carriage disappear over the brow of the hill. Behind them Hamish waited for Mary Jean to join him for some ploy they had planned for the rest of the day. Bruce patted her hand as he let her go. His thoughts dwelled on Raju and Faye Felicity. Once again Bruce was indebted to his Indian friend. Whatever he had said to Mary Jean during the short time they had spent together this morning had brought the final vestiges of antagonism crashing down and away. He felt certain his daughter would now be ready to reason it out together, and they would be restored to their usual camaraderie.

His mind switched to a remark made by the beadle this morning, when he, Cairnglen's minister, had arrived at the kirk, fully resplendent in MacAlister dress kilt and sporran and ministerial collar, to perform the wedding ceremony for his friend.

Willie Gillespie had muttered, "Yon furriner?" When Bruce challenged him, he would only say, "Not for me to say, Reverend, but ye micht be hearin' fae the kirk session!"

Thinking, *Oh no, not again*, Bruce had quickly absorbed himself in the celebrations.

Now it came back clearly to his mind, and he called to Hamish and Mary Jean. "I'll change clothes and go to the kirk for a wee while." This was not unusual for a Saturday afternoon, nor were the responses.

"Aye," from Hamish.

And from Mary Jean, "All right, Daddy."

He did not go directly to the vestry cum office but stood outside for a few minutes. This would serve the double purpose of bringing Willie to find out what he wanted and would also give him the opportunity to take a closer look at his church

building. Faye Felicity had described it as built of Carsehill sandstone and probably late seventeenth century, miraculously surviving what she had termed as "the maniacal rush of the Puritan
menage." The moldings inside were dated from a more recent
period, she had said, and he did know some of that history,
although details escaped him for the moment. Something latent
within leapt as he stood in the nave, looking into the sanctuary.
Man doing his utmost to please God was recorded here in these
ancient stones. The sunburst above the pulpit took on a new
dimension, and he wanted to get on his knees and join his own
worship to that which had gone before.

He raised his arms in an instinctive movement of praise just
as the voice behind him said, "Were ye needin' something,
Reverend?"

Bruce had forgotten about Willie. When first introduced to
this zealous guardian of things sacred, he had explained to the
man that he would not wish to be disturbed every time he came
into the kirk, but if he needed the beadle, he would enter by the
front door rather than going directly into the vestry, from the
side. Today he did wish to speak to Willie, but had been so
absorbed in a new admiration for the place it had slipped his
mind.

"It's yourself then, Willie? Yes, I do wish to ask you something. I'm not a man for saying one thing and thinking another,
so I'll out with it and ask you to explain your remarks to me
earlier, before I performed the wedding ceremony of Mister and
Mistress Smith."

"It's no' ma place to say."

"Come, come, Willie. If it's not your place to say, then why
did you say it at all?"

The man glanced at a spot above Bruce's shoulder. "They're
sayin' that the secret weddin' is against the Scripture, an' they'll
be callin' a session meetin'."

"By *they*, I take it you mean the elders, and if the wedding is
a secret, how do so many know about it?"

"They're sayin' yon furriner shouldna' be mairriet tae a white
lassie even if she is an English wummen." Knowing from ex-

perience that logic and common sense did not enter the picture,
Bruce waited for more.

"They're sayin' he's likely been mairriet mair than oncet, and
if he dees, she'll be cremated wi' him."

A startled gasp escaped Bruce. "Is that all they're saying, or
is there more of this, of this *rubbish!*" Biting his tongue, Bruce
recalled how every word, embellished and mutilated, would be
used against him later.

"Och, naw, Reverend! They're sayin' a blight'll come on the
cattle now that a cow worshiper has cast eyes on them. I dinna'
believe that masel'!"

"Thank you, Willie, for the vote of confidence. Will it help
you to understand if I tell you this man is a wonderful Christian
and has been so all his life?"

Willie scratched his head, not comprehending at all. He
doffed his cap and turned to leave. "Will ye be wantin' ony-
thing else, Reverend?"

"No, thank you, Willie. I'll be inside for a wee while, but I'll
see you in the morning."

"Aye. I'll awa' then."

Walking to the front, past the Mannering Heights pew, where
Lady Mannering would be seated on the morrow, Bruce stood
for a time to glance over the partition to another separate pew.
The Galbraith family of father and daughter would no doubt be
there tomorrow also.

"Gunpowder Galbraith!" was the name given to Mr. Drummond Galbraith, Esquire, by the townspeople. Undoubtedly
one of the "theys" Willie had been quoting.

Clearing his mind by the simple method of reciting Psalm 119
from memory, Bruce went directly from that worshipful portion
of Scripture into prayer.

⁓·◦⊰⦗ 8 ⦘⊱◦·⁓

"Today's reading is from the Acts, chapter eight, verses twenty-six to forty." The elder intoning the Scripture happened to be Mr. Drummond Galbraith, Esquire, this morning, and if thoughts could burn, the preacher seated away up there in his pulpit chair would be a heap of ashes by the time the long passage reached its end. Regulars in the congregation had already surmised this was going to be no ordinary Sunday, and even the visitors, some of whom had standing room only, and that behind the twenty rows of designated and ten rows of public pews, also sensed something. This week the Cook's Tour from the inn included a group of the Good Templars from Edinburgh.

The reading over, the congregation settled as comfortably as possible to listen to the glorious words of Charles Wesley as the choir rendered all eight verses of "O for a Thousand Tongues." When Bruce rose to make his address, the shuffling and whispering ceased and a hush descended. His first words were a repeat of verse two of the hymn. He thanked God doubly, first that singing was again allowed as part of the services, and second that the hymn, not chosen by him, went so well with his message's theme. Thinking the Holy Spirit had chosen perfectly, as always, he launched into his sermon.

"My gracious Master and my God, Assist me to proclaim, To spread through all the earth abroad, The honors of Thy name. Amen."

Accustomed to their minister's unorthodox entry into prayer, the resident congregation of Cairnglen was not surprised, but some of the visitors exchanged glances. All that was soon forgotten as the theme of today's sermon broke on them.

"Maybe Philip should have looked again at this black man struggling to understand the words of Isaiah the prophet! Do you think so? Why is this passage in there at all? Holy Writ makes one more mention of this same Philip further on in the book of the Acts of the Apostles. Here he is described as an evangelist as well as one of the seven. So much then for Philip's credentials, meaning his right to interpret God's words for the seeker. More important, Philip was led by the Holy Spirit to go to that place where the Ethiopian would be."

Willie cringed in his seat by the back door, thinking: *Oh, my, we're in for it the day*, as Bruce continued.

"Here I must apologize to every man with skin of a darker shade than my own, than our own. Such a one, or such a phenomenon—meaning something out of the ordinary to us in Scotland—is hardly mentioned in Holy Writ. Or do we think only pale faces are mentioned because only pale faces matter to God?" Until now he spoke in his even, peatty tones, but suddenly he began to speak more loudly. Thumping the pulpit with his clenched fist, he winced in agony. He'd forgotten the old injury again.

He thundered, "No, a thousand times, no! Different races and kinds are scarcely mentioned in Scripture, because God scarcely recognizes them as differences. In His sight we are all the same. We all matter. Philip cared nothing for the color of the man's skin when he climbed into that chariot. It is my contention that he never even noticed. He was too intent on explaining Isaiah's words to the Ethiopian seeker. The Holy Spirit had sent him for that purpose.

"Do we think the Holy Spirit doesn't send or guide men today, because they don't appear or are taken up as Philip was? Does that mean God doesn't act through His people in our time? Certainly not! Without apology or false humility I say I believe I've been sent here as your pastor and shepherd, and certainly I pray God I've fulfilled that call. But there is another call I fear I may have neglected until now!" His eyes roved over his flock as he said the last phrase. Some of them shuffled uneasily under his gaze, but a few sat enthralled.

"Evangelist! The picture in your minds this very minute is likely one of a fiery speaker on top of a soapbox on a street corner in Edinburgh or Glasgow!" Concerted gasps drew Willie's gaze away from the preacher for a second, but he returned it at once, sure that nobody was going to leave this kirk while the MacAlister was speaking, and he wasn't done yet.

"*Evangelist* means that, too, of course, but it also means much, much more. It means the teller of good news! It means the bell ringer who brings in the poor in spirit from the hedges and the fields. It means, as the angels sang at His birth, 'Behold! I bring you glad tidings of great joy.' It means the joy bringer, the bearer of such superlative news as the world has never before heard."

He quieted for a moment as if to absorb this himself, closing his eyes. When he opened them again, his smile was dazzling. "That is what Philip did! Let me read that bit again, and just because he did, listen now, hear what happened, '. . . And when they were come up out of the water . . . and he [meaning the dark-skinned Ethiopian eunuch], went on his way rejoicing.' You see, Philip had told him about Jesus and His love for all the world! Philip had told him how Isaiah's words foretold a Savior whose blood would be shed, whose body would be whipped and scourged for the sins of that world—how that blood, being shed, would be for all mankind, for all of us seated here, even you, even me. Philip had told him of the resurrection of the Lord Jesus Christ and that He is risen, victorious over hell and death.

"Hallelujah! Why should he not have been overjoyed after hearing such news? Yes, he should, and so should we. We also know of that great resurrection day.

"We, too, should be rejoicing, but first, let us see to our hearts. Now I speak not only about the different species of man whom our Great Creator made in His image. I speak of denominations, of creeds, of different spellings of the same names, yes, even of our clans. 'Tis glad we are that the dark clouds of the Inquisition are gone. They are gone, are they not? We must do more than pray about that. We must search our own hearts and make sure. Make sure such days are gone, never more to return. Before closing with verse two of the hymn again, I'm going to ask something I have neglected to ask for far too long. If anyone listening to my voice, young or old, is not sure of having received that cleansing from the blood and through it His so great salvation, I beg of you, see to it today, this very hour, indeed before another minute goes by. Next week, even tomorrow, might be too late!"

Willie rushed forward to start the organ bellows. Everything was unusual this morning. Fancy him wanting to end with a song! The choir leader ignored Willie and struck a note with his tuning fork, and the powerful words again poured forth. Something had happened to the singers, and an observer could have noted they now meant every word. However, no one was observing, each one busy with his or her own thoughts. A commotion brought some eyes open, but it was only Drummond Galbraith rushing from the kirk, closely followed by his daughter, haughty skirt swishing the bare floorboards. They almost collided with Lady Mannering, who, her eyes blinded by her tears, was rushing the other way. One of her attendants held her arm to lead her up to where Bruce now stood at the bottom of the pulpit steps, his hands stretched out toward her.

Willie the Beadle brought the note to the manse door next morning. He didn't know what it said, but he had a good idea. He waited for a reply. This was addressed to "Mr. Drummond Galbraith, Esquire," and Bruce had written: "I will be pleased to meet you in the vestry at seven o'clock this evening, as you request. Bruce MacAlister."

"A masterful sermon, Reverend, masterful! Maist needed for thae sinners."

Bruce nodded and waited. He knew this man; this factory

owner had not called him here to congratulate him on his sermon. More was coming.

"We havena' heard the likes for many a year in Cairnglen."

Bruce spoke up. "I regret that, and I promise you it will be different from now on."

"Now! Now! I'm not complainin' about the sermons in the past. They've been fine, just fine. The complaint is for the now. Masterful as I said, and no doubt meant for ignorant sinners and not for your faithful congregation."

"It was meant for everyone, including you and I. As the Word says, 'He that hath an ear, let him hear. . . .' "

"Aye, that can work both ways, Reverend. For ye or against ye. I'm here in obedience to the Word myself. Correct me if I'm wrong, but does it not also say somewhere that if two folk have a fault between them they should discuss it privately?"

"That is correct. 'Twas Jesus' own words, recorded in the Gospel of Matthew, chapter eighteen and verse fifteen, I believe. Have I trespassed against you then, Mr. Galbraith?"

"Aye, you have that. . . . Apart from your rantin' in the kirk yesterday and gettin' Lady Mannering so excited that my daughter, who's a friend of the daughter at the manor, tells me that they had to send for Doctor Shaw. But I said, apart from that altogether, you've been at the rabble rousin' again!"

Bruce's brow wrinkled in genuine perplexity, but he awaited further enlightenment.

"Ye may look puzzled, but ye're kennin' fine what I mean. They laborers in my factory heard o' the sermon on 'all men being equal,' and they're at it again with their demands. Ye'll mind of a similar situation a few years back?"

Bruce did "mind" only too well. In that particular sermon he had inadvertantly used the word *explosive*. Seemingly the man standing in front of him had not forgiven that slip; however he still had not reached his reason for requesting an interview.

"The point of the matter is this. Somebody went at once to O'Mulligan and told him of your words, givin' the impression that you are in favor of a rise in wages to equalize pays." If the factory owner had taken a glance at the minister's face, he might have recognized the signs—blue eyes flashing fire, brows fur-rowed deeply.

His first real clue might have been the voice picking up a different timbre: "Equal to what, Mr. Galbraith?"

"The Irish laborers want the same as the tradesmen. 'Danger pay' they call it, but that's naught to do wi' us the now."

"Nothing to do with us? I don't understand. Isn't that why you wished to speak to me then?"

"I'll take care of that. I want you to retract what you said about all men being equal. That's a most misleadin' statement, and ye ken fine it's no' true."

"No, I do not know that. I certainly know that God, in His infinite variety, has created each one individually. But in His sight, spiritually speaking, all men are indeed created equal."

"That's right! That's what I mean. Admit to the men at the meetin' the morrow what you just said. *In God's sight* and *spiritually speaking.* If you explain that to them and take back what you said about the black folk and the Catholics and all being equal."

"Wait a minute, my words are being twisted now, as they were when I preached on the talents. I can retract nothing I said yesterday, although I will speak at your meeting to clarify some of what I did say."

Slightly mollified but by no means satisfied, Galbraith turned to leave. "Right ye are, then. If you say the right words, ye'll not be sorry, but on the other hand—"

Bruce gazed at the man, his glance as cutting as his voice. "Are you threatening me, sir?"

"Not at all, not at all! We'll wait 'til after the meetin' the morrow."

Bruce sat on, listening to the sounds of Willie speaking to Galbraith as he escorted him from the building, but hearing nothing. Yes, he would speak to the factory workers, and what he had to say would surprise them even more.

9

Describing it all later, Bruce could never be sure whether it was the earth-shaking blast of the explosion or the flash that filled the sky, lighting up the whole glen, that woke him. Hamish claimed that a terrible thunderclap, loud enough to wake the dead, was his first inkling. Whatever it was, they met at the foot of the stairs, moments later, and raced for the door, pulling on clothes as they ran. Mary Jean, her long nightgown billowing out behind her, followed them quickly. All waited while Bruce located the direction and the source of the disturbance.

"It's the factory, of course, and there are more buildings waiting to go up! Hamish, you stay here with Mary Jean. I'll have to go. Help'll be needed as well as comforting, I'm afraid."

Mary Jean screamed, "You're not to go and leave me!"

He turned to her, his tone unusually sharp. "Yes, I must. It's my place to go. Do not make things worse, Mary Jean."

"My friend, Dorrie Henderson, her daddy'll be there. He's a night watchman at the works." Mary Jean, a dreamer and a lone person at heart, nevertheless had one special friend in the Cairnglen school: Dorrie Henderson. Yes, Dorrie's father did work the night shift at Galbraith's.

A bit hesitant, Bruce glanced at Hamish, as they both sat on the bench, lacing their boots. Mary Jean was buttoning her own as Hamish spoke, "You'll need me to help as well. She'll be fine at the Henderson's. I'll take her there first, and Mary Jean, you'll need to let us go then."

"Aye!"

The Henderson house was in turmoil and not altogether because of the happenings outside. Mary Jean hesitated at the
door. The noise from within was terrifying. Hamish had left her
at the end of the street. Those company houses had no garden
in the front, and the doors opened directly off the street.

Mary Jean had been here once or twice before, and she liked
Mistress Henderson, who reminded her of Gran'speth in some
ways. But she had never stayed long, as the other children were
noisy and messy. She felt sorry for her friend and had invited
her to the manse, but Dorrie could never come, because she
always had to watch one or more of her wee brothers and
sisters.

A month ago, just before they went away for the holidays,
Mary Jean had remarked to Dorrie that her mammy was getting
fat. Dorrie had looked at her strangely and said, "She always
gets fat, and then we get a new brother or sister!" Mary Jean
had said no more at the time.

Screams met her ears now, and as the knock on the door had
been ignored, she opened it cautiously. A huddle of terrified
children overflowed from the big bed on one side of the fire-
place, while on another similar bed Mistress Henderson lay
screaming without pause.

Dorrie spied Mary Jean and ran to her side. "She's havin' the
bairn, and the works 'sploded, and my daddy might've been killt!
He aye said it would blow up someday." Mary Jean's eyes were
big as saucers in her small face as Dorrie kept talking. "Oor Jimmy's awa' to get Mistress Keenan."

"He might not so be killed, Dorrie. Is your Mammy all right?"

"She's awright. Mistress Keenan aye comes. She'll tell us to
go to sleep, an then we'll wake up, an' we'll have a bairn an'
she'll tell us whit it is. Mary Jean, you look funny. Whit's
wrang?"

"I've never been. I mean I haven't seen that before. Maybe I
should go back home?"

"Don't go. You didna' tell me what ye came for, but I s'pose
your daddy went to the works, an' yer uncle as well."

"Aye!"

"That terrible big bang started it—my mammy's pains, I mean. There she is again. I wish Jimmy would hurry up wi' Mistress Keenan." The human mound on the bed started moaning, and the moans grew in volume until her terrible shrieks filled the room once more. They seemed to fill Mary Jean's very mind. From the other bed echoing screams came from the smaller children.

An older boy, whom Mary Jean knew to be Jimmy, ran in. "The midwife's at the works. Her man says they need her to help the doctor. I'm away as well, Dorrie. Mind you, I work there masel'." He made for the door again as he spoke.

"But Jimmy. What aboot Mammy?"

"You ken whit to dae, Dorrie, and Mary Jean's here, I see. She can help ye." With that, he disappeared.

The moans from the woman had subsided again, and Mary Jean was startled to hear a small weak voice say, "I heard Jimmy, and I'll tell you lassies what to do. There's not much time. Dorrie, you show Mary Jean where the milk and the loaf is. Warm it up and make them some saps. They'll go to sleep then. That's it, aye." Mary Jean followed Dorrie to the press under the window. They both did as the woman had directed, and sure enough quite soon the little ones were asleep.

Mistress Henderson called out again, "Now, Mary Jean, you've never seen a birthin', but you'll see one the night, because Dorrie'll need your help. Dorrie, ma wee hen, reach under the bed for the box. Everything you'll need is in it. Oh my, it's startin' again, and the bairn'll be here any minute."

In the emergency of the moment Mary Jean forgot everything and just did all that Dorrie told her to do. Not until her friend announced, "It's a wee laddie," did she stop to think. She had handed cloths and other items from the box as Dorrie demanded, and now it was a huge pair of shears. A gasp escaped her as Dorrie cut what looked like a thick piece of skipping rope and then tied it off. Next she picked up a slippery morsel and thrust it at Mary Jean. It wriggled and immediately joined in the shrieks.

"You haud him, and you can gi'e him a name as weel. We've nane left."

"David John, son of thunder!" She whispered to the yelling infant, and now she didn't seem to be bothered with the noise for the wonder of it. Amazed, she pulled her glance from the miracle in her arms and looked at the clock on the mantle. Six o'clock in the morning, and daylight was creeping through the tattered blinds on the window. For the first time since entering her friend's little house, she thought of the catastrophe that had brought her here. Her daddy and Uncle Hamie, and Dorrie's daddy, too, what could they be doing?

A bustle at the door brought everyone awake except the exhausted mother on the bed. They all waited, silent now, for the door to open and for what that might bring. They gazed, fascinated, as the latch began to move, oh, so slowly.

Bruce had prayed as he ran, his thoughts chaotic. "O Lord, I don't like this at all. The day I toured the factory buildings, I knew there was more they weren't showing me. I heard once that the powder mills had been condemned, but the owners—and the workers, too—had pleaded in seventy-five that if it had stood for thirty years with no explosions, so it could stand for another thirty. Sean O'Mulligan warned us that the buildings were too close to each other, and a blind donkey knows that, but we couldn't or didn't do anything about it. Lord, I just pray no one is maimed or killed. O God, I don't know how to pray. Help us, Lord Jesus!"

Men and women poured out of the town, falling in behind him and some beside him. One of these, puffing and blowing but still managing to get a word out, gasped, "I've kent this would happen, and I was right, Reverend!" Bruce twisted sideways, but the slight Irish lilt told him the voice belonged to Father O'Mulligan. The statement needed no answer, so he merely nodded as he ran. His thoughts exactly, but futile now. He noticed the priest had taken time to don his collar and cassock, while he felt most undignified, shirtless under his house jacket and wearing the Indian cotton trews presented to him by the happy couple—was that only the day before yesterday? They had reached the huge factory gates and they slowed to a walk as they spotted the crowd milling about aimlessly.

Hamish ran up to join him just as the gatekeeper announced, "Tha main buildin's awa', and they're keepin' folk back fae the other buildin's, as they could go up like a box o' matches ony minute." The words were barely out before another earsplitting explosion rent the air. For a while, the two preachers were busy quieting the women and some of the men.

A voice Bruce recognized could be heard, raised above the din, in an argument with the guardian of the gate. "My daddy's in there, an' my mammy's bad!" Suddenly the lad—Bruce now saw it was Jimmy Henderson—ducked under the gatekeeper's arm and tore across the yard.

"Jimmy Henderson, you come back here!" The man yelled but made no attempt to chase the lad.

Bruce pushed his way to the front. "Is there nothing we can do to help put the fires out?"

"There's nothing to be done. Mr. Ogilvie says the men are doin' all they can an' the fire brigade, too. Reverend, you'll do fine if ye just talk to the ones here at the gate. I canna take responsibility if ony mair go in."

"What about first aid?" It was the priest speaking, and the spokesman leaned on his staff as he answered.

"Doctor Shaw's in there along wi' the district nurse. The doctor's big carriage and horses is ower there in the trees. So far I've had no reports of casualties. They're either a' deed or naebody's hurt. I think masel' they all got oot, and they're dowsin' the other buildin's. My orders are to let nobody else by me."

The preachers looked at each other, and Bruce voiced their single thought: "That's too dangerous. They should let it go!"

At the moment a shout came from the crowd as a group of men came hurtling toward the gate. A few women were scattered through them, and the meaning of this was clear, even if the shouted words were lost. Bringing up the rear came Dr. Shaw and Mr. Ogilvie, each bearing someone up. All seemed to be on their feet at least.

Ogilvie's words rang clear, "Get away! Get away! It's ready to go, get yersel's away."

Some of those on the fringe turned to flee, but Bruce waited, along with Hamish and O'Mulligan. He prayed silently, "Dear Lord, show us what to do."

One of the first to reach the gate was Jake Henderson. He stopped short when someone called out, "Did ye see yer laddie, Jake?"

"My lad's no' workin' the night shift. Och, he wouldna' . . . ?" Bruce reached the man.

"Yes, he did, Jake. Where would he be most likely to go? I'll find him for you while you get home. Your wife needs to know you're safe."

"Aye, but I should go for my lad."

"Let me go for him. Just show me where."

"He would go to the main factory, where I usually am, but it's blazin' like hell! Excuse me, yer honors! He'll not get near it for the heat, and the peat underneath is burnin' now as well, but if I know my Jimmy, he'll try." He turned to run back but collapsed in a heap at the gatekeeper's feet.

Bruce ran off in the direction indicated, praying he would not be too late. His heart missed a beat when he saw sparks flying and landing on the building closest to the gate, and at the same moment he caught sight of Jimmy running his way. Next moment the lad lay on the ground, ground already as hot as any furnace. Bruce knew the soil was peat mixed with coal. Lead had also been found here. It could smolder for weeks, maybe months. He grasped Jimmy under the arms, and Hamish, who had been right behind him, took the boy's feet. Bruce glanced backward.

"They say everyone got out. That seems a miracle to me!"

"It'll be a miracle, right enough, but we ken they can happen. Now we'll have to hurry away ourselves."

"I just hope they have an exact count of names and numbers. This young fellow is suffering from heat and exhaustion. A bit undernourished, too, I'm thinking."

"Aye!" They ran back to the gate with their burden. Dr. Shaw directed them to a place where they could lay the boy down while he examined him. The crowd had thinned a bit, and the priest lingered with the others. Rising from his knees, the doctor gave orders for Jimmy to be placed in his carriage beside his prostrate father.

"Get away home now. Nothing more's to be done here."

No sooner had they finished than another crash rent the air. Those remaining turned to run in a body. A lone voice from the rabble shouted, "One more to go, and they're all away." His last words were drowned out as the loudest crash of all lit up the sky for miles.

"Were it not so tragic, it would be a glorious sight!" Bruce ventured the remark as he and the priest ran along the path together.

O'Mulligan answered grimly, "To me it is a glorious sight. No deaths, I hear, and we're well rid of it. 'Twas an eyesore and an eruption waiting to happen, an' that's the truth. Old Galbraith's goin' to have to think up something else to make his fortune, and we'll be havin' a few new rules for him to go by."

The procession wound its way back to the town, falling in behind Dr. Shaw's carriage. The fireworks display was ended.

Cheers had gone up after Mr. Ogilvie finished the roll call, finding none missing. No one complained about equal pay or danger money this night. A sober crowd knew not where its next pay would come from, and most realized that the smell of prosperity would fade with the winds as the fires died down and went out.

Ogilvie knew that tomorrow the fire inspector would arrive, along with insurance folks, and there would be work for a day or two for the able bodies to dig ditches and channels to direct the waters of the Dochart River to cool the underground fires. The cooling-down process would take a while, as the combustible peat and ironstone coal could burn for years, if not brought under control. But all that could begin tomorrow. Nobody was dead. If Galbraith's engineer wondered where his boss could be, he kept it to himself. Galbraith was his own man and often left town for days at a time.

Abruptly those at the head of the long procession of townsfolk stopped, halting the others. A horse was galloping along
the path at full tilt. The rider pulled on the reins with a cruel
tug, and the lathered horse rose on hind legs, panting and
snorting as Miss Evelyn Galbraith leaned forward in the saddle.

Her mouth opened in a snarl of rage. "My father, you bunch
of selfish dolts, where is my father?"

The workmen stared at one another, bewildered.

Ogilvie stepped up to the heaving animal. "We've not seen
him, miss. I'm surprised he's not with you, but now that you
mention it, he should've been here. Has anybody else seen the
gaffer?" He swept the crowd with his arm, and a small man
stepped forward.

"A seen him on his horse when A came off ma shift at ten. A
was late leavin', an' A thought the gaffer was just oot for a
canter."

The girl on the horse slashed her whip at the air, spooking
the horse so that it again rose on its hind legs. Those closest
moved back swiftly. "No doubt you've made sure everyone else
is accounted for?"

The men shuffled their feet, exchanging guilty glances.

Bruce and the priest had remained at the back of the crowd.
He wanted no dealings with Miss Evelyn Galbraith, but now
Bruce felt it was time to intervene. "If your father is missing,
Miss Galbraith, I'm sure we can organize a search party at once,
but before we should risk getting too close to the embers we
should make certain he is not at home or visiting."

"My father is not at home, or why should I be here now? Nor
is he out visiting at this hour of the morning, Reverend MacAlister. I'll thank you to mind your business while my father's
employees take care of searching for him. Ogilvie, see to it at
once. He could be lying hurt and helpless somewhere."

Dr. Shaw, blackened and singed, the same as everyone else
who had been beyond the yard gates, called out, "Miss Evelyn,
let me assure you no human being could still exist within five
hundred feet of yon buildings. We took the count, and if nobody knew your father was about, then how can we tell now?"

"Dr. Shaw! Please explain what you mean."

"I mean, either you're mistaken that Drummond was here, or else he's—eh—no' alive. He couldna' survive in yon blaze. The main offices and storehouse were first to go, and Ogilvie assures me nobody's ever in there at night. If your father was here, and none o' the night shift saw him, either comin' or goin', then I'm sorry to tell you—" His meaning was very clear this time, and for moments no sounds came from the crowd.

Suddenly the woman on the horse screamed out. "If no one else is willing to go and find him, then I'll have to go myself."

The doctor reached for the animal's head, while Bruce stepped closer. "If you insist, Miss Galbraith, we will form a search party, but I agree with the doctor that to go through the gates will not only be futile but dangerous."

"I do indeed insist. All of you here who are employed by my father will return to the factory and make a thorough search for him."

Father O'Mulligan stepped up then. "Sorry, miss, that would be too dangerous. We cannot risk it."

"And who asked you? You Irish bog crawler. Your opinion is worth even less than the Reverend MacAlister's to me. Come along, Ogilvie, and you, Gallagher." No one moved.

"I see. I'll have to go alone then, and if that doesn't show you up for a bunch of cowards! Please unhand my horse, or I'll have no hesitation in riding over you." The doctor jumped as she raised her whip again. As the animal leaped, Bruce was thrown to the ground. Horse and rider disappeared in a cloud of dust in the direction of what could now only be described as seven heaps of smoking rubble. Raising himself ruefully on an elbow, Bruce turned his glance skyward. The sun was beginning to rise, but it would not be seen much today, as clouds filled the horizon to the west. More rain was on the way, and it never had been more welcome.

Hamish and the priest helped Bruce to his feet. "Are ye all right, Reverend?"

"Fine, Father. It'll take more than that to damage this highlandman. What are you thinking—about Galbraith, I mean?"

"What I'm thinkin' is not for public ears. Somebody should catch that daft wummen afore she kills hersel'."

He need not have worried. Evelyn Galbraith stopped short of the gates. The sight meeting her eyes was one of utter destruction and desolation. They were right. Nothing could still be alive within. The tears that coursed down her cheeks now were not for Drummond but for herself. No longer could she doubt that her father had perished with his factory. His parting words rang loud and clear in her mind: "No matter what you might hear in the night, don't dare venture out until morning."

She would have obeyed implicitly, except for that hysterical maid, who had come screaming to her bedroom, "The world's comin' to an end, miss, just like ma granny said it would, and the maister's nowhere in the hoose!"

10

"**I**'ll keep the Hendersons here for a wee while. The lad's eyes are worrying me, and the father got the worst of the first blast, being the closest to the warehouse when it went up. His lungs could be affected." Dr. Shaw had built a shed at the back of his house, which he used at times for patients who needed to be watched while awaiting transport to the hospital in Strathlarich.

During the entire bone-shaking journey to the doctor's house, Jimmy had been weeping and moaning, "I canna see. Oh, Mammy, I canna see!" His father had still not fully regained consciousness. Two other men had complained of sore eyes, and another had hurt his back when part of a roof beam had hit him as he ran.

The doctor spoke to Bruce and the priest, after they and Hamish had helped move the injured inside. He was still talking: "It's a fair wonder there are not more casualties, and a good job it happened in the middle of the night, when so few were working. The warehouse was all locked up at night, and Henderson merely walked round it to make sure there were no prowlers about. Another wonder is that the ones working were three buildings away from the main warehouse and had time to get away after we got there."

Bruce was waiting to leave, and the priest, too, was getting restless. "I'll just go and explain to Mistress Henderson. My daughter is at their house."

"I'll come with you. They are part of my flock, you know."

Hamish had other plans. "I'll be staying here to help the doctor and the nurse. They might need to move the folk that's hurt. After that I'll go directly to the manse."

So together the two men of God arrived at the Henderson door. Not a sound came from within as Father O'Mulligan reached for the latch. Before lifting it all the way, he stopped to say, "There's too many coincidences for my likin'. Would you not be agreein', Reverend?"

"I agree there are quite a few, yes. What point are you making?"

"Nothing I can be sure of at the moment, except that no' only is Galbraith missing, but my upstart cousin Sean, the big union man, hasn't showed his face either. He usually is in the forefront of any excitement, even when he hasna caused it! Och, no, he wouldna'. What would you say to you an me meetin' later on the day, after we've both had a bit rest, and takin' a walk round the Galbraith works—or what's left o' them?"

Bruce's brow furrowed. "Should we not tell Constable Moffat first?"

"No, just you and me 'til we see what's what. I'll not let on to Sean, either, should I see him. He's too fiery and would cause more trouble. I think there'll be trouble all right, but I want to have a look before the inspectors and the insurance and all them get busy."

"I'm not sure it's right. Moffat should be consulted or at least told."

"You're not a coward, I know, so—"

Bruce still wore his frown. "If there's something to discover, it'll surface, without us poking and prying."

"I might as well tell ye I'm worried about Sean. Could ye consider it as a favor then?"

"All right, in the morning. Och, it's morning now. When we've had a rest and a bite, then. I'll meet you at the works' gate." He pushed the door open.

They sat on the edge of the bed, eyes like saucers, and behind them five more pairs of eyes stared out of faces still bleary with sleep. At sight of the priest, Dorrie let out a yell and rushed toward him. Before he could stop her, she was pounding with all her meager strength on his legs.

"My Daddy's no' deed, he's no', nor oor Jimmy eether. They're no'! They're no'!"

The other occupants of the bed set to screaming in echo, and Mistress Henderson sat up wearily, rubbing her eyes. The infant by her side also began to howl as Father O'Mulligan thundered above the din, "What have I landed in then? Is it Bedlam and not a dacent Catholic house?"

The noise did not abate, and Mistress Henderson, recovered somewhat from her ordeal of the night hours, took a hand. "Shut yer faces!" Instant silence rewarded this, except for the newborn, who still had to learn to heed that voice and tone. Its owner turned to the men in the doorway. "Come in, Father, and you, too, Reverend. Dorrie mask a drop tea."

The priest waved his hand. "No tea the now, thank ye, mistress. I'm here to tell ye yer man's just a wee bit winded, an' he's at the doctor's. So is Jimmy."

She glanced at him sharply. "Jimmy's winded an' a'? He wasna even supposed to be there."

"Well, he's at the doctor's. They'll both be home anon. Don't ye be worryin' now. Let me look at my newest parishioner." He picked up the swaddled infant in an expert hand, but the mother was not to be so easily put off.

"Reverend MacAlister. Whit's wrang wi' ma Jimmy?" Bruce's face clouded. He turned to Mary Jean, who had not moved or spoken a word since they entered, although her big, expressive eyes spoke volumes.

"I'm sorry, Mistress Henderson, but we don't know yet. He complained of his eyes hurting, and Dr. Shaw wanted to examine them."

"Oh, I see. He'll not be blind?"

"We pray it won't be that serious and that it will be temporary."

Father O'Mulligan had deftly changed the squalling infant,

and it stopped long enough for him to say, "A braw lad ye have here, Kate. What'll ye be namin' him?"

"Wee Mary Jean gave him the name. It's David John. We'll see whit ma man thinks o' that first, though. We've four of each now."

She lay back on her pillow as Bruce stepped forward. "You're tired. Mary Jean and I should be on our way home. Thank you for letting her stay here while her uncle and I went to help at the factory."

"I was oot o' it maist o' the night, but I mind oor Dorrie sayin' what a help Mary Jean was to her. Baith lassies did a grand job. Will ye take a drop tea then?"

"Some other time. Come along, Mary Jean. Good-bye Mistress Henderson, Dorrie, Father."

The priest gave the child to his mother. "I've changed my mind. A cup of tea would be fine. I'll help myself. Dorrie can make a bit breakfast for the other bairns. Reverend, you'll mind what I said?"

"I will."

They were out and walking swiftly along the street before Mary Jean spoke. "Where's Uncle Hamie?"

Bruce explained before asking, "You helped at a birthing, darlin'? Were you not frightened?"

"Aye, Daddy, a wee bit, but then we had no time to be frightened after, well, you know! It's the biggest miracle, is it not?"

"It is that, my pet, but there have been many miracles this night. So you named the baby David John. How did you pick that name, Mary Jean?"

"He was roaring from the minute he came out, and the 'splosions were so loud, I thought he should be called the Son of Thunder." They smiled at each other, but Mary Jean had a question. "Daddy?"

"Aye, Mary Jean?"

"How did wee David John get inside Mistress Henderson?"

Bruce felt the moisture break out on palms and forehead. They had kept up a steady pace as they approached the lane leading to the manse, but that did not fully account for his perspiration. He supposed no parent was ever ready for this question, but her timing could not be worse. Knowing she was waiting and that their rule of no pretending was always in force, his inner groan turned to a prayer for wisdom and the right words just as Hamish hailed them.

"Bruce! Mary Jean! Haud on a minute." He was puffing and panting along behind them.

Just before he came close enough to hear, Bruce looked down at his daughter, "Can you wait for your answer, pet?"

"Aye! Daddy, I'm sleepy. Can I have a cradle carry?" The three arrived at the manse with Mary Jean seated on the crossed arms of her father and her uncle.

Amazement lit all three faces when they saw the jaunty cart standing under the coach-house arch and they recognized the occupants. Raju and Faye! Allowing Hamish to take Mary Jean's full weight, Bruce ran the last few yards. What could have brought them back so soon?

11

"**M**y wife and I have decided we're not running away to America. Neither one of us truly wants to do that." Raju gazed fondly at his radiant bride for a second, and then, as if the sight were too much for him, he turned back to Bruce and Hamish.

They were gathered in the manse's immense kitchen. Mary Jean had been packed off, protesting, to bed, after Hamish had served them all with a good, hearty breakfast. Remarks had been few until now, as the obvious state of Bruce and Hamish's soot-blackened faces, clothes, and hair, smudged, too, on Mary Jean, had told a lot about their activities during the past hours.

Bruce replied, "Back to Calcutta?"

"Not at once. We'll stay in Glasgow for a while." Faye spoke now, and again Bruce stole a glance at her. What a difference happiness can make! It lit up her whole personality, making her beautiful.

"All right. When you left for your honeymoon on Saturday, I understood you would be coming back in about two weeks for a few days and that you would then be taking passage. You intended to avoid embarrassing or hurting any family or friends who might not have understood. Obviously you've changed your minds, and I assume you are here now to tell us how and why."

Raju picked up the story. "You know about Cook's Tours I believe?"

"We do. There's one comes here every week during the summer. The Trossachs are known as the highlands in miniature and—" The couple started to laugh, and Bruce grinned ruefully. "Yes, I was about to give you a discourse on the area. Tell me, Raju."

"When we arrived at the Station Hotel, in Oban, one of these groups had just come from another train and apparently was booked to stay the Saturday night at our hotel. I had just signed the register as Mr. and Mrs. Ralph Smith!" He stole another glance at his new wife before going on, "The lobby was teaming with folks. Americans and Londoners and who knows what else? The desk man punched his bell, and a dark-skinned fellow came forward to take our suitcases. I was warning him away, when my wise wife here nudged me.

"The man took the bag and led us to the room. After placing it on the floor, he crossed the room and deliberately closed the door, remaining inside and facing us. We watched in amazement and some annoyance. We wanted to be alone. I was just going to ask him what he was doing, when he said, "Mr. and Mrs. Smith, is it? I could have sworn it was Mr. and Mrs. Raju Singh!""

The narrator stopped for breath while Bruce and Hamish sat up straighter in their chairs. Hamish had been dozing, thinking, *Another one with the mouth full of big words*, while Bruce's mind had slumped into a semicomatose state, for want of sleep.

"Yes, Bruce, I see you've guessed. It was one of the brotherhood from Glasgow. He was not a hotel employee at all. In the bustle, the clerk had paid no heed when this man came forward to serve us. It turns out he travels with the tours as a guide and a general factotum. After assuring us he would not reveal our secret, he went away.

"Faye and I didn't know whether to laugh or cry. Soon, however, we reached the mutual conclusion that the Lord was telling us something. There and then we decided. The name change doesn't matter, but the reason for it does. We also decided to come and tell you first. So here we are. Next morning we told Harry—his last name is unimportant, but he is a half-caste from the Bombay area. His father, a Black Watch private, claimed him and smuggled the boy to Glasgow before he was posted to the Crimea, where he was killed in action. The brotherhood inherited him. By the way, he might never have noticed me in the crowd, had I not visited the brotherhood last week to make inquiries about your Jeremy!"

Again Hamish sat up to listen. "Whit aboot Jeremy?"

"They've discovered he was one of a batch of young men—and girls, too—kidnapped recently from the prisons and the streets and bound, not for the army or Egypt, but for one of the Arab countries. Inquiries are going on, and we should have more information soon."

Engrossed in the tale, no one noticed the small, nightgown-clad figure enter the room and stand listening, until she screamed, "A white slave. I just knew it. Jeremy's been sold as a white slave. Oh, Daddy—" The scream turned to a wail of woe as she ran across the room and hurled herself at her father. At first Bruce was not sure if this could be a reawakening of her anger at him, but quickly he realized she was seeking reassurance. Her vivid imagination saw Jeremy in some dreadful situation, and the tender side of her nature could not abide the idea of her good friend being hurt.

While Bruce soothed his daughter, the other three watched in solemn silence, even Hamish inactive for once.

At last Mary Jean's sobs began to subside, and she was able to compose herself with the help of one of her daddy's big white hankies. She blinked her eyes, washed clear as crystal by the tears, at Raju. "He's not dead then, Mr. Smith?"

Raju clasped his hands together in the symbol of prayer and truth. "He's not dead, Mary Jean. In fact our information tells us, that apart from his freedom being taken away, he is being very well treated at present."

"Yes, maybe, but he'll want to be at Mains just the same."

Hamish and Bruce nodded agreement at this childish statement. The hall clock chimed noon, and Hamish rose rather stiffly. "I'll sort the guest room for ye's." No one remarked on this as he left the room. He turned back at the door. "Maybe we should a' have a bit sleep the now and talk some mair efter!"

"So what will you do now?"

"Well, we're going to bring everything out in the open and take the consequences. The first thing we'll do is resign from the missionary society. Then we'll tell Mistress MacIntyre. Her response to our news will decide if we go to Yorkshire or whether we will merely write a letter, informing Faye's family that she is now Mrs. Ralph Smith, with no other details. Whatever happens, we will stay in Scotland for a while."

Faye had kept her eyes glued to his face all the time he was speaking, her pride and happiness open for them all to see. But Bruce had more questions. "And what will you live on?"

"As I said before, I have been studying the camera arts for a few years now. It may be that I can find work or even start a small business. Of course I'm a teacher, and my wife's a nurse, but who would employ—?"

"There's something I would like to remind you of before you say any more, Raju. 'Tis this. You have spent many years in a country where the caste system is very much in force—not only among your countrymen, but in the army and the tea companies, and—face it honestly now—also among the missionaries. I believe we are more tolerant in Scotland. Make no mistake, the class system is much in evidence, but as for your skin being brown, I think not many people will notice or, no offense, mind you, even care. Did it ever occur to you, Faye, that your family could fall into that category and may be less affected than you imagine? The small fuss we had here was merely a one-man vendetta against myself. I've lived through those before, and I can handle Cairnglen!"

The couple sat quite still, very close together, hands clasped tightly.

"Now, speaking of photography, when may we expect to see the pictures of the wedding?"

Raju laughed in delight, just as Mary Jean and Hamish stepped in carrying a tray with coffee and cake. "The great chieftain wants to see himself in his kilt and clerical collar combined!"

Even Hamish smiled at this, while Mary Jean and Faye got a fit of the giggles.

Bruce tried to look offended but quickly saw the joke. "All right! All right! I'm as vain as the next one, I suppose you mean. When?"

"Quite a while yet. We have to finish out the roll, and then they have to be developed. It could be two or three weeks yet."

Faye and Mary Jean had an understanding. Earlier the older woman had explained how her husband, although he could not guarantee it (and she had taken time to look that big word up in the dictionary for Mary Jean), was sure the message received through the brotherhood about Jeremy was good news.

Now Faye poured the coffee into the tiny demitasse cups Hamish had produced from the display cabinet, and Mary Jean served the cake. Into the midst of this happy domestic scene Father Dennis O'Mulligan stumbled. No one heard him as he half ran, half staggered to the open front door. Hearing the commotion in the hallway, Hamish rushed out, closely followed by Bruce and the others. The advent of the unexpected visitors had almost removed last night's catastrophe from their minds.

Bruce reached the priest first. "Calm yourself, man, what's got you in such a state now?"

The priest managed to gasp, "I ran all the road!"

"Never mind telling us what we guessed. Tell us what for when you catch your breath."

" 'Tis my cousin Sean. She's killt him!"

The group exchanged horrified glances, and Hamish muttered, "He's haverin'."

"Tis the truth I'm telling ye, Cormack. That besom o' Galbraith's shot Sean, and I came here to stop a riot."

"Have a sip of this coffee, Father. You're making no sense." The nurse in Faye took charge, and surprisingly the man obeyed as she led him to a chair.

He gulped the hot coffee and then, after carefully wiping his mouth with his sleeve, began again. "Here it is then. When you, Reverend, failed to come this mornin' as arranged, I went round to get Sean. A few other lads came along, and we went to look at what's left of Galbraith's works. I had a feelin' Sean was not his usual self, but when he started to rant and rave about the possibility of Galbraith havin' set the fire himsel' for the insurance, the other lads took up the shoutin', and nothing would do but they maun march to the big hoose to confront him. Miss Evelyn somehow got wind that they were on the way. I tried to stop Sean but he's—was—a thrawn Irishman." The priest turned away as his emotions surfaced. The room was hushed as they all waited for the next part.

"She stood on the steps, holdin' the shotgun aimed at us. Sean was shoutin' that our business was with her father, but she never spoke a word, just pulled the trigger and—" The large man began to shake, and Faye moved to his side with the cup of coffee. He stared blankly.

"I don't suppose ye have a drap o' something stronger? No. Och, sure an' I'll be fine in a minute. Somebody ran for Dr. Shaw, but before he arrived I had time to get down beside Sean. I knew he was done for and prepared to give him the last rites. He managed to catch my hand, and I leaned in to hear his confession. Soon the doctor arrived in his carriage, and he shook his head at the sight of Sean. The other men said not a word, just followed us back to the town. Sean was dead before we got there. Whilest I went to tell Sean's wife and bairns, the union men called a meetin'. When I came out of the house, a crowd had gathered, and the men were in an ugly mood. One spark, an' they'll be up in smoke, and that explosion'll be worse than the other, because there'll be more killin' if we dinna stop them, Reverend."

"What are you suggesting I can do, Father? If you and the constable can't stop them—you did summon Constable Moffat, did you not?"

"I didna' need to summon him. He was there on the fringes, but he's mair feart than the gentry who've a' disappeared."

"Of course I'll come with you, but I scarcely think the crowd will listen to me either. Where is Galbraith, anyway?"

The priest looked off into the distance before replying, "Some are sayin' he's skipped and faur away by now. Others are sayin' he got killt in the blast after settin' the fuse hissel'."

"What do *you* say?"

Still without looking at Bruce, the priest mumbled, "The last is maist likely. He wouldna' benefit from insurance if he ran away to hide somewhere."

"Unless he didn't know about any of this."

"He'd know!"

"Is there a way we could find out? If we could say for certain he was dead, then we could tell the men enough people have died. I'm sorry to hear about Sean. You must be grieving sorely, yet you've come all this way to prevent further bloodshed. Has the law done anything about Miss Evelyn?"

"Not yet. I wonder if they will. About Sean it can't be helped now, and I'm determined to stop any more violence before it happens. Did I notice a vehicle in your close?" As the priest began to regain his customary assurance his brogue lessened in proportion.

"You did indeed! My friends here, Mr. and Mrs. Smith, hired it from Strathlarich Town. What are you planning?"

So it happened that the men left for Cairnglen while Mary Jean and Faye Felicity stayed at the manse. Exhausting the subject of the awful things happening in Cairnglen, the two began to discover each other. "I think I'll be a nurse, too, when I grow up. Mistress Henderson said I was a good helper when she was birthing David John."

"Yes, you would be a good nurse, but you've plenty of time yet before you have to decide."

"Uncle Peter—I mean Dr. Blair—said I should be a doctor. Some lassies are able to do that now. But he's, well, he tells stories." They were seated on the back steps enjoying the sunshine.

"Mary Jean, do you remember much about the times when you went with your daddy and uncle round the coast in your boat? What was its name again?"

"Revelation. Aye, I do remember. I liked that fine. We've still got the *Revelation.* She's docked in the sea loch by Aribaig."

"Have you now? And do you still go out in it, I mean, her?"

"Aye! Sometimes another minister comes here, and we go then."

"Are you going this year?"

"I don't know. We had our holidays when Uncle Hamie got a sore head. It's all mixed up. Harvest has to be done at Mains with no Jeremy. I think we'll not be going this year."

"You're all very fond of Jeremy, are you not?"

"Aye!" Mary Jean turned her head away, and Faye's eyes filled as she thought of this child of Jean's—losing her mother before she knew her and now what seemed the irretrievable loss of her friend.

"Trust Raju and his friends, Mary Jean. It may not be that soon, but I'm sure Jeremy will come home someday."

"Aye!" The monosyllable closed the subject for the time being, so wisely Faye kept quiet.

Mary Jean's next remark came in a whisper. "The priest's own cousin, Mr. Sean O'Mulligan, where will he be the now if he's dead, Mistress Faye?"

Faye almost groaned. Her work in India had often been with children—children much different from the ten-year-old confronting her now, with her big, clear eyes reflecting, at the moment, the topaz ornament she herself was wearing. In Calcutta children were so used to death that they never remarked on it or seemed to notice. Mary Jean moved on the step, keeping her eyes on Faye. "Help me, Holy Spirit," prayed Faye. Evasion would be pointless and could lose the child's trust.

"I'm not sure, Mary Jean. When we don't know people and whether they've believed or not, we cannot speak for them."

"My friend Dorrie says if you're only a wee bit bad you go to a place called purga . . . purga—"

"Purgatory. Yes, this is the belief of some. It is not what we believe, though, as it is not mentioned in the Bible."

"But, if Mr. O'Mulligan believed in it, he could be there, could he not?"

"How can I say he will or will not be in a place I do not believe exists, Mary Jean?" The puzzled frown, so like her father's, furrowed the small girl's brow, and Faye could almost see the next question forming. But before it could be voiced, they had another interruption. Engrossed in each other, neither Mary Jean nor Faye had heard the sound of approaching hooves until they were confronted with a horse and rider emerging through the archway. Faye leaped to her feet, and Mary Jean was already standing when the horse was reined in. It reared as the rider pulled it up cruelly.

Even without hat or coat, the horsewoman who dropped to the ground from the elegant sidesaddle could not be mistaken for other than who she was. Mary Jean whispered aside to Faye, " 'Tis Miss Evelyn Galbraith!"

Faye caught her breath as she recalled the Sunday when she had first visited Cairnglen. This person had been in the pew, along with an older man whom Bruce had later informed her was the owner of the factory. Here she was, then, the woman who, according to the priest O'Mulligan, had killed a man a mere three hours ago.

They waited until the strange visitor spoke. "I wish to see the minister, if you please."

"I'm sorry, but he was called away. Could we help you with anything?"

"No, thanks, not unless you know where my father is or you can bring that fool of an Irishman back to life."

Ignoring the last part, Faye answered the question. "We don't know where your father is. In fact, without guesswork, I'm not even sure who your father is or who you are, either, for that matter."

"Evelyn Galbraith! My father owned the factory—now in ruins, as my life is, too!"

"I'm Faye Smith, and I—"

"Yes, well, I've no time for the social graces just now. I need help, first to find my father and then to convince the policeman that it was an accident when my gun went off and killed that trespassing Irishman."

"Won't you come inside and be seated? Reverend MacAlister

may be back soon." Mary Jean glanced curiously at Faye but made no comment.

Miss Galbraith was looking from the horse as it covetously eyed the succulent vegetable garden, Uncle Hamie's pride and joy, then glanced back to the two females on the doorstep. "I will come in after I tie up this mare."

Mary Jean piped up, "There's the stable. It's empty."

A ghost of a smile crossed Evelyn Galbraith's tense features. "That will do fine." She followed Mary Jean's pointing finger, leading the animal.

Soon she returned and was ushered into the back kitchen; she almost fell into the first chair she came to. Wisely Faye did not demur or insist on using the "company" room.

The woman's next words brought further surprises. "I'm nearly demented. First the explosions and fires, then my father disappears! All the servants have run away on me, and now I've killed a man. I never meant to do that. They'll be coming to arrest me soon, and I don't know where to go or what to do." As those sad words displayed facts already known or suspected, the two listeners refrained from remarks.

Evelyn Galbraith spoke with very little emotion and no true sign of remorse as she continued, "MacAlister's always preaching about Christ's followers being charitable. *Love one another*, you know? I'm here to challenge him on that and to claim sanctuary and protection from the angry mob which, I have no doubt, will soon discover my whereabouts."

Mary Jean's eyes had resumed normal size as Faye took stock of the position. Twice, during her years in the Calcutta mission house, they had been besieged by angry rioters. Faye knew that, no matter what ignited a riot, logic and reasoning went to the winds. She picked up on one phrase. "Your servants all ran off, you say?"

"Yes, the cowards!" She glanced round the kitchen. "I could take a glass of something." Mary Jean walked to the sink and began to work the pump. As the water gushed she heard the uninvited guest continue, "I took the time to lock the doors, and the gateman said he would stay at his post for a goodly reward. Why do you ask, Mistress Smith?"

"It seems to me the first thing must be—apart from the imminence of the law—to find out where Mr. Galbraith can be. Would you consider the possibility of his being a coward, too, and running away?"

"Never! He feared no one or nothing, except maybe—"

"Except?"

"Except bankruptcy."

"Was that a near possibility?" Faye's direct gaze bored into the other woman.

"Of course not. Not that he ever discussed the business with me, although I begged him many times."

Faye insisted, "It was a possibility, though?"

"I'd better tell you the truth of it, as far as I know."

"Maybe that would be best."

No other sounds disturbed the quiet room as Evelyn Galbraith told the story of the night before the explosion.

"So you promised your father you would keep quiet, no matter what you saw or heard?"

"Yes, I was puzzled, but I didn't know he would not come back himself."

"I would say you've been under quite a strain these past few days, Miss Galbraith. What do you think will happen now?"

"If I may stay here until somebody arrives, and the policeman comes first, I'll go by what he says. The same applies to MacAlister, but if the mob—" She shuddered but quickly rallied. "This house seems well furnished. Is there a—"

Mary Jean had kept her gaze fixed on the visitor. Faye roused her by saying, "Show Miss Galbraith the tiring-room, Mary Jean." As the two left the room Faye's mind whirled. What would happen next? What would Bruce do, and more important to the bride of less than a week, what would her new husband have her do? Giving sanctuary could put them all in jeopardy, but Bruce MacAlister's history showed him in jeopardy many times. That he would accept the challenge, ignoring the threat to himself, she could hardly doubt. Raju would stand by this highlander, whom he admired so much, as would Hamish, of course. Maybe this would be a seige.

Mary Jean came back then. She walked over to the window, pushing the footstool in front of her, and soon she sat perched on the windowsill. A moment passed silently before she said, "Mistress Faye, I see more smoke away over there!"

Faye ran to see for herself, but she felt she knew before she saw.

A shriek came from the doorway. "It's Rathven Hall. I never thought they would go that far. Oh, I should not have left. If Father's really dead, and I've shot and killed another man, then I should have stayed and allowed Rathven Hall to become my funeral pyre." Her voice had risen several decibels, and Faye spoke sharply, "Please be quiet. How can we be sure? Anyway, a fit of hysteria will avail you nothing."

"I can be sure all right, because my home is the only building large enough to cause such a blaze except for Mannering Heights, and that lies in the other direction. . . . My life is finished, and I'm done for."

Mary Jean still knelt on the window ledge, but Faye knew the child well enough by now to realize she heard and understood every word. However, she was still a child. "I'm hungry, Mistress Faye. Could we not have our tea?"

Evelyn Galbraith began to laugh, the sound truly hysterical now. Faye stepped up to her and lifted her hand to strike, but the woman regained control at once. "I'm not having a fit. But it is amusing is it not? Rome burned while Nero played his fiddle. Rathven Hall burns, and Polly put the kettle on and we'll all have tea."

This kind of cold, hard sarcasm went much deeper than the simple hysteria Faye had been prepared for, and unless the woman broke soon, allowing healing tears to flow, she would become ever harder. Mary Jean had the right of it. If Rathven Hall was truly alight, the menfolk could be there for a long while yet. She would busy herself with what any good wife should be doing—making the tea.

"An excellent idea, Mary Jean. We'll make some tea. You set

the bowls on the table, and we'll have some of that soup your uncle left simmering on the stove this morning."

"That's the most ridiculous suggestion I have ever heard. Here I have a pack of wolves on one side of me and the lions on the other, and you want to ply me with your soup. As if I *could* eat a bite!"

"Oh, I meant it for Mary Jean and me, but you are welcome to join us, if you wish."

"Daddy and Uncle Hamie are home, and Mr. Smith as well."

Faye rushed to the door. Sure enough, the trap was rattling at full speed across the dirt road. Raju held the reins while Hamish sat beside him. But there was no sign of Bruce.

Jumping from the still-moving vehicle, Hamish ran to Mary Jean. Before she could ask, he called, " 'Tis awricht, Mary Jean. Your daddy's fine. He was called to Lady Mannering's. She's been took bad."

Raju had unhitched the horse and was leading it into the stable just as his wife reached his side. "You'll find another horse in there, my love!"

He smiled at her without remark and kept walking toward the stable door.

12

"**R**aju, didn't you hear me? I said—"

"I heard you, my dear. When Miss Galbraith could not be found, Bruce and Hamish put two and two together and guessed she would be here. Knowing she would not have walked, I assumed there would be a horse. We didn't want to broadcast the fact. Since we are being watched, I'm trying to act normally."

Faye steeled herself not to look round as she followed him through the stable door. "What else is happening in Cairnglen, Raju?"

"The Galbraith residence has gone the way of the factory. In no uncertain terms the gateman assured us there was no one inside at the time. This was definitely arson, but we can be thankful no more deaths have occurred. Although its members showed the utmost valor, the fire brigade was inadequate for the task there, as it was at the factory the other night."

"What about Bruce?"

"Oh, a servant came from the manor house—Mannering Heights, Bruce calls it—to fetch him. The dowager is ill. Seemingly it is not unusual for her to do this and Bruce says she more than likely wants his version of the activities in her town." Raju tethered the livery horse to a hook on the wall. The other animal glanced up and nickered but quickly turned back to the bundle of hay protruding from the manger. Raju reached in to retrieve some for the second horse and rinsed his hands in the pail of water before turning to his wife. He pulled her close.

"We've had a blissfully quiet honeymoon, I must say, sweet one."

She snuggled closer. "*Blissful?* When we are allowed to see each other, yes; *quiet,* no! Do you think this is a picture of what our life will be like?"

"Who knows? With Bruce MacAlister for a friend, anything can happen, and it's beginning again, I believe."

As sounds of angry shouting penetrated their haven, Faye sighed. "Hold me for one more minute."

"I'll hold you forever, but at this moment, friend Bruce needs us to fortify the kila."

A sea of angry people surrounded the manse, but except for more angry shouts, no action was under way. On one side Father O'Mulligan's oratory seemed to put a measure of restraint on the mob, while on the other side Constable Moffat stood slightly apart, flanked by his special constables. He had ordered one of his men to send a telegraph spinning across the wires for reinforcements, and until those forces arrived, the policeman would only observe. He wanted no more violence. Confused and not altogether sure why these men had come to the manse, the constable merely marked time.

The mob, with a sprinkling of women among the men, had spotted the jaunty cart as the priest took up a stance in it to address the crowd.

"Nothing is to be gained by waiting here, I tell you. You should all disperse to your homes, and we'll have a meeting tomorrow."

Angry mutterings grew louder, and one voice answered, "A lot o' good your meetin's have done so far. Yer cousin's deed, and nae money comin' in for ony o' us. We'll a' dee o' hunger afore long."

"That's because you got impatient, Sean included. . . ."

But the crowd was beyond reason. "Speakin' ill o' the deed he is, and him his relative and a priest an a'!"

A woman's voice piped up this time, "Shame on ye, Faither. Ye should be conductin' Sean's wake an' no protectin' his killer. Have ye no respect?"

"Respect does not concern me at this moment so much as

trying to avoid any more wakes—no matter who for. I might ask you, Mistress Murphy, what respect have you? Out here instead of at home with your bairns." But he was drowned out. The crowd's anger and lust for revenge were out of control.

It had all started a few hours ago, with what had been, to some, more a lark to get Galbraith to show his face than a serious attempt at justice. When the big Irish leader had gone down under the Galbraith woman's gunshot, the whole situation had turned ugly. Not long after Sean had been declared dead another had placed himself in leadership. Some of the soberer workers had advised caution, but they were quickly outnumbered, and the second march on the Galbraith residence had begun. This time they had encountered no resistance, and a rebel, more daring than the others, had broken into the kitchen and scattered paraffin about. By the time the police and the fire brigade—the latter still working on the factory grounds—arrived, it was too late for the main house. All they could hope to do was restrain the fire before it reached the stables and the gatehouse. The gardener's cottage, a short distance from the residence, had also been safe. But Rathven House became a heap of rubble within the hour. Bruce and the others had arrived just then, and the crowd had gotten hold of the idea that both Galbraiths were at the kirk manse. Now the mass of townsfolk, intent on some kind of answer and seething with righteous indignation, waited there.

At Mannering Heights, Bruce had begun to lose patience with Lady Mannering. Hearing the first message, he had thought, *She's crying wolf again,* but when word came from the doctor that she really could be dying this time, he had not dared risk it. Indicating to Hamish that he would be back as soon as he decently could, he had allowed himself to be driven to the big house on the hill.

If he had ever been asked what style of home he preferred, between Mannering Heights and Rathven Hall he would have chosen the latter. Early Victorian clutter described the Mannering residence, while Galbraith's home showed a clean, more defined contour. Bruce sighed. What a waste, and all in such a short space of time. The changes wrought by those flames—and the more he thought on it, the more inclined he became to agree with O'Mulligan that arson was involved in both cases—would affect the lives of dozens, no, a hundred or more families. He realized he was trying to summarize for what he suspected was Lady Mannering's way of getting his opinions on the matter.

At seven o'clock that night Bruce walked home from the manor. Avoiding the town by skirting through the woods, he entered the manse lane from the back way. He had declined the use of a vehicle, and the quietness in the wood seemed to deny the violence of the past few days, but as he approached the manse all illusion of the ordinary vanished.

Two vehicles jostled each other under the coach arch, while the backyard had been transformed into a livery stable yard. No folks were visible from here, so Bruce, uncertain what awaited him, opened his kitchen door.

Almost comically, they were lined up facing the door. Mary Jean spoke first: "Did you see all the horses, Daddy?"

"Aye, I did that, my pet, and I'm not even going to try to find out why they're here."

Faye moved to his side. "You'll need some food?"

"No food. I had some at the big house. Is there any reason why I need to stay up now? What I want is sleep, if nobody else does."

He walked toward the stairs but stopped at the sitting-room entrance as Faye spoke again, "Miss Galbraith's in there, sleeping on the davenport. I gave her a mild potion. She was hysterical—the quiet kind, which is worse."

If Bruce was surprised, he did not show it. "Is there anything else I should know before I go to my room?"

"The priest, O'Mulligan, is sleeping in your bed!"

This time his laugh was short. "If I hadn't just left Lady Mannering, soundly asleep in her own bed—not dying, I might add—I'd ask you whereabouts in the manse *she* is."

Raju moved then, with Hamish close behind. "You're right, Bruce, you need to rest. Hamish has a place ready for you in the other wing."

Hamish nodded, adding, "Would ye no' be wantin' some tea or cocoa?"

"Nothing, thank you. I trust, seeing you're all concerned about me, that you've had food and sleep yourselves? Hamish, lead me to that bed, no matter where it is. I'll see you all in the morning."

"Reverend, are you wakened?"

"Aye, I would say I must be now. Is that you, O'Mulligan?"

" 'Tis me, right enough. I have much to say to you."

"What time is it, man? Why, it's not even daylight."

"Ten past three in the mornin'. Just before dawn. The darkest hour."

Bruce groaned. "Spare me your philosophy." He struggled to sit up and reached for his bedside table. Belatedly remembering he was not in his own room, he discovered a table of some sort stood there, and he fumbled for a match to light the lamp. Hamish had placed his Bible within easy reach, and he picked it up.

"Could I talk to you for a wee while before you start to readin'? I came the now because the house is still sleepin'."

"I doubt if Hamish is sleeping, but what is this about? I got all the news before I left Mannering Heights. The servants there know as much as we do."

"They don't know the half of it, MacAlister, nor do you!"

Bruce peered at the man seated on the chair between the bed and the window. "Could we get on with it, then, whatever it is?"

"Aye. If I tell you Galbraith is certainly dead, what would you say?"

"I'd say I'm not too surprised, but how can you be sure?"

"Sean! The big eediot was prowlin' about outside Rathven Hall gates on the night of the explosions. He saw Galbraith come oot the back way. Neither daughter nor servant was wi' him, but he was mounted on that great black horse of his. Sean followed him, although he was on his own two feet. Galbraith seemed in no hurry, so Sean found it easy to keep him in sight at a distance, without being seen or heard himself."

"Wait a minute, O'Mulligan, how can you know all this?"

What sounded like a sob broke from the priest, and a moment passed before he answered, "Sean told me. It was part of his last confession." Bruce sat up, wide awake now and thoroughly interested. The other man continued, "Sean followed until they got to the works. He watched, expecting the owner to go in the main gate. They all knew of an opening in the fence, but Sean was amazed to see the gaffer make for it. He left the horse tethered outside. By now Sean was suspicious."

Bruce interrupted again, "He told you all this as he lay on the ground, gasping out his last breath?"

"Not all. He had told his wife some of it, earlier."

"Did he confess why he followed him in the first place?"

"Not him, but I surmised our Sean would have been up to some mischief of his own. Anyway, Galbraith did use his key to go in the main warehouse. Sean watched through the window, and when he saw what Galbraith was doin', he ran in to try and put a stop to it. The crazy man was emptyin' a keg o' the powder and scattering it aboot the floor. He got such a fright when he saw Sean, at first, but then he rallied and threw the empty barrel at him. Sean dodged it and jumped the smaller man. They struggled until Sean went down with a punch to the stomach. He got up quick enough, in time to see Galbraith just lightin' a fuse. Again he rushed him, and this time Galbraith went down, hitting his head on a barrel as he went. He lay quiet. The fuse was well lit and too close to the scattered powder. Sean kent fine what that innocent-looking powder can do, so he turned and ran for his life. He got as far as the fence before it blew. Galbraith must have had it well enough planned for the timing, but he never got out. Sean rode the horse a wee bit on the back road, then thumped it, to send it on its way home, while he ran back to join the crowd in time for the count."

Bruce could think of nothing to say except, "Why are you telling me this now?"

"Because I ken I can trust you, and someway it has to be settled that Galbraith is as dead as Sean is. The unplanned justice of the whole thing amazes me. Sean could not have lived with his feelin's of guilt that, no matter what Galbraith was up to, he should have tried to drag him oot. Neether one o' them was up to any good. Then there's the daughter. I'm sure she suspects her father is dead. The horse must have got back to the stable, but all the servants were watching the fireworks, so Miss Evelyn would have put it back into its stall and tidied up the mess herself so's nobody would know it had been oot." The priest began to tell him of the goings-on at the manse.

"It all sounds so far-fetched to me; yet aye, I suppose it could've happened much the way you say," Bruce said, when the other man's words flagged. He pondered for a few more minutes. "What's to do now? I was too tired last night to even ask how the mob got quietened down."

"The police! Moffat does have a bit more backbone than I would have gi'en him credit for. Your friend Smith talked to him, and then he came over to join me in the jaunty cart. He told that crowd how a special squad would be arrivin' in the mornin' and would demand the names of the ringleaders. If they dispersed quietly the now, he said, his own information would include that the ringleader was dead. He also said it was his duty to take the Galbraith woman into custody."

"Did he then? Take her in, I mean."

"Not yet! He's still here though. He sent the special constables away with the crowd, to make shure they did disperse peacefully, and I understand your Hamish—"

Bruce broke in, rather rudely, for him, "I know! I know! Found him a bed for the night. Where will this all end?"

"I pray the violence is already ended. The morning will bring sobering thoughts of where their next shilling is comin' from. What the town'll do for work only the Lord knows."

"Speaking of the Lord, I'm for praying this very minute. Then I'm going to take my grandfather's advice. If I canna' make a better o' it, I'll not make it worse by greetin'."

He lay back on the pillow. Aware that the priest was still in the room, he prayed silently; then as the balm of peace flowed through him, he knew his rest to be over for the time being. A shimmer of daylight edged its way round the curtains that were partly drawn over the window, and he sighed. The sound roused O'Mulligan, who had been having his own private communion.

Bruce spoke. "The truth must be told!"

"I thought you would say that, but I hesitate, because, after

all, Sean is, I mean *was*, my cousin, and I have broken the
confessional. The family could suffer badly, and he is dead.
What good can come of blackening his memory?"

"Assure yourself he did all he could without dying himself. It
was not cowardice that made him challenge Galbraith in the
first place. He could have run then. Besides, most of the men
know enough about explosives to realize time is of the essence
once a naked fuse is lit. As for his family, I see it as your duty,
as the nearest kinsman, to take them far away from here."

"You're quite right, of course. I'll just have to take the consequences of my own betrayal of my position as father confessor."

"We've to consider what's best for the whole town. I see no
benefit from going into that. He did tell his wife, and you, as
adviser more than priest, must tell only enough of the truth to
be of benefit. Within God's laws of conduct and the laws of the
land, we must act and with honor."

"What should happen now?"

"I believe matters will be taken out of our hands when the chief
constable arrives and the insurance folk come. You and I will no
doubt be called into a counsel of some sort, and there you must
disclose what you've told me about Galbraith. After that, it's a
case of wait and see. As for Miss Galbraith, in light of the new
circumstances, the verdict will favor her a bit more. Come on. I'm
done with sleeping for this night. We'll go and see what Hamish
has for eating. I'm starving, and you should be, too."

The priest's face cracked in a ghost of a smile. "Begorrah, and
I am that. I believe I could eat a horse, now it's off my mind. My
stomach's thinkin' my throat's cut, so it is." As the priest turned
away Bruce moved from his bed toward the water basin on its
stand. He splashed his face and donned his clothes. Together
they left the room.

Reaching the other wing Bruce exclaimed, "That Hamish!
I've to be up a lot earlier than this to beat him. Do you smell the
ham frying?"

13

Everybody in the house had smelled the ham frying, and soon a motley group gathered round the manse kitchen table. Faye and Raju joined them just as Bruce started to ask the blessing.

Hamish waved the couple to seats and got up to serve them, but Faye objected, "No, no, Hamish, we can serve ourselves."

Bruce swept the table with an amused glance. A policeman, a Roman Catholic priest, a woman who was technically a prisoner, known to have killed the priest's own cousin, Hamish seated beside a wide-eyed Mary Jean, Raju and Faye Felicity, and he himself, forever dubbed the preaching hielandman. His smile, a trifle grim at first, relaxed somewhat. His prayer as always, to the Holy Spirit to bless and guide, must be his beacon, whatever the rest of the day might bring.

First the day brought the law of the land bearing a warrant for the arrest of Miss Evelyn Galbraith. A woman warden led her away, silent now after one final outburst in which she had clung to Faye. Faye's promise to visit her soon calmed her down. The next deputation came from the Roman Catholic Church, seeking Father O'Mulligan. He and Bruce shook hands solemnly, promising to keep in touch.

The day also brought a large bundle of letters, along with the *Inverness Courier*. Not desiring to take part in the domestic routine and noting that Bruce was only interested in his mail at the moment, Raju picked up the newspaper and disappeared into the sitting room.

A sudden longing for the Mains at Aribaig almost overwhelmed Bruce. His mother's letters always sent his thoughts
winging back to the old days, when Dugald would scrutinize
their post and guess the contents before the gully knife slit the
envelopes open. Andrew would gently admonish, while
Gran'pa Bruce smiled in the background and his mother
brought the tea. Shaking off his moment of weakness, he slit
open Granny Mac's carefully sealed envelope.

My dear Bruce:
    Loving greetings as always to yourself and Mary Jean,
and include Hamish, too. Matters have been rather quiet at
Strathcona House since you left, and you must excuse an
old granny for her flights of fancy, but maybe you can help
me explain the following: Letters keep arriving here for
Faye Felicity Gordon. You'll remember Faye as my dear
friend Isabel's daughter. The family lives in Yorkshire. Oh,
I'm rambling on, and you'll know fine who I mean.
    As for the flights of fancy, is it possible you know more
than the rest of us about Faye Felicity? She stayed here
with me for a few days, about three weeks ago, but she
was so jumpy I was becoming concerned about her. Then
she left quite suddenly. It wasn't clear to me if she intended to visit you and Mary Jean or go back to Yorkshire
or even London. Now these letters assure me she is not in
Yorkshire, and if in London, not with the missionary society. Could that, by any stretch of my imagination, mean
Cairnglen? I realize the young woman always was of in-
dependent spirit, but I hardly think that without due cause
she would go off to places absolutely unknown, never ad-
vising those of us who care about her. She was greatly
agitated about your Jeremy, and her visits with Agatha
Rose were distressing, I know. What do you have to say?
    One more thing, before I close. Another letter lies here
awaiting the addressee. Someone named Ralph Smith. It
appears to be from the American Embassy in London.
There may be no connection, but it is all extremely pro-
voking.

My letter is quite taken up with this subject, I see, but I will briefly give you my other news.

George Bennett pays me regular weekly visits, which I welcome. He says he is going to settle down now that he is over seventy. I don't mention my years to him—or anyone else for that matter. George also says that he has made his last journey to America, but I doubt that very much. He is as hale and hearty as ever. He will be writing you himself.

A. R. smuggled a note to me. She is worried about Peter. He has taken to drinking heavily. More distressing news, I regret to say. I'm taking the liberty of writing, by this same post, to his father. Remember how Dr. Blair, Senior, beat the "demon drink?"

I said "one more thing," but that is not so! Cook Mac-Laren has given notice. Her legs are troubling her. She will return to her daughter's place in Saltcoats. I thank my Lord every day for Betsy Degg. Both send their love to you and yours, as I do.

Beulah MacIntyre

P.S., Bruce, If F. F. is really planning what my fanciful (might I say even romantic) imagination thinks she is, and you have any contact, tell them they'll have my blessing. Life is too short and can be too grim at times for us to hold any kind of prejudgment.

Love—Granny Mac

Faye and Mary Jean came back into the kitchen as he finished reading. He thumped the table for attention, calling Hamish and Raju. Handing the lengthy missive to Faye, he said, "Read it to them. I'll be out on the moor, not too far!" He added the last as Hamish threw him a startled glance. Though Mary Jean clamored to go with him, he remained firm. "I'll come back for you, pet. I'll not be long." Without more ado she subsided. Granny Mac always sent Mary Jean her own letters, and today she had found another closed envelope inside hers, written in very childish printing, from Douglas Blair. He had addressed it

to Mary jean MacAlister, Aribaig in the Hilands, Scotland. It
said:

> Dear MJ i wish i was big and i wude run away to see you
> my dady is still angry and doing funy things mamy is
> crying and my wee sister laffs a lot. Stirling and me fite
> evry day and Fessie did that again yesterday. im fed up so
> i am and glad we are going to bording skule soon i wish i
> cude cum to see you furst. cude we be pals agane? from
> Douglas Blair. ps i sade a prare for jeremy i hope hes not
> ded.

It had taken Mary Jean quite a while to decipher the mean-
ings, and by the time she finished the note, tears streamed
down her cheeks.

Faye and Raju waited politely, and Uncle Hamie did what he
always did when trouble loomed. "I'll make some o' that choc-
olate coffee you brung." When he returned with the brimming
cups on a tray, Mary Jean had composed herself, and Faye
started to read Bruce's letter.

Raju, who had been preoccupied with what he had read in
the newspaper, laughed aloud as she finished. "We should
have known not to try to pull the wool over Mistress MacIntyre's eyes. Now all our subterfuge is in vain. I completely forgot
about giving the American Embassy her address as my British
domicile because I didn't wish to involve the missionary society
or Bruce until we had talked with him. Oh, my!"

"I should have known better, too. She is a born romantic. She
helped Bruce and Jean elope by turning a blind eye to what she
must have known Jean was up to." Most of this flowed over
Mary Jean's head, and Hamish had lost interest. They moved
together, gathering up the cups on the way. Mary Jean wanted
to go to her own room. She had things to do.

The married lovers made for the window seat going over this
latest development. The happenings this week in Cairnglen
had engulfed their attention, but now their own situation
loomed large again. Auntie Mac could be trusted to say no more

until she heard from Bruce, so they must now consider Faye's parents and how they should break their news.

The discarded newspaper screamed its headlines to an empty room.

Guy Fawkes or Joan of Arc? [*OR BOTH!*] Cairnglen, one of Perthshire's most prosperous small towns, both industrially and touristwise, lies a ghost of its former self tonight. The buildings, forming the "Galbraith Explosives and Engineering Works," literally blew to smithereens, all in less than an hour, on Monday night. A count of heads showed no workers missing, and except for a few minor burns, there were no serious injuries either. The occurrence will mean a loss of livelihood for some one hundred families.

One mystery still remains unsolved. The owner of the works, Mr. Drummond Galbraith, was not available for comment, and rumor had it that Galbraith may possibly be the only fatality. As this issue goes to press a gang of workmen, led by a known agitator for safer conditions and better wages, Mr. Sean O'Mulligan, is on the way to the absent owner's mansion to demand audience with him or to find some answers to their questions about the future. The outcome promises to be interesting, to say the least, and your *Courier* reporter will be on the job to bring you full details as they develop.

STOP PRESS: Cairnglen. Miss Evelyn Galbraith, daughter of the owner of the fateful explosive works, reported elsewhere in this issue, shot and killed the ringleader of the group of agitators threatening her home today. The victim is a cousin of the parish priest!

Returning from the short, lone sojourn on the moor above the manse, Bruce glanced briefly at the report of what he already knew. Then he picked up a long, dun-colored envelope, still lying on the table. Intent on the one from Beulah, he had ignored the rest of the bundle. The typewritten Aribaig address had been crossed out and *Cairnglen*, written in by his mother.

On the top left-hand corner a long line of names still had him wondering. Feeling more like Dugald then ever, he opened it.

His exclamation again brought him everyone's attention. "A matter to my advantage! Well, well. A pity I can't go at once to find out what." All eyes were still on him as he continued. "Fitzhugh, Hardcastle, MacKnight, and Wardrop, Solicitors-at-Law. My, but that's impressive. But Carlton Place, Glasgow? The letter says to attend in person. I've no immediate plans to go to Glasgow. In fact not before Christmas."

Faye spoke up, "It does sound important, though. Could you not see your way—"

"No, I could not!" He turned away with the abrupt statement, and those who knew him best recognized the subject was closed until he brought it up again himself. Gathering up the other papers, he left the room, this time going to his study. Faye and Raju gaped at each other. This was a different Bruce MacAlister.

Before they could comment, he was back. "Forgive me, please. My behavior is utterly inexcusable, I know."

Faye opened her mouth to respond but caught her husband's warning glance in time.

"It's Peter! Lord knows I've tried to understand and have been in much prayer for him, but I'm getting no peace. What should I do?"

Only then did Raju move. He rose from the window seat to stand beside his friend. "If you're getting no peace, then perhaps you have to try again. You'll be risking another rebuff, but it may be what you must do."

Bruce stared, hearing the words, but obviously far away in thought. At last he responded, "Yes, I must, you are correct. But I do have a few matters to see to here first. Then I will go to Glasgow."

One of the "matters" was the town-council meeting. This auspicious group had called an emergency meeting and invited Bruce, along with others who held positions of leadership in Cairnglen, to attend.

Before leaving for the town, however, Bruce summoned his

extended family for a private council. "The town meeting starts in less than an hour, so Raju and Faye, you first."

"Well, Mistress MacIntyre's letter has brought us back to the reality of our own situation. We'll go to see her at once and face her with the truth, most of which that astute lady has already guessed. Then we will take her advice regarding Faye's family. We have the feeling she will advise openness there also. Whatever else happens, we will return to Cairnglen and take up your kind offer of living in the other wing of this house, until we receive further directions."

Bruce then made his announcement. "I'll be going with you as far as Strathcona House, and then I've this business to attend to." He held up the buff envelope. "After that, I'll be seeing Peter again. Some of the ideas I have in mind cannot be discussed just yet, but will depend on the results of my journey. Mary Jean and Hamish, well, I've not quite decided yet. We'll just wait and see."

14

"**M**iss Mannering, gentlemen, I call this meeting to order, if you please." The town clerk tapped the tabletop with his ruler as he spoke, and those present quieted at once, except for the Honorable Priscilla Mannering, whose opportunities to talk without her mama interrupting came so seldom, that, when they did, she couldn't stop. She always had so much she wanted to say, especially to Reginald Galahad Payne. Reggie was Cairnglen's one and only lawyer and a most dignified member of the town council.

The two, or rather Priscilla, had been deep in a discussion about the annual highland games, to be held in Callender next month. Certainly, she had concluded, the works' explosion created a nuisance, but nothing should stand in the way of the games. Payne's face reddened as he realized every other eye in the room was upon Priscilla and him as the clerk waited for her to stop speaking.

When this did not happen, the clerk raised his voice, "We have some very serious matters to attend to, so I will ask for your complete cooperation. Would the secretary please read the minutes of the last meeting?"

Reginald stood up, flourishing the typewritten sheets. Rambling through the finicky details of the last meeting, his mind strayed to how much had transpired since he had written the words. Finished at last, he sat down, and the meeting would have continued at its usual leisurely pace had not Dr. Shaw thumped on the table.

"I've not got the time to sit through all this palaver. Can we get to the main business?"

"Order, please. Your pardon, Doctor, we still must tend the town's other concerns."

The doctor leaped to his feet. "Without the Galbraith works, will we have a town? I vote we get to that first."

"With all due respect, Dr. Shaw, I must remind you that you have no vote in this body." Spluttering some, the doctor seated himself again, and Bruce threw him a sympathetic glance. His own thoughts had been wandering. Now that his decision was made to go to Glasgow and confront Peter, among other things, he was impatient to get under way. Should he leave Mary Jean with Hamish, or should he take her to Aribaig? His mother's latest letter did not hide the fact that she pined for Jeremy. His thoughts switched to the newlyweds. They were still in doubt as to whether to go to Granny Mac's or Yorkshire first.

"Are you opposed, then, Reverend MacAlister?" With a guilty start, he realized that the group round the table had their hands raised in agreement to something he had missed entirely. He, like Dr. Shaw and Constable Moffat, had no official vote but were allowed to venture opinions in this manner.

Dr. Shaw hissed at him, "Raise yer hand, man!"

Bruce obeyed.

"That makes us unanimous then."

The scrutineer wrote busily, and Dr. Shaw leaned close to whisper, "We've been elected as pro-tem council members. Pay attention, Reverend." Bruce nodded shamefacedly and set his mind on the proceedings for the remainder of the meeting.

"Already the town is feeling the want of the rates. Ninety percent of our revenue comes from the Galbraith Explosives and Engineering Works. The other ten percent, well, we who are sitting here now indirectly depend on the works." The chairman was stating indisputable facts, and the others waited, resignedly. "Unless someone here has an alternative suggestion, we'll have no choice but to close the town!"

Suddenly everyone was speaking at once.

The clerk rapped the table. "Order! Order! I believe Constable Moffat has a statement to make. May I remind you that this part of the meeting is strictly confidential and that by your upraised hands you promised to abide by this rule."

Constable Moffat wiped his brow before beginning, "It is my duty to report to this body that the chief constable sends his regrets he cannot be here in person, and I'm authorized to speak for him. Mr. Drummond Galbraith, the owner of the late works we speak of, is missing, but until remains are found or a year has passed, he cannot be presumed dead." Reginald waved his hand, but the clerk ignored him as Moffat continued, "His daughter, Miss Evelyn Galbraith, is being held in protective custody, for her own safety at an undisclosed place, pending the assizes in September." He sat down in silence while his words penetrated to already-dazed minds.

"The chair recognizes Mr. Reginald Payne."

"I cannot disclose the source at this time, but evidence is available to confirm that Mr. Galbraith is indeed deceased." Gasps all round the table greeted this, and Priscilla gave him a glare that might kill. Obviously he had not confided this news to her.

"Thank you, Mr. Payne. The question here is still the same. What can we do that will be best for the town? Dr. Shaw?"

"What about insurance? Surely—"

The chairman turned to Reginald again.

"I cannot disclose anything further except to say this: Make your plans discounting insurance."

Bruce raised his hand.

"The chair recognizes Reverend MacAlister."

"Could we table any definite decisions for say a fortnight? Could we not manage that long without the, er, rates?"

"You may or may not know, Reverend, that the rates are payable twice yearly in March and September. I presume I need not remind you of the date. We are always overdrawn at the bank for the last few weeks of each period."

"That would still give us a few weeks, just the same?"

"Yes, I daresay, but—"

It dawned on Bruce that the man in the chair was also a shareholder in the bank. An unworthy thought about the interest, possibly charged the town, for the "few weeks" of grace, crossed his mind as a voice, unheard at the meeting until now, spoke, "May I speak to that, Mr. Chairman?" It was Ogilvie the works manager.

The clerk nodded.

"A few weeks might be possible for the town, but what about the folk? Most of them go from hand to mouth as it is, and the best of them will only have put by enough for two or three weeks at the most."

Priscilla Mannering spoke then. "I have my mother's permission to say that Mannering Heights will provide relief in the form of soup and bread in this emergency."

The clerk was eyeing Bruce even as he thanked Priscilla profusely for her mother's generosity. "Did you have something specific in mind, Reverend MacAlister, when you asked your question?"

"Nothing too specific yet, but I've an idea in the making. I have to go to Glasgow on a private matter. If any decisions can be held in abeyance until I return, I should have something more definite to say then."

"Our choices are few. Where can most of the townsfolk go?"

Ogilvie spoke up. "Some of the tradesmen are goin' already, but it's only too true that most of them will have no choice but to wait it out, whatever comes."

"Order, please. Before I sum up, does anyone have anything relevant to say, first?" Silence met his words. "Right! Here is the situation. The town will form a relief fund, and Lady Mannering's soup kitchen will commence immediately at the Heights. The ratepayers will be advised of a meeting, the date to be confirmed, but no later than one month from today. Those of us with solid suggestions—and by that I mean with pounds to back them up—will bring them then. Any further business? No? Meeting adjourned."

15

Cairnglen's telegraph boy, perched proudly on his new bicycle, swerved dangerously as he passed the hansom cab on the rough road leading to the kirk manse. Pedaling faster, he yelled at the driver, "Get a bicycle built for two, afore that auld nag dees on ye!"

Eddie McCartney had more on his mind than a cheeky laddie. Besides he had a lady in the cab. Not a fancy one, mind you, but still with a refined way of speaking, Edinburgh with a touch of a highland brogue he guessed.

So Elspeth arrived at the manse exactly five minutes after her son received the telegraph announcing her arrival. No letters had come from him since his return to Cairnglen, but the strange envelope she had forwarded to him, along with yesterday's report in the *Courier*, had prompted her to gaze at Andrew appealingly.

"Dinna look at me like that, Wife." He had said, "Go and pack yer valise. Gran'pa and me can starve for a day or two."

Indignant, she replied, "You'll not starve, and I'll not go, when it's so close to harvest time."

"We're givin' the oats another week to ripen, prayin' for no more rain in the meantime. Away you go!"

So here she was.

An ecstatic Mary Jean had been hugged, Bruce's furrowed brow smoothed by her fingers, and Hamish's hand shaken. All that remained was for her to be introduced to the couple standing politely by the parlor door. Bruce hesitated. Had the message arrived sooner, he could have asked Raju how he should explain their presence here.

But that astute fellow had taken the initiative. Leading Faye, he walked forward. "How do you do? I'm Ralph Smith, and this is my wife, Faye Felicity. Hitherto, we were known as Raju Singh and Faye Felicity Gordon. Even if we had not met before, I would know you anywhere, Mistress Cormack." His words astonished her, but his manner set her at ease.

"I'm sorry, but our previous meeting had slipped my mind. You went off to India, I recall."

"Yes indeed, but we will excuse ourselves now, as you have family matters."

Bruce held up a hand. "Don't rush off, Raju. You can hear this, too. Mother's coming has solved one of my dilemmas. That is, if she can stay the week." Elspeth nodded, delighted to be needed but still puzzled by the presence of this couple.

Bruce was explaining, "I take it, Mother, that you are aware of Cairnglen's catastrophe? Yes, and you know already about the misunderstanding with Peter. All that brings me to this. I'll be going to Glasgow—on the morning train, I hope. The Smiths will be going at the same time.

"Part of my reason is to try to talk to Peter again, before it's too late. Another reason is to raise some funding for Cairnglen, for a new industry—photography. No, wait, I'll speak no more of that now. You can all have your say after. Meanwhile these two can make their peace with friends and relatives, and Mam, you can stay here with Mary Jean and Hamish." Silence greeted his announcements, and even Hamish, who had started up to make the tea, stood at the door with mouth agape.

Elspeth spoke first, "May I ask, Son, where you are going to get your funding and what—?"

"Sorry, Mam, you may ask, but forgive me if I say I'm not telling any more until I return."

"Oh, I see. Well, Mary Jean, will you show me where I'm to sleep? Is it the same room as last time?" Mary Jean glanced from her father to Uncle Hamie. The Smiths had Gran'speth's usual room.

Hamish spoke up, "Ye'll want to be on this wing, Elspeth. I'll help ye get it ready." The three left the room together to sort out the domestic arrangements.

Raju gazed at Bruce, his thoughts in stunned turmoil. Faye said nothing but clasped her husband's hand tightly. At last Raju whispered, "Am I dreaming, or did you say an industry to do with photography? My love, tell me if I heard aright?"

Faye smiled. "Not dreaming. Just receiving answers to our prayers." She had her eyes on Bruce.

"You would be willing to try it, then, my friends?"

"Willing, yes, I should say most willing." He gently removed his wife's hand and stood up. Going toward the window, he turned to gaze out at the darkening sky. His shoulders began to shake as the others waited. Presently he composed himself.

"Thank you, Bruce MacAlister." Faye laughed joyously as Bruce reached for her husband's hand.

"We've a long way to go, but I've the feeling the Lord is with us in this plan. Now we should find out if there's some food and prepare for an early start. The train leaves at seven o'clock."

Raju and Faye had spent some of the time, while Bruce was at the meeting, preparing an Indian-style meal. The packet of spices and herbs, which went with Raju everywhere, had been used lavishly to disguise the only kind of rice available from Hamish's shelves. The party seating themselves to enjoy a rather late, but exotic, supper was cheerful enough. Elspeth, not sure she altogether approved, nevertheless joined in. After all, she could gaze at her beloved son, the minister, and she had Mary Jean by her side.

Bruce shifted the portmanteau to his left hand. He stood just inside the arch of Glasgow's Central Station. The city was having one of its days when the rain never ceased. Though he watched the cabbies vie for business, he made no move to hail one yet. Should he first stop at Strathcona House, or should he go directly to see George Bennett? He knew in either place he would be welcomed with open arms and heart, despite his unannounced arrival.

A familiar voice broke in on his thoughts: "It's yersel', Reverend MacAlister!" He turned to see Benny, the porter, standing behind him.

"Ah, Benny, how are you?"

"Ah'm fine. Whit aboot you?"

"Well enough, Benny. Have they not made you station master yet then?"

"Not yet! Not yet! But I did get a bit of a promotion. I don't need to sweep the platforms or the waitin' rooms now. My job's to post the arrivals and departures in the upstairs windows. That's where I was when I saw you. Never mind aboot me. I've heard your toon had a calamity?"

"Indeed, yes, and you heard the truth." Reminded of his reason for being here, Bruce half turned back to the arched openings to review the dismal scene. The crowds had thinned out a bit, and one lone cab awaited his bidding.

Benny stepped up. "You'll want that cabbie, then. Micht we be seein' ye at a meetin'?"

"I doubt it, Benny. I must return in a day or so, but I'll be seeing George, although I've told no one I'm coming."

"You'll not faze Mr. Bennett or Mistress Oliver, either. In fact they'll be that pleased to see you."

"Yes, they're kind, but I dare to think Mistress MacIntyre will be pleased, too."

"I'll hail yon cabbie, then, an' I'll have to awa' back to my own duties. The London train leaves in ten minutes, and I'll be postin' the next train from the east."

"Bless you, Benny. I'll be giving George all my news, and he can pass it on to you, if you're interested."

Benny had signaled the drooping vehicle, and now he held up a giant umbrella, seemingly produced from nowhere. "Aye, I'm interested right enough. The Lord's blessing on yersel' and yours. I'll be praying that all goes well with you. Nae need to remind ye that when we acknowledge Him in a' oor ways, He'll direct oor paths." He snatched Bruce's bag and hustled him into the damp interior of the cab.

"Good-bye, Benny. Well met!"

Benny's words echoed as he gave the cabby the address of Strathcona House. Had Bruce forgotten that portion of Scripture? Murmuring softly, he repeated the well-known phrase in his own personal way: "I, Bruce MacAlister, acknowledge You, Lord, in all my ways. I place myself in Your hands now. Please direct my paths."

A strange girl opened the door to Bruce's knock. They stared at each other for a moment before the maid spoke, "Yes?"

"I'm Bruce MacAlister. Is your mistress at home?"

"I'll see." To his amazement the door slammed in his face, and he was left standing on the step. The drizzle had turned to a downpour, and he pulled his hat down and tucked up his coat collar. He could hear Betsy's voice raised in a scold before the door was flung wide, and he was unceremoniously pulled into the lobby.

"Gracious sakes, Reverend Bruce. That silly Maggie should've kent your name. Here, let me take your hat. You're soakin' wet, so you are. Maggie, stop yer snivelin' and take the reverend's coat to the kitchen. Where's Mary Jean, sir?" Half laughing, Bruce waited until Betsy stopped for breath.

"It's quite all right, Betsy, and Mary Jean's not with me this time. Pleased to meet you, Maggie. I could do with a cup of tea. Betsy, is Mistress MacIntyre at home?"

"She is that, but she's in her bed. If you go into the drawin' room, Maggie'll bring you some tea whilest I go and tell the mistress you're here."

"In bed? She's not ailing, I hope."

"No' ailin', just restin'. The doctor says she's to rest mair now. I serve her an early luncheon, and she rests for two hours after it. As ye ken, she's an awful early riser."

"Let her finish her rest, Betsy, and never mind the drawing room. I'll have that tea in the kitchen, while you tell me all that's been going on here. I can hardly believe it's only six weeks since we were here, and Cook MacLaren's retired in the interval!"

Maggie McLaughlin was soon initiated into the actual person of this Reverend Bruce MacAlister, of such legend that she almost felt she should curtsy as if to royalty.

Quickly Betsy brought Bruce up-to-date on the news of Strathcona House—how Cook MacLaren had retired right enough, after thirty years with Mistress MacIntyre, but not without leaving Betsy all her recipes; how Mr. Bennett visited regularly once a week. Paddy McShane was away to Ireland. Finally she stopped in the middle of a sentence, to look directly at him. The new maid had left to spend her half day in the town, and just the two of them sat now before the roaring fire.

" 'Tis fifteen years since ye first came to that door, Reverend Bruce. I mind o' it as if it happened yesterday."

A cloud of pain darkened his eyes for a second, and Bruce's brow furrowed.

Betsy continued, "Ah dinna want to offend ye, sir, but she's grievin' again. 'Tis Miss Faye this time. Dae ye ken ocht tae ease her mind?"

"I think I do, Betsy, I—"

She held up a hand. "Say no more to me, then. I hear her movin'. I'll tell her ye're here." Betsy almost ran from the room, leaving Bruce pondering what he would say to Beulah.

"So I was correct in my assumption? One thing grieves me, and that is how Faye Felicity thought I could not be trusted."

"No, no, Granny Mac, she was more anxious not to burden you with a secret she didn't want her parents to know of. She laughed that you almost guessed."

"Now they're off to face the Gordon clan anyway, and together."

"Everything's together now. Yes, I saw them onto the train for York. I've never met her parents or any of that family, except Agatha, of course."

Again his eyes clouded, and Beulah sighed. "No good news for you from that quarter, I'm afraid, Bruce. 'Mr. and Mrs. Ralph Smith' you say they are calling themselves?"

"That's right. It will simplify matters for them. As we know, Scotland is better than most countries regarding racial prejudice, but it does still exist. If they're going into business, they'll need to be wise as serpents while being gentle as doves."

"Tell me more about this photography business. You say a brand-new factory is to rise like a Phoenix from the ashes of the old one."

He smiled at her. "Do I detect a hidden poet, Granny Mac? That's good! Maybe Raju will call it that, although he and Faye might not care for the idea of a mythical creature's name."

"From my knowledge of those two—and don't forget they've both spent time under my roof—the myth won't bother them. The concept of new life rising from the burnt embers of the old is more than myth. It is grounded in our faith. Elijah, Moses, Peter, John, the Upper Room tarriers."

"Wait a minute, you lost me somewhere."

"Fire is a destroyer, we know that, but it is also a purifier and a refiner. We can use that imagery and take it into the spiritual. You've been through it; I've been through it. Both of us the better."

Bruce's laugh now held a hint of bitterness. "I can't deny I've been through it, but as for being the better for it? That's a hard one. I've had to come to terms with it, and I agree that God worketh all things for good, but I cannot claim to be a better person for it."

"You wouldn't, of course, and that's part of it, too. Let us be practical now; you have other business in Glasgow?"

"Yes, this letter here. Shall I read it to you?"

"Indeed not! I'm not past reading for myself. Where are my spectacles?"

Bruce smiled, his good humor quite restored. "What's that round your neck?"

Ignoring this, she read the solicitor's letter and passed it back to him. "To your advantage, eh? When are you going?"

"It's too late today, but first thing tomorrow. If this *advantage* they mention is money—but no, I'll not conjecture, and we'll say no more about business until I've been to see them.

"Betsy has become cook, she tells me, and I do believe I smell roast beef?"

"Yes, you do that, but it'll not be ready for a while yet. Tell me about Mary Jean. She was so upset when she left, but her letter here seems to indicate she's over it somewhat. She also tells me of her experiences on the night of the explosions. For a ten-year-old she writes well, if briefly."

"She wrote it while I was packing my bag this morning. I didn't give her much time, and she had one other letter to write as well."

"My, but she's canny for her age, just like her mother."

-⋯∘⊰{ 16 }⊱∘⋯-

The sky had cleared miraculously during the night, and Bruce glanced up at the statue of Sir Walter Scott, where it towered over George Square. This place held so many memories for him: the day he had arrived in this city for the first time and stopped at this very spot to get his bearings for Strathcona House. Later that day, when he and Peter met Jean and Betsy under the statue, Jean had thrown Peter's hat in anger, the wind had caught it and whirled it high, to land on Sir Walter's granite head. His mind wanted to balk at the next memory, but it insisted. Jean and Betsy again had been waiting under the statue, and Raju Singh had brought him here for the tryst with Jean that led to their elopement.

Quickly he forced his thoughts to change direction, and Bruce began to visualize this morning's coming interview. His note, left yesterday, when he'd had the cabbie wait for him, had merely requested that the lawyers let him know if today was not convenient. Since no word had come, the next hour would tell him what this was all about. Seated on the upper deck of the tram car, he allowed his thoughts to accept the possibility that maybe, just maybe, the advantage could mean money. If so, he prayed it might be enough to help Cairnglen and Raju get started without debt.

"Do you swear on this Bible that you are Bruce MacAlister, at one time of Mains Farm, Aribaig, in the County of Invernesshire?"

"I am he, but I will not swear on the Holy Word."

The lawyer sighed. "How am I to be sure of who you are if you will not swear an oath?" Bruce didn't answer, and after a slight hesitation, the man slipped the Bible back into his desk drawer. "At least show me something that will identify you."

Bruce reached into his breast pocket and brought forth a second envelope. His mother had suggested he bring his ordination certificate, for she had foreseen the possibility of what he had just encountered.

The other man examined the paper, then handed it back. Waving Bruce to the upright wooden chair, he settled himself into his leather armchair and linked his hands together. "Well, Reverend MacAlister, the news I have to relate will give you a clearer understanding of why I had to be absolutely certain it was you. A valuable client, Dr. Angus Archibald Alexander, recently deceased, has named you as sole beneficiary in his will."

The words, spoken so casually and without emotion or sentiment, took a moment to sink in. Then Bruce stood up and turned his back on the lawyer. Dr. Angry dead! And leaving him something in his will? It was hard to believe that such a man could be dead. Why, the last time he'd seen him, his old professor had told Bruce he could be reinstated to the kirk. The man had been vibrant with life and vigor as he planned a voyage to America for an international conference. Other memories of this same man flashed before his eyes. Bruce saw him striding off through the heather with Hamish, the day after he had told Bruce the kirk had rejected him. The same purposeful stride had crossed the corridors of the university, during those years of learning. Beulah's analogy last night came to him now as he realized that the subject of this "advantage" had been instrumental in the firing of the vessel that was he, Bruce MacAlister.

Bruce faced the desk again, and the other man, the Fitzhugh of the letterhead, spoke in a kindlier tone, "I'm sorry! I thought you must have known of his passing."

"No!" Bruce's thoughts churned. "We never really got on. I wonder why he did this?"

"Dr. Alexander leaves no known relations. Having never married, he died childless. I can tell you, Reverend MacAlister, although not a great fortune, it is still a substantial sum." Bruce's image of a few hundred pounds disappeared as the other man continued. "After death duties and other expenses— which we have kept to a minimum, I might add—the net total is in the region of ten thousand pounds."

Bruce reached for the chair and sat down heavily. His brow furrowed into its ploughed-field pattern, but he remained speechless.

His informant did not lack words, however. He was going on and on about safe investments, and how the reverend could leave all that to this very firm.

"I'll take it. I've an immediate use for it, and it's the Lord's bounty and provision for this time."

It was the lawyer's turn to be speechless. He turned several shades of pink as he expostulated and spluttered. Sitting up straight in his chair, he at last found words: "Please reconsider, Reverend. We have the soundest investment plan in the country, with absolutely no risk and—"

"I'll take the money. I'll be returning to Cairnglen the day after tomorrow. I'm a minister, as you know, and have a sermon to prepare and deliver on Sunday. Och, man, I don't mean you'll hand me all that siller in sovereigns before I go. Just make it negotiable with some ready spending money, and I'll be back on Friday morning to get it."

He left the inner sanctum and the still-fuming solicitor. In the outer office a startled clerk was rising to answer the frantic ringing of Fitzhugh's bell, and Bruce told him, "I think he'll need a cup of tea!"

Without waiting for a tram, Bruce strode along Duke Street, paying no attention to the strange glances from passersby. Often, in Cairnglen or Aribaig, he walked about in homespuns and clerical collar, but apparently what was unremarkable there was not so here. Fitzhugh had handed him a sealed envelope, and he had absently stuffed it in his jacket pocket. What he felt the need of at this moment was a friend with whom to share this amazing news. *Peter!* Of course. Glancing around vaguely, to get his bearings, he realized he had walked all the way to the Broomielaw Bridge.

As if in answer to his thoughts, an almost empty tram trundled up, and he read the destination without surprise. He didn't wait for it to stop but leapt on the running board. The conductor had a few choice words to say, but when he noticed the collar, he turned it into a joke. "In a hurry to get to heaven, Reverend, are you?"

Bruce replied, "Oh, is that where we're bound? I thought we were just for the Gorbals."

A few women, shawls loosened on this bonnie morning, shared the tram and the joke. Bruce's earlier journey had not been so quiet, that tram being filled with chattering girls on their way to work at the numerous factories and workshops. He leaned back on the wooden bench, thinking this was not the place to read his letter. The swaying vehicle was merely the means to an end. Bruce recognized he was again clogging his thoughts with trivia to keep back the rush of feelings ready and waiting to overwhelm him.

The conductor was addressing him, "Here we are then Reverend. Heaven, or in other words, the Gorbals terminal. I take it ye dinna want to go back wi' us just yet?"

The street had hardly changed in the twelve or so years since Bruce had last been there, yet when he glanced upward, he noted more than a few newer buildings. Also the street sweepers were at work where before rubbish and debris had been left to rot on the cobbles and gutters. A clock struck the hour, and he automatically pulled out his watch. Exactly noon. Unless Peter's routine had changed drastically, he would, at this very moment, be threading his way through a waiting room overflowing with suffering humanity, to the outer door of his clinic. Then he would cross the street to the hostelry for a hot pie and. . . .

Here Bruce's thoughts blocked again. Twelve years was a long time, and Peter *did* have a private practice. Also Granny Mac had warned Bruce that his friend had taken to the drink this past while. Almost wishing he had gone back with the trolley, Bruce caught himself murmuring, "The battle is the Lord's." Reaching the corner of the street, where the clinic used to be, he turned in to it. At that precise moment Dr. Peter Blair stepped through the doorway.

"Well! Well! Well! If it's not the highland laddie himself? Come to see how the lesser beings are surviving, no doubt?"

With shock and horror only too evident on his expressive face, Bruce recoiled. The man was drunk? Immediately he caught himself. "Peter, my friend, it's good to see you."

"Sorry, but I canna say the same about you. You're smug, do you know that? Smug! As my American friend would say, you're a stuffed shirt. Thass funny is it no'? A stuffed shirt. Or should I say I stuffed skirt. Ha, ha, ha! Thass funny, is it no'? Like the goose we had for dinner last Christmas. Funny! Funny! Funny!" He doubled over at the immensity of his joke, and Bruce reached instinctively to catch him.

With surprising dignity, Peter brushed the hand away. "Leave me be. When I need your help, I'll ask for it. There'll be two moons in the sky when that happens. Now, if you'll excuse me, I've business to attend to." He stepped off the curb to cross the street. Bruce followed.

The occupants of the hostelry barely glanced up from their varied activities. The host stepped forward. "The usual, Doctor, man?"

"The usual, Murdoch. Ye've a famous name. Did ye ken that?"

"Ye've mentioned it a wheen times before, Doctor. Will ye have a hot pie? The missus just took them fresh fae the oven."

"No pie the day, Murdoch. I've had a scunner of a mornin'. None the better for a recent encounter."

"I'll have one of your guid wife's famed pies, Murdoch, and a pot of tea." For the first time the landlord noted the figure stepping up from behind Dr. Blair.

"It's yersel', Reverend! Katrina, it's the Reverend MacAlister! Bring him a pie and a pot o' tea. How are you, sir?"

"I'm fine, Murdoch. I trust I find you and Mistress Murdoch the same."

"Aye. She'll be oot in a minute. You'll recall she's fae Mallaig and aye enjoys a crack wi' ye. Katrina, what's keepin' ye, wummin?"

Bruce glanced at Peter. He had slumped into a corner of a booth. His eyes held a glazed look. Bruce decided he could spare a few more minutes in polite talk before joining his angry friend.

Greetings over, Bruce directed the loquacious woman to place his food on the table in Peter's booth. He sat down, uncertain what to expect, but the other man seemed oblivious now and sat with his head on his hands, staring blankly at the empty containers in front of him. A tankard of ale and two full glasses of whiskey had disappeared in the interval. Bruce commenced eating the delicious pie. A crusty loaf, the kind his mother often baked, and a crock of golden butter, as well as the giant pot of tea, accompanied the pie.

Using the last crust to soak up the gravy, having ignored Peter after the anguished first glance, Bruce was wondering what to do next when the well-remembered voice let out a roar, "What does a body have to do hereabouts for some service? Wear a backwards collar and a saintly smile?"

Murdoch hurried over. "Wheesht, Dr. Blair. I'll bring you food, if you want, but no more drink. Ye've had enough."

"*I'll* decide when I've had enough! There are other hostelries, you know, where a man can have what he's willing to pay for without a sermon or being watched by the saints themselves." Peter stood up, and in doing so swept the table with his jacket sleeve, sending the ale tankard and the glasses flying.

Bruce jumped up and caught hold of his friend's arm. "Please, Peter, will you not sit for a minute and let me talk to you?"

"I've nothing to say to you and nothing to hear from you either, sir. So if you'll just go away and mind your own business, I'll get back to mine."

"All right, if you can walk to the door in a straight line and on your own gait, I'll leave you alone for the now; but if you can't, then I won't leave until we've had a talk." The other man eyed Bruce glassily and gazed directly into his face. Suddenly he crumpled and and fell back into his chair, his head on the table.

The landlord, who had been standing by, came at once. "Help me take him to the back. I've a couch he can lie on 'til he's sober enough to leave."

"Has this happened before then?"

"Aye, but only the once. I sent a boy to the clinic, and they shut it for the day. We can do that again, if you like, Reverend."

"Yes, we'll do that, Murdoch. But I'm afraid this is more than just drunkenness. I believe he's on the verge of a breakdown. I'll get a cabbie and take him to a place where he can get help."

The landlord looked frightened. "Not to the asylum, Reverend, he'd never forgie me for that, nor you either."

"No, not to the asylum, Murdoch. It's to a friend's, a mutual friend who lives on Duke Street—a Mr. George Bennett. If you'll arrange to shut down the clinic, say for about a week, I'll do the rest. I'll send to Burntisland for his father, and I'll get a message to his wife as well."

"My, Reverend, I'm glad that you're here to take charge. He's oot o' it, richt enough, and worse nor thon other time. I'll away then and do the necessary."

If George Bennett was surprised to see them, he hardly showed it, and in short order they had Peter tucked into a bed in the very room that Bruce had occupied at one time. His housekeeper, Mistress Oliver, as spry as ever, was quickly dispatched to fetch George's personal physician, a member of his congregation and completely trustworthy not to be judgmental. Peter was still unconscious when the doctor finished his examination.

"Intoxicated, of course, but there's something else, bordering on dementia, I would say, based on what you tell me. God willing, we've got to him in time. I've a prescription here, and that, along with faithful and fervent prayer, should divert the worst. He'll be out for a while yet. When he comes to, he could be violent. I've another suggestion, George: Mister and Mistress Velvet. They could be here when he comes to himself and would be just right to handle him. You know them, George, from the assembly?"

George nodded, his concern for Bruce uppermost. "Maybe Reverend MacAlister should not be here when he wakes up."

"That would be my advice."

Bruce, who had waited and listened during all this, now stepped forward. "I'll away, then. I have other matters to attend to. First, I'll go to see Mistress Blair and then I'll send word to his father. As long as Peter's going to be all right, I'll stay away from him until his father sends for me. Thank you, George, for being, as always, a good Samaritan."

"Not at all, Bruce. We know who the good Samaritan is, and remember, Peter's my friend, too. Will you be staying long in Glasgow?"

"I'm going back to Cairnglen on Friday. I had hoped to spend some time with you first, but—"

"We must still arrange an hour or so. I could slip away to Beulah's when things settle down here and the Velvets take charge of Peter."

"We'll see. Meanwhile I'm away now to see Agatha Rose. Pray she'll not get the vapors until I've explained."

"We should all pray before you go. Dr. Grant, will you say a word of prayer?"

Far from getting the vapors, Agatha Rose so reminded Bruce of her aunt Faye that, had the circumstances not been so heartbreaking, he would have been amused.

"I've known something would give way sooner or later. I'm thankful to God you were with him, Bruce."

"Aye. But me being there made it sooner, I fear. Are we in agreement, then, that he's better left where he is for the time being?"

"Yes, but will he stay there? He'll create a rumpus the minute he comes to himself."

Bruce gazed at this young woman who had so captivated his friend. She was showing a different side to her nature today. He had dismissed her from his mind as frivolous and hysterical, but he realized he had done her an injustice.

"It's more serious than that, Agatha. When he comes to at George Bennett's, we must pray he will allow Dr. Grant to look after his immediate problem—and then, possibly a nursing home."

"He'll not agree willingly, Bruce, but if we get his father here before he regains his full reasoning then, maybe—"

"How can we ensure that?"

For reply Agatha picked up the bell from the small table by her side. At once the maid appeared. "Jenny, I want a telegraph sent to the doctor's father in Burntisland. Here is the address and the message. You know what to do?"

"Aye, missus!" The girl hesitated at the door.

"What is it, girl?"

"We were wondering what to do about dinner the night?"

"Just take the telegraph, and I'll tell you in plenty of time about dinner." The maid disappeared again, and Agatha Rose turned to Bruce with a ghost of a smile.

He answered her unspoken question, "They're expecting me at Strathcona House, but I could drink a cup of tea. Where are the children?" He had noticed no sign of them since his arrival at the Carlton Place house, half an hour earlier.

"I expect them home at any moment. This is the day Nanny takes them to the park. The boys ride their bicycles, and we have a contraption fitted on Nanny's tricycle with a seat for Felicity. She likes to be in that so—" He saw the telltale flicker of her lips as she faltered.

Bruce stood up. "I don't mean to distress you further, but what about Felicity?"

"We all know—that is Nanny and the boys and I—that your Jeremy was not to blame for what happened that day. But everything got out of control so fast, and Peter will not face up to it or discuss it. At the present time Fessy is never without one of us, and I have had special clothing made so that she can't . . . she can't—" The tears, building for the past hour, spilled over, and Bruce reached to pat her shoulder. She dabbed her eyes and took control again. "Enough of that, and they'll be home soon. What shall I tell the boys about their father? Douglas will understand, but Stirling could make a fuss."

"They're almost seven years old now, are they not?"

"Eight, next month."

"Agatha Rose, I've always found the truth to be best. For eight-year-olds, that should just mean telling them that their father has been taken ill and will not be home for a few days. If they want more than that, I'm sure the right words will come. Which reminds me, I have a letter here from Mary Jean for Douglas."

This time the smile transformed Agatha's face. "Oh, yes, I helped him smuggle one out to Auntie Mac for her. We only knew your old home address then, as Peter was always the correspondent. Later on he read out of the paper the report about an explosion in your parish. He thought it highly amusing. Oh, I'm sorry, Bruce, but you did say—"

"Never mind all that now, my dear. Before the children arrive, I've been so taken up with Peter and all I almost forgot to give you the news about your Auntie Faye."

At those words, amazement turned Agatha's mouth to an O, and she cried, "Auntie Faye? Grandmother Gordon's been so worried about her. Where is she? What's happened?"

"Nothing bad. Now don't get upset again, but I have their permission to tell you the news!"

"They? Who are *they*, and what news?"

"Give me a chance then. Your auntie is now Mistress Ralph Smith. I have it on the best of authority, as I performed the marriage ceremony myself."

"*Ralph Smith?* I've never heard of him. Did she meet him in India? On the ship? She stayed here for such a short visit, and we hardly talked—I was so worried about Peter and our Fessy."

Bruce sat silent for a few minutes. "You could say she met him in India, but they met for the first time about twelve years ago, here in Glasgow in Strathcona House. Before Jean and I were married in fact."

She stared at him blankly, and then: "Oh, my! Oh, my! He's changed his name! Where are they now, Bruce?"

"On their way to Yorkshire. No, I'll correct that. They will already have arrived there. At first they were going to run off to America and never reveal his true identity, but neither of them really wanted that, I'm glad to say." He decided not to mention any of the tentative plans for Cairnglen. Agatha had enough to absorb for the present.

At the door a flurry announced the arrival of the children with their nursemaid. Jenny arrived, breathless, at the same moment, gasping out that the telegraph was on its way. Together the twins burst into the room. Douglas rushed up to Bruce at once, but Stirling hung back, his eyes wary.

"Uncle Bruce," yelled Douglas, "where's Mary Jean? Did she get my letter? Did you see that big explosion? How—"

"Whoa there, Douglas. Let me answer one thing at a time. Mary Jean's at home in Cairnglen. She got your letter, and I have her answer here for you, and yes, I did see the explosions. How are you, Douglas, and you, Stirling?"

Douglas grabbed the proffered envelope and sat down at the window to read it. Stirling had still not spoken but was glowering at Bruce.

His mother admonished him, "Stirling, your manners?"

"How do you do, sir? Mother, is something the matter? Where's Father?" Just then the maid entered with the tea trolley, and saved from answering, Agatha busied herself with cups and teapot.

Douglas rejoined the group, requesting, "May I please be excused to my room? I must answer Mary Jean's letter so that Uncle Bruce can take it back with him, Mother."

"You may be excused, Douglas. Have some cake first, or better still, take some with you."

Stirling had still not moved. "Sit down and have some tea and cake, Stirling."

"No, thank you, Mother. I want to know what's happened. Why is Reverend MacAlister here, and where's my father?"

"Stirling, you are being very rude. Your father is ill. Oh,

don't worry, he's in good hands for the moment. I've sent word to Grandfather Blair and—"

The boy leaped across the room, one small fist clenched and uplifted, and began to punch Bruce's legs. "It's all *your* fault. Why can you not leave us alone? Every time we see you, something bad happens."

Horrified, the mother called out sharply, "Stirling! How dare you speak to our guest like that? Stop it at once!"

Bruce caught the pummeling hands. "It's all right, Agatha, I can speak for myself. Would you mind excusing us?"

The outraged mother opened her mouth to protest further, but something about Bruce's expression halted her words. Finally she responded, "I'll see about dinner then."

Alone with the irate boy, Bruce held on to the clenched fists with a firm but gentle grasp. "Stirling, would you please explain what you meant when you said it was all my fault?"

The boy's face twisted away from him, and the small body shook with rage. He made no reply.

"If I have done something to hurt you or your family, Stirling, it was most certainly unintentional." Still no response, so Bruce kept talking. "Did your daddy never tell you the story of how you boys got your names? I'll tell it again anyway.

"All the years when we were friends and student boarders together at Strathcona House, we told each other how we would call our firstborn sons Bruce and Peter, respectively. Then one day we were trying the names, and while Peter MacAlister sounded fine, Bruce Blair did not, and MacAlister Blair would have been confusing and too much of a mouthful, so we excused each other from the promise. When he discovered there were two of you, your father decided to name you after famous towns. By then Mary Jean's mother was dead, and I thought it most unlikely I would ever have a son." Some of the tension had drained from the boy, and Bruce knew he was listening in spite of himself.

"You're hurting my arm."

Bruce let go at once, fully expecting the lad to rush from the room.

"Are you sure my daddy's not dead?"

"I'm sure. He's not very well . . . but—"

"He's drunk, isn't he?"

Here was the dilemma Agatha had foreseen, and Bruce was alone in a tight spot. If he said yes, he would be disloyal to Peter; if he said no, he would be lying. He did something he and Mary Jean had promised never to do to each other—answer a question with a question. "Where did you get that idea, Stirling?"

"I heard Nanny tell the milkman the day our Fessy, I mean— Oh, never mind that now. Where is he?"

"He's at a friend's house. No, not Strathcona House, another friend. Your mother knows." A scuffle at the door, the sound of a loud slap, then a screech, caused Bruce to call out, "Come in."

Douglas came in, closely followed by his mother and his little sister—the poor wee one who, all unwittingly, in the fullest sense of that word, was the cause of this whole mess.

Bruce's heart throbbed with compassion for the child, for his friend, and for the family. He walked over to Felicity and picked her up in his arms. She snuggled down without a sound as he stroked the silky blond head.

The twins gazed wide-eyed at Fessy, who never behaved this way. She astounded them further by speaking out some words clearly and logically, "Fessy likes uncle!"

At that moment Agatha reverted to normal and burst into tears.

The children's nanny had removed them quietly, and once again Bruce was alone with their mother.

"Twice now I've been packed up and ready to leave him. Both times he begged me to stay, and each time he promised faithfully to stop drinking. But he couldn't keep that promise. Last Sunday I went into his study to ask him if he wanted some food. He sat at his desk with a half-empty bottle in front of him. Several bundles of papers lay piled on the desk. When I asked what he was doing, he swept the papers into the wastebasket with a curse and dropped a lighted match into it." Bruce tried to conceal his shock at this, but she was paying him no heed as she went on, "Only Jenny and I were in. Nanny had taken the children to church. Peter was slumped forward, and I rang the bell. Between us Jenny and I managed to contain the blaze. I told the girl it was an accident, but she, well, I'm sure she knows better. No one smokes in this house, and she had heard Peter rage and threaten at other times."

"Does Peter's father know about any of this?"

"Not all, but I'm sure he suspects."

"Well, we will know more, when he arrives, what we should do. Were the papers important?"

She turned away. "Just some old letters. He does tend to be a squirrel with them."

"Mine among them, I suppose?"

"I'm sorry, Bruce."

"Well, Agatha, I don't think I can do much more here. You and your faithful staff will manage fine. I'll look in on Peter on my way to Strathcona House. No doubt the senior Blair will take command tomorrow."

She nodded and silently held out her hand.

A brisk five-minute walk brought Bruce from Carlton Place to George's home on Duke Street. Noticing a few strange carriages lined up in front of the house, he surmised a gathering of the assembly to be taking place inside, so he slipped round to the back door. A quick consultation with Mistress Oliver assured him that Dr. Blair was still sound asleep and that the Velvet couple were installed in his room.

"Mr. Bennett called a special prayer meeting, and we're trustin' the Lord for answers." The cook nodded in agreement as she dealt briskly with a bowl of eggs at the massive table. Apparently the meeting would include a meal.

Bruce thanked both ladies as he took his leave. "He's in the best of care, and I need have no concerns."

"Pray, Reverend, only pray!"

*   *   *

Bruce pondered the phrase, "Only pray," as he quickly covered the streets leading to Strathcona House. *Why do we place the diminutive only in front of* pray? He wondered, chuckling. It certainly would not be diminished prayer in George's house tonight. Peter indeed could not be in a better place.

Bruce's mind switched to the morning's episode with the solicitor. Could that have occurred just a few hours ago, or was it all a dream? He felt in his pocket for the letter. No dream this. Now would be as good a time as any to read it. The clock in the square struck five as he sat down on the bench for the second time this day.

Dear Chieftain:

When you read this I'll be gone from the life we know and discovering for myself the next one—the one we've spent our days trying to portray in order to bring in the harvest, as Christ commands us. The Gospels are filled with analogies of multiplication, and we, as teachers of the Holy Word, use that as a theme while we watch the lines of newly ordained march out of the university. Some fall by the wayside, some land on fallow ground, and a few, like yourself, become what I believe Christ wants us all to be, true seed in a fertile place.

From that first sighting of your face, tight with apprehension yet glowing with the inner zeal of true dedication, I recognized you to be one of the few chosen. God's anointed! Somehow I was to be to you the devil's advocate. Your light (or should I say Jesus' light) shone through it all. Many times I wished to beg forgiveness but could never do it. Posthumously I do it as I write, and you read this missive, for I am ever the coward.

My prayer, as I write, is that you will accept, in the spirit it is given, a small token of my esteem, in the form of the legacy. This would have been for my son. Although we never knew it, you were my son in Christ. Use it to further make His glories known. I am aware that your whole life is geared toward that goal, so allow me to share in your great exploits in this continuous way. Your father in Christ.

A. A. Alexander (no longer angry!)

A couple, out for an evening stroll, looked at him strangely before hurrying on. He reached for his hankie. Of all the happenings this day, reading the professor's letter had almost unmanned him. He blew his nose and dabbed at his streaming eyes. Not almost!

As he sat on, Bruce noticed it was one of those rare evenings where the sun seemed in no hurry to go down. The air had been washed clear by yesterday's rain, and the grass fairly sparkled. This oasis of peace and quiet in the heart of the bustling city, even this very bench, seemed to vibrate with renewed memories.

Uppermost in his mind was the memory of what had taken place many miles from here: his strange wedding and the nuptial journey with Jean. She and the old Peter, along with Raju, Paddy McShane, and a reluctant Betsy Degg, had planned the elopement, but afterwards, he himself had taken charge.

Sending the others on their way, he had arbitrarily hired Paddy McShane to drive them to Wemyss Bay, where waited, as he somehow had known it would, a steamer bound for Rothesay. Vividly now he recalled moments that, eight years ago, when Jean died, he had tried to shut away forever. Now he shivered as a stray breeze sprang up to affirm the memory of how his kilt had whipped round his knees as they had stood close together on the deck of the *Maid of Kintyre*, his right hand on the rail, covering Jean's left, where the ring, produced so appropriately at the correct moment by Peter, had rested. He had winced when she brought up her other hand to squeeze his, and a small, involuntary groan had escaped him. Immediately she had been all contrition as she saw the deep weal, still very raw from the vicious swipe of the professor's cane only a few weeks before.

The rush of memory brought her very words to him now: "Oh, darling. I didn't know you were hurt. What happened?"

Reluctant to tell of it, even to this woman who would very soon now be truly a part of himself, his innate honesty forbade making up a story, so he had explained it all. Then and there that impulsive wife of his had taken the painful hand and raised it to her lips, covering it with kisses before he realized what she was up to.

Later on, in their modest hotel room overlooking Rothesay Bay, she had begun again to smooth and gently kiss the puckered weals, until he stopped her. Placing her wet cheeks between his palms, he had gazed deeply into her eyes. "Never mind that the now, my bonnie Jeannie. I seem to have something else on my mind." Laughing in delight, she had obeyed him.

Seated on the bench still, Bruce's groan was unmistakable this time, and he glanced quickly about. No one was near. Folding the letter, he carefully returned it to the envelope. *How strange our memories are,* he thought. *Here am I, reading Angry's posthumous letter, and you'd think I'd go off into a dream about him and his classes, but instead, I go into those long-buried memories of Jean and I together.*

He rose from the seat. His *why*s to God had been asked and partly answered in that other long-ago day, or dark night of the soul. Time now to return to the present and whatever he might have to face on the morrow. No matter what else happened, the day after that he must prepare to return to Cairnglen and his parish responsibilities.

Betsy Degg awaited him with mounting anxiety. "The mistress has been worriet aboot ye, Reverend Bruce, and I'm worriet aboot her. She's waitin for you to join her for dinner."

Feeling guilty and slightly concerned, yet unable to move out of his state of fatigued euphoria, Bruce murmured an apology as he hastened to wash up and prepare for the meal and the questions that would surely follow.

However, after Betsy and her helper cleared the dishes, Beulah leaned back in her high winged chair, having allowed him to say only that he had come into a bit of money and that Peter would be all right.

"On the subject of inheritances, Bruce, I wish to speak of my plans for Strathcona House and yourself, but more for Mary Jean."

He rose to protest. "Granny Mac, you must not—"

"I must and I will. Usually when you visit me, you are surrounded by others, and much as I love my great-granddaughter,
she does tend to pull my attention away from other essentials.
Please indulge me, Bruce."

He subsided at once.

Later, as he lay in bed, gazing at the familiar ceiling, sleep
slipped far away. He tucked his arms behind his head and
deliberately pondered the situation. Granny Mac, the indestructible, would be eighty years old in a few weeks. One of her
strongest desires was to be still alive at the turn of the century,
when she would be ninety. She denied feeling old, though she
had admitted a few breathless moments from time to time.
Bruce resolved to quiz Betsy about this in the morning.

Meanwhile Granny Mac had revealed the contents of her will
to him: Mary Jean would inherit Strathcona House, and except
for a single piece of jewelry coveted by his absent, newly rich
mother-in-law, its complete contents. He sighed.

His thoughts veered to Peter Blair. He truly had done all he
could in that dramatic situation, for the present, although he
would talk to the elder Blair before leaving Glasgow. Bruce also
intended to pay a visit to a wee shop he had just happened to
notice when he got out of the tram in the Gorbals. What had
caught his eye was a sign in the dusty window that read: PHO
TOGRAPHY.

-·◦◦{ 17 }◦·◦-

Rising early as always, Bruce slipped away without disturbing the household, leaving a short note for Beulah. His knowledge of the habits at the Bennett domicile assured him Mistress Oliver would be about her morning preparations for George's breakfast, so he quickly made his way there. Fog, dripping from his hat brim, daunted him not at all.

As he had guessed, a hearty breakfast was under way, and when he agreed, with little persuasion, to eat some, Mistress Oliver set a place at the kitchen table beside a roasting fire.

"I'll not stay long this morning, but I did want the news of Peter."

"His father has already been and will come back later this mornin'. He left a message for you wi' the maister. Will you not wait? He'll be risin' soon enough."

"No. I have business I want to see to this morning, but I'll be back by about one o'clock. Did Peter sleep the night through?"

"Like a babby, and still at it. Oh, here's Mistress Velvet. She'll tell ye."

Recognizing Bruce as a preacher who had spoken at their meetings more than once, Mistress Velvet proceeded. "Och'n he'll be chust fine. A week or twa's rest wi' nae whiskey at all, an' he'll be a new man." Wondering how this could be managed, Bruce's brow furrowed, but the talkative lady had more to say. "His faither had a guid blether wi' Dr. Grant, and betwist them, they've got a rare cure hatchin'. It's not that yer freen's a true tippler, ye ken, but he could be, if left long enough."

She turned now to Mistress Oliver. "I'm to feed him some gruel wi' some o' that nature's remedy sprinkled on it. He's still sleepin', so I'll hae ma ain breakfast an' then ma man'll be doon for his." Mistress Velvet appeared to enjoy her breakfast, as well as her other meals, and Bruce caught himself thinking, *She's well named, with that velvet-smooth skin and candid eyes.* Peter was in good hands.

Draining the teacup, Bruce stood up, dabbing his mouth with his hankie. "My friend's in the best possible place, and I have much to do this morning. I'll be back later, Mistress Oliver, if you'll mention it to Mr. Bennett."

"Aye, indeed, and I will that. Wrap yersel' weel. 'Tis a dreech mornin', Reverend Bruce."

Their joint prayer for the meal had included a request for clear guidance for the day, so Bruce, fortified with good food and with the blessings of the ladies ringing in his ears, felt better than he had for many weeks now. Although the pangs following Jeremy's disappearance still nagged, he had a new peace about it. The fog was clearing a bit, so he decided to stride it out to his next place of call.

"What would I have in this midden of a shop to interest the likes of you? A minister and all!" The bushy-browed man, with the sourest expression Bruce had seen for some time, faced up to him, for all the world resembling one of Gran'pa Bruce's bantam cockerels. Bruce had to turn away to hide his smile. "Your sign brought me in. I'm needing some advice."

The look grew even fiercer as the man absorbed the words' meaning. Very few sought his advice, and he had learned not to trust those who did.

The dark, dingy shop reeked of pipe tobacco and dust, and Bruce sneezed. The man wiped a chair off with a doubtful-looking rag before inviting Bruce to sit. "I haven't much time, ye ken, as I've a paper to get out."

Bruce came directly to the point. "We need some advice about setting up a photography business."

The man's shout of laughter disturbed a dog nestling in the inglenook, and it padded over to Bruce for a sniff at his feet. He patted the long shiny ears while he waited. "My, but you're the bonny wee dog. Are you related to Prince Charlie?"

The laughing ceased abruptly. "He's a purebred *King* Charles spaniel. Have ye any objections? Come on, Jude, out ye go." The two vanished through the back, and Bruce glanced about, more curious than ever.

The only clean article in view was a black, shrouded object standing about five feet tall in the window corner—the camera. Purebred dogs and cameras! Clues to the person who was now returning to the shop by the sound of it. This should be an interesting interview.

Dog and man entered, in that order, but apparently Jude was to be fed before any further discussion could take place. Satisfied at last, the man perched himself on the edge of the cluttered counter. He leaned over to search for something. Finding a battered old clay pipe, he placed it between his teeth but did not light it.

"Photography, is it? What would you be wantin' wi' that information? Unless ye're in one of they camera clubs."

Without further delay, Bruce launched into explanations, but he was stopped almost at once. "I'm Barnabas Hill, jack-of-all-trades and master of none in publishing a newspaper. I write it, edit it, take the photos, sell the advertising, such as it is, set the type and printer's dummy. I crank the press, and then, when it's dry, I set it and deliver it masel', so ye see, on paper day, I'm gie busy. Who are you?"

"Bruce MacAlister, pleased to meet you, Mr. Hill."

"Are ye now? Well, ye'll maybe not be so pleased when I tell ye ma paper, *The Glasgow Pursuit*, is maist radical in its editorials."

"At the moment I'm only interested in the photography, although I would be happy to take a copy of your paper back to Cairnglen to read."

"Cairnglen? Cairnglen? That's where the gunpowder works blew up! So that's it."

Bruce nodded, more puzzled than ever.

"Continue, man, am I to guess every step?" Without interruption, he allowed Bruce to outline the still very elusive plan. By the time Bruce finished, Hill had lowered himself into another chair by the fireside. The pipe remained unlit.

"There's maybe a dozen things wrong with your plans!" His brogue had strangely disappeared as he talked now. "Number one, money. You'd need at least six thousand pounds just to begin the building and another five or six for equipment and materials." Bruce smiled. Two days ago this news would have ended the discussion. "Have you got that much?" Bruce nodded once as the other went on. "Second, the best materials needed are in terrible short supply. I have a contact in Sweden who can get me some, but that's just a trickle compared to what we would need."

Noting the *we* without comment, Bruce waited.

" 'Tis the ingredients for the formulas I'm talking about. With them we could make our own. Let me consider a bit. Aye, it's just possible. Have you a hundred pounds on you?"

"Not with me, but I could get it very quickly. Why?"

"Ask no questions, and you'll be told no lies. I've an idea, but I'll not say too much the now. Come back this afternoon with the money, by then, I'll know. Another thing. You'll have to trust me and not be asking questions every minute. Now I do have to get my papers out."

"Of course. I'll be off then, until this afternoon."

Thinking over the strange morning as he found his way to the tram depot, Bruce spared a moment to glance over at the clinic. A sign on the boarded-up door explained the obvious.

What could Barnabas Hill's story be? That he must have known better days came through in his speech and some of his actions. Then there was the dog; the man treasured it more than his own life.

As he boarded the tram in a more sedate manner than he had yesterday, Bruce was rewarded with a smile from the selfsame conductor. When he paid the halfpenny fare, the fellow quipped, "Ye could live to be an auld man yet, Reverend!" Bruce laughed, but his thoughts were far away.

A cashier's check for five hundred pounds awaited Bruce in the outer office of Fitzhugh, Hardcastle, MacKnight, and Wardrop, Solicitors-at-Law, along with a letter stating that the balance would be deposited in the bank of his choice within the week. He named the bank and left quickly.

The Bank of Scotland, where Granny Mac dealt, was Bruce's next stop. The startled teller had to go to the vault for such a large amount, when the bank had just opened, but he asked no questions. As he stepped from the impressive building, Bruce caught a glimpse of Betsy posting a letter in the big red box on the corner, but he did not hail her. Letters must be on the way to Yorkshire and to Boston, in the United States, with all the latest developments as far as Beulah knew of them.

Bruce arrived back at the dingy little shop just as a policeman and a pair of bailiffs were leaving. One of them was shouting, "It'll be the worse for you, Hill, if you keep insultin' her majesty's servants as they carry out their duties."

The three rushed past Bruce, where he stood in the doorway, trying to puzzle this one out. He ducked his head to enter. Barnabas sat at the counter, his ready chatter halted for once.

Bruce risked a question, "What happened?"

Hill focused his attention, noticing him for the first time. "Och it's yourself, Reverend. I'll tell you what's happened. I knew it would, someday, but why the day? Anyway, I was takin' the papers round the newsstands, and I stopped to make inquiries regarding the matter we discussed earlier. I took a bit longer than usual, and when I got home, they three were waiting for me."

"What did they want?"

"They've done it already. Shut down my operation. Soon they'll be back with the nails and the signs saying OUT OF BUSINESS. If I tamper with that, I could land up in jail. You see, some of the things I write, with photos of some well-kent faces, are not liked by everyone who reads the *Glasgow Pursuit*. The day's edition had some braw illustrations. Photies I took unbeknownst to the important folk in them. That's neither here nor there. They can shut my press down, and they'll be back soon to do it—and my bit shop."

"Your shop, too?"

"Aye, the landlord warned me as well. Mind you, I'm sure he's being paid to get rid of me by tripling the rent last month, and I haven't given him the money yet. This paper was to do it, but now I don't know. Here, read this for yourself while I look after Jude; he's been fair neglected the day. Come on, boy."

Bruce kept to himself his thoughts that Jude was the least neglected thing about this place, as he picked up the double sheet of newspaper.

"You're a temperance man then, Mr. Hill?"

"More *temperate*, I'd say." Noting Bruce's raised eyebrows, he grinned sheepishly. "Well, at least where the drinks are concerned."

"I must say I agree with the principles you have here. The pictures are most graphic to say the least, but still where would the libel be?"

"The picture of the gentry is of a duke and duchess—unnamed, I might add—gorging themselves at a dinner, along with some others of that ilk. The objection is how I've super-imposed a picture of a few native Glaswegians spending their coppers on a Saturday night."

"I see, but I'm trying to understand your reasoning."

"Reasoning! Reasoning! They flounce their righteous skirts at the slum drinkers, blaming the drink for the ills of the folk. Can they not see it's the other way round? The folk have nothing, nothing whatever. The drink gives them an hour or two of forgetting."

"While the gentry, as you say, seem to have everything, but they need to forget as well. What's your solution to that, then, Mr. Hill?"

"If you'll call me Barnie, I'll tell you the truth. I've no com-plete answer. Mr. Charles Booth has done a lot in the way of collecting facts and figures, and others have offered solutions—temporary, most of them—and we've come a long way, but it's not getting better." A loud hammering on the door interrupted the dissertation, and Bruce went to open up. The three men were back with reinforcements.

"May I ask what it is you want?"

The leader laughed scornfully. "You may ask, but I've a question for you first, yer honor. What business is it of yours?"

"My partner's business is my business."

A stunned silence filled the room. Then all the occupants, except a dumbfounded Barnie himself, began to speak at once.

"Partner, aye, an' the Queen of Sheba's ma auntie."

"If you're his partner, ye'll no doubt be paying the back rent o' sixty pounds." This man glanced at the others for approval of his smart remark.

In answer Bruce opened his wallet and removed six crisp, new, ten-pound banknotes. "We'll want a receipt!"

A bowler-hatted man stepped forward now. "What about the libel in his paper?"

"Can you prove libel?"

"He admits it."

Bruce turned to Barnie, who still wore a look of astonishment bordering on the comical. He shrugged. "If I retract, they'll not sue."

"Will you?"

"I don't see how I can, however. . . ." He stared at the intruders, who still gazed stupidly at the money. "You've stopped me for the time being, but someday I'll be back. Now, leave. My rent's been paid, and that makes these private premises."

The uniformed man stepped up to whisper in the leader's ear. One last attempt: "We're not sure we should accept this paper money. Sovereigns would be preferred."

"We have this receipt, and it's too late to change your mind. Rest assured this is good Bank of Scotland money."

The sounds faded as the men left, still grumbling. Bruce and Barnabas were alone again, with Jude back in his corner.

"What did you find out about the photographic materials?"

"If we have the money, I can have the articles sent to you."

"Listen, Barnie, you seem to have come to a standstill with your work here, and I've a feeling the boys in blue will be back on the least excuse. Why not come to Cairnglen with me, on an advisory basis? After all, I'm not even sure my ideas are feasible, and you can help me find that out."

"Advisory basis, for what?"

"A photography processing works of some kind."

Barnie had been stroking his dog's silky ears, but on these words he looked straight at Bruce. "You're serious then?"

"I'm serious!"

The other man glanced round the room. "I'll need a wee while to redd up!"

Bruce nodded. There was no denying that. "You will come then?"

"Aye!"

All was bustle at the Bennett residence when Bruce got there. Glancing at his watch, he realized it had been exactly twenty-four hours since he'd brought Peter here. Dr. Blair, Senior, and Agatha Rose had arrived, and a plan of action was under discussion. Ushered into the drawing room by Mistress Oliver, Bruce was greeted by the elder Blair.

"There you are, my boy. Agatha tells me you've been to the rescue again."

"Only because I was there and, I fear, precipitated matters."

"Och, 'twould have happened sooner or later. Better wi' you there than some others I can think of. I ken the signs.

"Here is my proposal then. I'll hire a locum for the practice—neglected anyway this past month—and a student to help me with the clinic. We think it's best to take advantage of Mr. Bennett's kindly offer of this place for Peter to recuperate at present. He's in good hands, and we'll look in every day. The boys can come and see him, too, maybe by Sunday." The doctor's many words did not hide from Bruce the deep emotion felt by this father who himself had struggled with and overcome the devilish alcohol.

Content to leave all the arrangements to the family, Bruce was not surprised as the doctor continued, "No offense, Bruce, lad, but I think it would be better if we postpone your own visit to Peter for a wee while yet. We'll let him come to himself, and then I'll have another wee talk with him and let him do the asking after you."

Bruce nodded. There would be nothing more for him to do here. He rose to leave. As he said farewell to Agatha she handed him two envelopes addressed to Mary Jean. His heart lifted. In their best script Stirling, as well as Douglas, had written out *Miss Mary Jean MacAlister, c/o Manse, Cairnglen, Perthshire.*

George accompanied him to the door. "I'll not delay you then, Bruce. I've a feeling you're up to some exploit that will include soul winning, no doubt. Keep me informed." The last held a mild and loving query.

Bruce smiled ruefully. "Seems a while since I've been soul winning on any scale, George. I've been lollygagging in the comforts of the Cairnglen Manse. I'm ashamed it took a near tragedy to bring me to my senses."

"We both know the Lord's ways are not our ways. He has a different method of counting things that are past our finding out. A time for everything, you know! God be with you then, and I'll await to hear what happens next. Meanwhile, we'll take good care of our friend Peter. He, too, is in the Lord's hands, although he is not so sure of it as we are."

"Betsy, when Mistress MacIntyre goes out nowadays, and Paddy's not here, who drives her?"

"She doesn't go oot much now, Reverend Bruce, but when she does and it's no' in Mr. Bennett's coach, there's the Thompson livery stables."

"Would they have something available for a longer journey and maybe a small flitting?"

Betsy eyed him shrewdly. "I'm sure they would."

"Don't look at me like that, Betsy. I'm not planning to move Strathcona House to the Trossachs! I've a new friend who is going to come with me and stay at Cairnglen for a while, to help me with a project I have in mind."

Betsy instantly became more cooperative. "I'll speer them for you then. The mistress is waitin' in the drawing room."

"No need for you to go out, Betsy, just tell me where it is. I'll go see Granny Mac first, though."

But the servant knew her job. "It'll not be a bother, sir."

In taking his leave of the old lady, after explaining part of his plan, Bruce promised, "I'll bring Mary Jean to spend Christmas with you. As always, it will be Boxing Day before I can leave the parish—if I still have a parish, that is—but whatever happens, I'll keep you well-informed. Now I want to hear no more of this 'I'm getting too old' business, just as long as you're feeling well."

"I'm well enough. I'll look forward to Christmas then. Meanwhile Agatha sent me a note requesting that she begin calling on me again. She did not need to ask, but I suppose. . . . I'll write and tell her to bring the boys and the wee lass, too. Bruce?"

He gazed again at this person who had meant so much to his beloved Jean. "Yes, Granny Mac?"

"I pray for your Jeremy every day. I feel assured in my spirit, that, although he may encounter much danger, he'll be home eventually and none the worse. Maybe even better for it."

Bruce felt his eyes wet. Impulsively he gathered the frail body to his muscular chest. He whispered, "Thank you, my dear."

Betsy knocked discreetly. She had come in earlier and left again, sensing this private moment. "The cairt's waitin', Reverend Bruce."

While the men loaded the wagon, supervised by a suddenly enervated Barnabas, Bruce leisurely strolled toward the clinic for a last look. Sure enough the boards were being removed from the door.

As Bruce entered the hostelry across the street, Murdoch greeted him hopefully, "'Tis yersel', Reverend. How is Dr. Blair? Is he coming back already?"

"Not yet, Murdoch, but he'll do fine for the now. His father will be overseeing the clinic for a while."

"My, but that's just grand. Can I fetch you something?"

Suddenly Bruce had an idea. "Would it be possible for your good wife to make up a hamper? I realize it's short notice, but

I just thought of it the now. Some of her pies and a loaf of bread? Enough for four hungry men traveling by wagon to Cairnglen."

"She'll be that pleased to do it. Would you be requiring something to drink as well?"

"No ale or anything of that ilk, Murdoch. If the others want any, they'll need to furnish their own."

Wisely the host made no further remarks on that score. Calling his wife, he disappeared into the back regions. Bruce waited until he returned, saying, "Enough for four men it is then, Reverend. Gie her half an hour."

With a heart lighter than it had been for many days, Reverend Bruce MacAlister began his strangely escorted journey back to Cairnglen. The question of where to house Barnabas Hill, his dog Jude, and the queer miscellany of furnishings, mixed with printing paraphernalia, he would solve when the time came.

18

There's a language wrote on earth and sky
By God's own pen in silent majesty;
There is a song that's heard and felt and seen.
In spring's young shades and summer's endless green.

Instantly awake, Bruce sat up and rubbed his eyes in a strangely childlike gesture. He had been dozing in the sunlight when the words penetrated his dreamy state.

Their cavalcade had skirted past the town of Luss and was stopped now, and the passengers and carters alike had enjoyed the splendid repast basketed by the landlord Murdoch's wife. Where they sat or lolled in the afternoon heat, the road dipped close to the shore of Loch Lomond, and Bruce had been day-dreaming of that day when he and Peter Blair had taken their first hike together on the hills on the other shore of this very loch. Barnie's recitation had jerked him into the present.

"John Clare! Why, Barnie, you're a man full of surprises."

"Surprised, are you, that I've had a bit of education, am familiar with some classics, and appreciate the arts?"

"Well, no! Not that altogether, but the poet wrote those words strongly believing in his Maker."

"And you've formed the opinion that I'm not a believer in God?"

"I never said that, Barnie. I haven't given it much thought. 'Tis your own private business."

"Oh, and I thought you preachin' men were always after converts."

"Put like that, it sounds predatory. No, that's the work of the Holy Spirit. Ours is to bring a person's interest to the point where he will want to know God for himself. When you start asking questions, that's where we come in."

"With all the answers, I suppose?"

"Not with *all* the answers, no, Barnie. More like with an introduction."

They sat on, gazing silently at the beauty of the scene that had inspired the quote and that so aptly described the surroundings, until Barnie said, "Shall we get on then? The carter's men are getting restless."

Bruce sighed. "Aye, I suppose so, but it's so peaceful here, and you've put me in mind of Wordsworth's: 'Rocks, rivers, and smooth lakes more clear than glass. Untouched, unbreathed upon.' "

At that moment the peace was shattered into a million fragments as the unmistakable sound of a gunshot rang out across the water. The lead driver jumped, an oath loud on his lips. They climbed into their places on the wagon, surrounded on all sides by Barnabas Hill's worldly goods.

That man began laughing. "Here we are then. My view from here is not so conducive to poetry. All this rubbish blocking it, wi' folks over there shootin' at the deer out o' season and for pleasure spoils it as well."

Bruce nodded. His own view was only partly restricted, and he could still see the loch from the back.

"We can change places if you like. I can see very well from here."

"Och, no, I'll copy wise old Jude here and have forty winks myself, if you've no objection."

"No objection."

The remainder of their journey proved uneventful. As they left the loch and neared the place where the river Dochart began its wild dash to the sea, Bruce's mind shot ahead to what he would say to the members of his extended household. Of course the "Smiths" would still be away, so he would only have to explain his actions to his daughter, his mother, and Hamish.

*   *   *

The stable bothy, unused for twenty years or more, was being "redd up." Hamish had opposed Bruce when it came to
bringing this stranger's motley belongings inside the manse. He
put his foot down when he saw the conglomeration of the printer's press, boxes and boxes of old books and papers, an ancient
brass bed, and a doubtful-looking chair, which he suspected
was more the dog's than the man's. A fragile old desk that
neither Bruce nor Hamish recognized as Chippendale and more
crates, the contents of which caused Hamish no curiosity whatever, followed. In fact Hamish's curiosity was at a low ebb, and
he became sure he did not want this man or his dog—although
the latter was no doubt the cleaner—about the place at all.

The carter's men unloaded in record time, leaving everything
under the coach arch, when Hamish had decided something
must be done at once.

Bruce joined him in the bothy. "Hamish, I've told you to get
some helpers before you start cleaning up in here. Wait until
morning, and go to the town to recruit some. We've the money
to spare now, and I'll not have you doing it yourself. Bring
Henderson, if he's well enough, and ask him to get some others
as well. At least two more. Some carpenter's tools, too, would
come in handy, as thon books will need shelves."

"He's to be here awhile then?"

"Who knows how long? A month or two, likely."

Hamish voiced more objections. "Yon contraption—printin'
press or whatever ye ca' it. That'll not go up the bothy steps."

Bruce had been thinking the same thing. "We'll see to that
when the rest is in place. Maybe we'll just cover it with a tar-
paulin for the time being. He's not so bad, you know, Hamish.
Could I ask you to be more cooperative?"

But Hamish could not be reconciled to this Barnie Hill. He did
not suspect the man of any wrong dealings, but there was something about him that Hamish could not "take to." With no
further words to Bruce, he turned and walked away.

*   *   *

On being introduced to Elspeth, Barnabas Hill gazed at her frankly for a full minute, until, flustered, she turned away. He explained his curiosity, "Mistress Elspeth MacAlister." Not waiting for her to remind him she was Mistress Cormack, he ran on, "Och, I should have known. You were Elspeth Munro, were you not?"

She gasped. "Yes, but how—?"

Still partly ignoring her words, he rose and began to walk about the room. Bruce and Hamish were outside somewhere, and Mary Jean was petting Jude, who seemed to be tolerating her attentions fairly well.

"Imagine! I was one of your father's students. I couldn't stick it, though, and left the second year. But you, I mind fine him bringing you to the classes, defying tradition and proving more unpopular than ever with his colleagues, but he cared not a whit. Beggin' your pardon, mistress, I'm imposing. It's just that I—"

Elspeth was laughing shakily. "It's all right, Mr. Hill. I know what you mean, but please—"

He wasn't finished for all his apology. "So you married the MacAlister! I see his likeness in the Reverend, but I should have guessed that would happen. How is the rascal?" Even as he said this, he remembered the introduction, and realized he was treading on sensitive ground. He stopped at last.

Elspeth spoke gently but firmly, "He's been dead these past twenty-five years. I'm Mistress Cormack now. Bruce, as you have detected, is the 'rascal's' son, as well as mine."

The man stood gazing down at her, his pacing halted. "Me and my big mouth. I don't know where to put myself, I'm that embarrassed, so I am."

"No offense, Mr. Hill. Maybe you would like to tell me about yourself."

"My story is not that interestin'. A year in the Crimea. Och, not being a hero at all, that horrible experience cured me of any youthful ambition toward the military life. I got a job with a newspaper after that, but they didn't care for my way with words; so to speak, they still don't. Then I tried to go at it on my own. The printed truth doesn't pay too well, mistress."

"It will prevail though, never fear."

"Aye, but there's more discreet ways of expressin' it. Dare I ask about your father, 'Hugh the Devourer of Students' as we radicals used to call him? I did hear he had to leave the bar on account of illness. I'm amazed any illness had the audacity to stop him."

Elspeth's look of pain vanished as quickly as it had appeared, but Barnie's reporter's sense noticed, and he cursed himself inwardly for his insensitivity to her feelings. She answered, "He's bedridden, but in no physical pain."

The man threw her another glance but said no more as Bruce came back into the room alone. The spaniel shook off Mary Jean's ministrations and padded up to him. Absently he bent to pat the dog.

"We'll make some temporary arrangements for your equipment in the morning, Barnie. Meanwhile, we'll pray it doesn't rain or blow a storm through the night. About sleeping—"

"Dinna fuss, Reverend. I saw yon stable and presume there's some hay in the loft. I'll doss down for the now and see about a place to stay in the town the morrow." He stole yet another glance at Elspeth. Without her permission, he would not divulge the fact that they had known each other before today.

"You're very pensive, Mam. Are you worried about them at the Mains?"

"No, Bruce, I have to confess to not giving them much thought. It's your Mr. Hill."

Astonishment registered for a moment, and then he laughed softly. "He is a curiosity, is he not?"

They were seated on opposite sides of the fire in the parlor. During his absence, Elspeth had spent one day baking, and mother and son enjoyed some of her special shortbread with a cup of tea before retiring. Everyone else had gone to bed.

"He's different, all right, but it's not that. I might as well as tell you. He knew your father and me before we were married."

"Can I be hearing you right, Mam? Did you say you knew Barnie Hill and that he's had some connection with the law school in Edinburgh?"

"I said that indeed, Bruce, and it's true. He was another student under your grandfather Munro."

"Well, imagine that! He certainly puts on an act of being an ignoramus, although I saw through that quite quickly. Making out the small presses were his only interest, which I couldn't believe! He never finished the course, I take it?"

"No, he says he left the year before John—that is, your father—and I did." She turned her head away, but not before Bruce saw the glint of a tear. This man obviously meant little to her, yet he had stirred up memories of more than thirty years ago, and she was reliving some of the pain.

Giving herself a mental shake, Elspeth forced the discussion into the present again. "What's he doing here, Bruce?"

For the the next hour Bruce brought his mother up-to-date on all that had happened in Glasgow. When he mentioned the legacy, she made a strange remark. "Gran'pa Bruce and I always thought he was more your friend than your enemy."

"Angry! My friend? Maybe after a while he tolerated me, but my *friend*? During the years he was my teacher, he was no friend, believe me, Mam." Bruce rubbed his hand in the familiar pattern. He had never told his mother about the incident, but she had known just the same. Years later, after Jean's passing, she had let it slip one day about an anonymous letter sent to the Mains, wherein the writer had informed the family of his injury. That person had also sent the princely sum of one hundred pounds, to help bring them all to Glasgow for his ordination ceremonies.

Suddenly Bruce clapped his hand to his head. "Och, no, it couldn't have been! Could it?"

"Gran'pa aye suspected. Who else could have known all the things the letter mentioned? And now this money."

"Who indeed?"

Both sat on, silent now, remembering, as Bruce absorbed the very idea and Elspeth pondered. She broke the quietness, "I want to match the ten thousand, Bruce."

"Match it? What do you mean, Mam?"

"When my father disowned me, my own mother put up with a lot. At first she agreed with him that I had, well, thrown my life away. But after I made the attempt at reconciliation, the day I brought you to see her and he, he—" She swallowed but rallied again quickly. "She changed her opinion, and she took some of her own money—apparently her father had arranged it so that it would always be hers, unless she signed it away, and she never had. Well she invested it in two trust funds. One for you, and one for me. Mine matured on my fiftieth birthday. Andrew will not touch it, so I would like a share in your photography works."

"I couldn't allow that, Mam."

"Oh, I'm not *giving* it to you, Son. I want to invest in this business, as I believe it has promise. I'll not be a silent partner, either. It will give me a new interest. Besides, it can only be for good—giving men jobs with a peaceful end product to bring happiness to folk. No danger of explosions. Or is there? I'm ignorant of the business, I'm afraid. I only know I like the concept."

"I'm ignorant, too. That's why I took this chance on Barnie Hill. He's most knowledgeable on the subject. You're just full of surprises tonight, Mam. Maybe we should sleep on all this, then. When Raju and Faye come back, we'll have a business meeting, with you and Barnie and a couple of the men from Galbraith's I've had my eye on."

"No meeting for me, this time. I'm for home to Andrew. But I'll be wanting to know every move you make."

Bruce gazed deep into the startling blueness of his mother's eyes, so like his own both from expression and color that he could have been looking in a mirror.

Elspeth pulled her glance away first. "I'm for my bed. Morning comes soon enough. Good night, Bruce."

"Good night, Mam. I think morning is here already. I'll just bank the fire before I go myself."

But that was not to be yet. Since the night of the storm, the stepbrothers had never quarreled seriously. However tonight, the moment Elspeth disappeared upstairs, Hamish walked into the parlor. His bone of contention—Barnabas Hill.

❧ 19 ❧

"**B**ut Hamish, even if he's as bad as you make out—
and that goes beyond all reason—we have to give him the benefit of the doubt and the chance to—"

"I'm no' sayin' he's bad at a', it's chust that I canna thole him.
I've seen his kind comin' and goin' on the ships in the docks.
Fu' o' talk and the grand ideas but nae gumption to do for their
own sel's."

Bruce pushed one hand through his hair in a weary gesture.
"He's not a drinking man, if that's worrying you. Besides he's
determined to find his own place in the town."

Hamish ignored the last part. "Och, that kind dinna need the
drink. He's a troublemaker. Already, in this very house, he's
causin' trouble."

"Something's causing upset, I'll grant you that. What are you
suggesting I do then? I've as good as promised him a job with the
new factory we're going to build. An advisory position, at least,
until we get started. The Lord—"

"Aye, that's it, the Lord! Have ye asked Him aboot a' this?"

"Not in specifics, but everything fell into place so smoothly,
I just thought it must be right."

They sat in silence for several minutes. Then Hamish said,
"I've a notion to go the Mains wi' Elspeth for a while. The
harvest is ready, an' withoot Jeremy. . . . Well, ye ken?"

If Bruce had been shocked earlier, he was much more so now.
For Hamish to go anywhere without him and Mary Jean was

unheard of. His not being able to "thole" Barnie must be very serious indeed. Bruce gazed at this man, whose experience for so many years had been in direct contrast to his own and afterwards so intertwined. He glanced away.

"If that's what you want, Hamish, it might be better at that. But as you reminded me earlier, we ought to pray, first."

"Och, I've been prayin'. A' the time ye were talkin' to Elspeth. It chust remains for ye to say."

"There's no more to say. We should both get to our beds."

"Aye. Guid nicht."

This unexpected turn of events completely astounded Bruce. Truly he had been taking his stepbrother for granted ever since the night they had escaped the storm together. Of course he had dragged Hamish's unconscious body ashore, but he knew the hand of God had kept him treading the black water and precariously hanging on to a bit of smashed wood from the dory. Later, when Hamish had announced his life now belonged to Bruce and, through Bruce, to God, he had accepted that as almost his due.

Bruce tossed under the blankets. What arrogance! Certainly he asked Hamish for his opinion about most things, and he left money management and the running of the household entirely to him. For other matters, though, he would arbitrarily say "we'll do this" without a by-your-leave. He had done it this time.

Bruce groaned a quick prayer, "Lord, show me." At first he got no answer, but soon peace began to flow through him as, one after another, Bible verses came to his mind. "No condemnation" and "All things work together for good to them that love God." Just as he drifted off to sleep he smiled as the verse, "His banner over me was love" floated like a cloud of protection above him.

Bruce's astonishment seemed mild compared to Mary Jean's dismay and Elspeth's utter amazement, when Hamish announced at the breakfast table that he would be going back to the Mains with Elspeth.

"Are we all going, Daddy?"

"No, pet, just your uncle. He wants to go and help with the harvest."

"But—?" She glanced from one to the other of her beloved family. Until that time when he was sick, Mary Jean had never known a moment of her life without Uncle Hamie being somewhere close by. Her daddy had to go away without her sometimes, but never her uncle.

Elspeth did not voice her surprise, beginning to guess the reason. She spoke now directly to her granddaughter, "Remember, we talked just the other day about growing up, Mary Jean?"

"Aye!" The child's lips quivered, but her eyes stayed wide and clear as she listened.

"Well, some of that's starting now. Nobody can have everything just the way she wants it all the time."

"But even if it's not hurting anybody else?"

"We don't know how far our actions reach, dear. What might not seem to hurt us might hurt somebody else. Gran'pa Bruce would remind us that God's ways are not our ways."

The men at the table—Barnie had not yet put in an appearance—managed to look slightly shamefaced. They had both listened intently as Elspeth tried to help Mary Jean understand that life did not stand still, even for her.

For once, Hamish was not bustling about with teapot and toast. Neither was Elspeth. But suddenly Bruce almost shouted, "What's all the solemnity? Hamish has decided to go home to Aribaig for a wee while. Less than a day's journey north of us. I cannot go the now, because of my responsibilities here and—" He stopped short. Should he let the child choose if she wanted to go to Aribaig with them or stay with him? With Hamish away she would certainly have to go with himself wherever he went. The three waited politely for him to finish his remarks, each guessing the struggle going through his mind. "Mary Jean, you will stay here with me."

No one said a word in resistance, but he thought he heard his mother whisper, "So be it!"

"Mary Jean, you and I will walk to the town and bring back the hansom cab. You'll be catching the one o'clock train, Mam?"

"Yes, I'll tidy up, then put my things in the valise. Will that suit you, Hamish?"

"Fine then, Elspeth. I'll not be takin' much the now." He rushed from the kitchen without so much as lifting a cup.

Mary Jean began to clear off the table, as she did most days, but Bruce stayed her hand. "Let Gran'speth do that. You go and get your coat and tammy on." She left, and he turned to his mother. "When Barnie puts in appearance, you'll give him some breakfast, Mam? He is my invited guest."

She threw him a grieved glance. "Of course, Son. As for Hamish, he'll be all right. Gran'pa Bruce and Andrew will be good for him the now."

"As you say, Mam, so be it! We'll be back with the cabbie in about an hour, and that'll be plenty of time."

They started off, and if Mary Jean was quieter than usual, her father paid no heed, as he was having his own thoughts. Returning in the hired cab, Mary Jean suddenly shouted, "There's the hunt. I thought they didn't go until after school goes in."

Their driver had a word to say about this. "Sir Mortimer has some freens fae America, and he's oot showin' them the road. There's some braw new horses an' a'!"

No further remarks seemed necessary, and the remainder of the journey was silent.

If Barnabas Hill had any inkling of the disturbance his presence had caused, he did not remark on it. Rising stiffly from his bed of hay when Jude licked his face, he delved into the hamper where a solitary pie and some crusts of bread still rested. Sharing it bite by bite with the spaniel, he refreshed himself at the water pump in the yard. Seeing no one about and having heard no sounds, he softly whistled to the dog. Then the two trotted together up the path leading to the heather moor. Clouds gathered on the horizon, but he guessed it would not rain for an hour or so. He would use this time to allow the fresh air to clear his fogged brain. Maybe in a place like this he could at last get

down to some real writing. As for photographs, his mind
teemed with ideas about that, too. Every turn in the path
brought another scene of beauty to his jaded vision. Stories,
poems, postcards; small, more portable cameras, there seemed
no limit. First, though, he would need to justify the big highlandman's trust in him.

His dreaming was cut short by a sudden commotion. At once
he recognized the set of lead hounds as they bayed and bel-
lowed their way through the gorse. Calling sharply to Jude,
who had been doing his own investigating of this strange ter-
rain, he decided it was time to turn back. Too late! The dog, like
the man, had awakened from the lethargy of life's drab routine.
The air, the food, everything in the surroundings contributed to
what happened next. Jude's ears cocked as some primeval hunting ancestry stirred deep within him, and before Barnie could
stop him, he was off. Screaming the dog's name, Barnie ran
after his scarcely recognizable pet, but the scene unfolding before him held an aura of inevitable destiny. A shot rang out.
The hunting party, supposedly only scouting the land, was ripe
to shoot, even to kill, anything that moved. Without a halt in
their progress, the riders continued over the distant hill, leaving
a raving Barnie, ready to fight off the savage hounds with his
bare hands. Fortunately, one of the beaters, bringing up the
rear, called off the hounds. Barnie, with no thought for himself
or the blood streaming from the shattered body of his beloved
pet, gathered it up in his arms as he would a child. Trembling
from the intensity of his emotion, added to the unaccustomed
physical exertion, his legs gave out under him, and he collapsed
onto the heather. Angus MacQuarie, the beater, a kindly man,
ran back to assure himself the stranger would be all right.

"I'm that sorry, mister, aboot yer wee dug. It's their first
outin' this season, and they're goin' daft. The maister has a new
gun and couldna' wait for his sport . . . and—" His voice trailed
away as he realized the stranger was paying him no heed, rock-
ing back and forth, holding the dead animal as if it indeed were
a bairn. Reluctant to go, yet knowing the hunt master would

take him off the pay list if he wasn't there at the end of the day, the beater turned to leave.

A hoarse shout stopped him. "What's the man's name? Did you say?"

Angus hadn't said, but he felt no compunction in doing so now. "Sir Mortimer Handley-Jones. He's an Englishman!" as if the last explained everything.

Angus stood another moment, gazing sadly down at the scene, then he reached into an inner fold of his cape, saying, "I've a wee flask here. Would ye take a drap?" But Barnabas Hill had already sunk back into his state of terrible mourning.

Bruce and Mary Jean had waved good-bye to the travelers. The cab had disappeared down the road, and father and daughter busied themselves with the jobs usually done by Hamish. Finally Bruce announced he would be in his study, working on tomorrow's sermon.

Mary Jean had ventured one question. "Where are Mr. Barnie and Jude?"

"They must still be sleeping in." But he wondered, too. The man had stated he was an early riser, doing his most creative work in the hours before dawn. "The minute he puts in an appearance, come and tell me, pet. Have you something to do now?"

"Aye. Gran'speth showed me purl and plain, and I'm going to knit a scarf for Angela." Bruce smiled as he walked into his study. Angela was the latest doll in her collection and no more needed a scarf than did Queen Victoria.

Mary Jean struggled to knit one more row before setting aside the miniscule scrap of would-be scarf. Nobody in her small world ever slept in until this time of day. Besides a dog always needed to go out for a walk. Daddy had not said she shouldn't go outside or to the stable. She would just wander over and rap on the stable door. If she heard no noises or barking, she would go back to her knitting.

Hardly had Mary Jean reached the pump when she saw them. Mr. Barnie, as he had told her to call him, was stumbling and slipping down the path from the moor and carrying something funny. Mary Jean gasped in horror as she recognized the bundle as Jude, and he was hurt. The man had seen the child, but he hardly recognized her, his mind was so stunned.

She cried out, "Mr. Barnie, what's wrong with Jude?"

He brushed past her with no apology. Tears blinded him, and Mary Jean followed slowly as he made for the stable door. She ran ahead to open the door, and then she stepped aside. The dog's head hung limply, and Mary Jean had seen enough dead lambs, even a stillborn calf once, to know that Jude was gone.

Gently placing his burden in the hay-filled manger, the man smoothed the tangled, feathery coat.

Mary Jean ran for the back door then straight to Bruce. He caught her up, at first not understanding a garbled word. "Hold on there, pet. I don't know a word you're saying. What do you mean? Have you been dreaming?"

"No, no! Come with me to the stable, Daddy. Mr. Barnie needs you. His wee dog is dead!"

Bruce didn't hesitate now but raced to the stable, with Mary Jean close on his heels. He prayed as he ran, "Lord, if this is so, help me with Your wisdom. I won't know what to say or do."

Those words in fact were his first ones to the stricken man: "Barnie, what can I say or do? I feel responsible for this terrible thing, yet I'm not sure I'm understanding what happened."

At last there came a slight response. Barnie had been kneeling in front of the manger, his hands still stroking Jude's silky head. He had also closed the staring eyes. Now he moved as he felt Bruce's hand on his shoulder. In a muffled voice he mumbled, "Not your fault, man. 'Twas that hunting party. Handley-Jones, the stalker said. I'll get him some way for this, so I will."

Bruce ignored the last part. "Hunters! Aye. We saw them earlier. They come from a place called Tomich. A few local folks join them, but they don't usually start shooting until later on. It's not—" He stopped before he said too much about the hunters. In this mood the other man might do something very foolish.

"Come on, Barnie. It's a terrible shame about your wee dog, but you can't bring him back. Come away into the house and have some refreshment. Have you even broken your fast today?"

"Och, yes. Jude and I had a rare feast: the remains of the picnic. Little did we know it would be his last before being sacrificed to the great god of blood sport!"

"I understand your feelings, but that kind of talk won't help matters. We've all had our sorrows to bear, but we have to keep going. Come along, Barnie."

To Bruce's surprise the man rose to his feet. "I'll get a clean shirt. Then I'll need to bury him."

"He'll do 'till you've recovered a bit. Mary Jean, go fetch a sheet from the linen press."

She dragged her eyes away from the dead animal and ran to obey, her normally bright orbs clouded with unshed pain.

Bruce turned back to Barnie. "For the sake of my wee lass, then, can I ask you to pull yourself together? She's awful sensitive."

They exchanged glances, and Barnie nodded. "Aye, I know." He was searching through his gladstone bag, and now he said, "He'll not be needing your sheet, Reverend, thanks just the same. I have his own rug here and his blanket, too. Together they'll make a fine shroud."

Bruce moved in to assist him but was waved back. "No, I'll do it. You're quite right though, he'll be fine there 'till I . . . I mean, 'till you and I have had a talk." His mind resuming its reporter's curiosity, he looked about for the others as they entered the house.

Bruce forestalled his questions. "My mother—and brother, too—had to get back to the farm. Harvesttime, you know?"

"Oh, I thought your brother stayed here with you."

"So he does, but we sometimes go to the Mains to help at harvesttime."

The subject was dropped.

⟶⊰ 20 ⊱⟵

"**B**ut why can we not go to Jude's funeral, Daddy?"

"First of all, we're not invited, Mary Jean. Anyway it's not exactly a funeral as we understand them." They were in the kitchen, putting together an evening meal. Bruce had discovered how busy his mother and Hamish had been during his absence in Glasgow. Jams and jellies, biscuits and pies, stock for soup, and even some jellied veal and potted cheese now graced the pantry shelves.

About an hour ago, with very little visible emotion, Barnie had announced that he was going to bury his dog. Bruce had offered no comment but stood behind Mary Jean, one hand firmly pressed into her shoulder. He need not have worried, as she had saved her questions for him.

"If it's not exactly a funeral, then what is it?"

"There's a difference in a way, pet. To Barnie, it's a private funeral in which he is saying farewell to a beloved friend. To others, it's simply the burying of the dead body of a dog."

"What is it to us, Daddy?"

"Well, we hardly knew Jude, and although we're terrible sorry he's dead, we cannot be mourning him in the same way as Barnie."

"What would Jesus do, Daddy?"

"We're not exactly sure of that, darlin', but we are sure of this much: Jesus knows all about it. He sees the wee sparrow fall, remember? And He grieved for His friends. Whatever Jesus does is in love, and we follow Him in that, as in everything. So if we show Jesus' love to Barnie and do not ask him questions, but wait until he tells us, that will be the best. Do you see, pet?"

"Aye!" The big eyes brimmed with tears, but she said no more.

A few hours later Bruce had another interruption. Mary Jean was already in her bed, sleeping soundly, he hoped. Barnie had not joined them for the evening meal, and they had kept to their plan not to bother him or try to coax him or push food at him. Suddenly the man appeared in Bruce's study, ready to speak or make some announcement. Bruce laid aside his pen.

Barnie's words brought more surprise: "You have a bathtub, I see."

"We have that. Mary Jean was in it a while ago, and I'll be having a turn myself before I go to my bed."

"Could I prevail upon you to let me use it?"

"Of course. Go now, if you wish."

"I will that, but I've a few things to say first." For a moment he turned away from Bruce's frank blue scrutiny. "Your mother will have told you that I knew her long ago!"

"She did indeed."

" 'Twas your father, John MacAlister, I knew best. A fine man but, if you'll pardon my saying so, a weak one. He had some fixed ideas on how Scotland—and even the very world— should be run. He got desperate, thinking how he could do nowt about it. We agreed on many things, but where he deeply felt the ills of the world, I said to hang with them. I've had enough to do looking after myself."

Barnie's face crumpled for a moment and Bruce thought he was going to weep at last, but no. "Disappointed with men, and one woman in particular, I just roved about, trying one thing and another. Writing's the thing for me, but even then, when I couldn't write how I wanted, I gave up on it. You know already that you came on me when I was at my latest endeavor.

"Funny enough, the drink never appealed to me as a way out. I knew a scientist once, who in a most graphic demonstration, showed us what a dram of whiskey does to a monkey's brain. I decided my brain needed no such deterioration. I had a photo of that demonstration, and I copied it in one of my papers. The Royal Society for Prevention of Cruelty to Animals beat me on that one. That's when I left Carlisle." He scratched his head and smiled sadly at Bruce. "Can you imagine the irony of that? Me, who loves the dumb animals more than the human ones—no offense, my friend.

"Anyway, this is getting long-winded. I started to say, since the days of the university and your grandfather Munro the Monster's lectures, I've traveled a lot of ground, but not in a career. Much as I loved my wee Jude, it's taken his death to show me I've achieved nowt. No, don't try to argue with that."

"I wouldn't agree with your evaluation, Barnie, but how can I help you?"

"You've a shine about you, man. 'Tis not 'religion' as I've thought I knew it. There's a peacefulness in you that I covet. Your mother's smeared with it, and your brother Hamish has it as well. Although I detect in him a more practical application o' it. For instance, I knew fine he took a scunner at me. Anyway, it took poor old Jude's demise to show me where my values lie, and I would like to hear about what it is you all have."

Discerning what Barnie had in mind, Bruce had already been praying for wisdom in how to answer this kind of request. "Well, Barnie, I thank you for those words. Money cannot buy what you describe, nor can it be forced on a body. You have asked to be told about it, but you still haven't asked to receive it for yourself. My advice for this moment, when your emotions are stirred so deeply by your loss, would be for you to watch and listen a bit more. For instance, come to the kirk in the morning. You'll meet all manner of folk there. In my own studying and reading of this book," and he held up his well-thumbed study Bible, "I have concluded that although Christians are called saints many times, they were and are very human, with their faults and feelings that come with that packet. In fact, the only perfect one is Jesus Christ Himself. Why not just come and see?"

What Barnie saw when he came, amazing Bruce by appearing in a black suit, tie, and a spotless white shirt, was not the most settled congregation to be held up as an example of Christianity at work. Cairnglen's depleted economy, plus the latest rumors about a possible new industry, had brought folks from far and near. The Bible reading was taken from 3 John 2, and as Bruce got up to speak, he repeated the last line with emphasis.

" 'Even as thy soul prospereth!' Many of us here today have come with a feeling of anxiety, maybe even of dread for the future, gnawing at us. Now, that is most understandable and I have been through some of that myself since the last time we gathered together here. But the text we have today is one of hundreds in the Holy Book that give us a clear description of how to live without anxiety.

"Far be it from me to say we have nothing to be anxious about. The Lord Himself knows we appear to have much. What I am saying is the opposite way round. In the first rule of five specific ways I will point out how to help our souls prosper so that the rest of that verse will also come true. They are Jesus' own words, in fact, as He says, 'Be anxious for nothing.' Thank God He doesn't leave it hanging there but goes on to tell us ' . . . But in everything give thanks.' Get rid of fears by giving thanks, even for adversity!"

Bruce stopped to drink from the small pewter cup left for that purpose. He dabbed at his brow with one of his giant hankies before continuing, " 'Not easy' you say, and I agree. It can only be done with Jesus' help. 'Behold!' He says—in our language that would be like 'pay attention now'—for I am with you always!' No limits, no special conditions attached, no certain places or specific times, but *always*. That's a big word and another reason to give thanks, thereby prospering—or blessing, if you like—our souls again.

"Here in our beloved Scotland, we have a favorite Psalm. 'Tis the Shepherd Psalm, the twenty-third. Take one verse for my third rule today. 'He, the Lord, restoreth my soul.' So, we don't have to struggle to do that ourselves either. He'll do it. He promised! A good Scot always keeps his promises, but Jesus surpasses all nationalities and traits, even our very best. If we, who are evil from birth, feel obliged to keep our word, how much more then will the Lord of Creation be obligated to keep His?

"Another Psalm brings us the fourth ingredient in the recipe for soul prosperity. It is in Psalm One Hundred and Three. I've requested the cantor to read it out loud in full for us the now. Mr. MacGregor."

The man, who had been listening as intently as every other person in the shaded lovely building, shook himself and began, "Bless the Lord, O my soul: and all that is within me, bless his holy name. . . . "

Bruce took the moment of respite to have another sip of the water and to pray that his words were reaching fertile ground. Once again he repeated the last line. " 'Bless the Lord, O my soul.' David, our Old Testament shepherd-king, a forerunner of Jesus, is telling—no he is *ordering*—his soul to bless the Lord. Three times in these verses we hear the words, 'Bless the Lord, O my soul.'

"But David's Psalm doesn't stop with the telling but continues to show us how to do this. With all that is within us we bless Him. It gets easier as we remember to ' . . . forget not all his benefits' and when we hear about His healing all our diseases; but best of all, He forgives us all our iniquities. In that *way* He redeems our life from destruction, even to crowning us with His—not our—loving-kindness and tender mercies.

"On top of all that comes the next promise. ' . . . Who satisfieth thy mouth with good things, so that thy youth is renewed like the eagles.' Most of us would like to have our youth renewed, or be given the ability to mount up with eagle's wings. From this passage we must conclude that God's Holy Spirit will endow us with like abilities when we serve Him above and beyond the call of duty. As the great prophet Isaiah says, ' . . . They that wait upon the Lord,' shall renew their strength. . . . In today's text, we see that we can bless His Holy Name for that promise." He gazed again at his listeners.

"I'm not going through every verse. You've heard it before

and know from my past sermons how to apply those good things to your own lives. Take verse ten though: 'He hath not dealt with us after our sins nor rewarded us according to our iniquities.' Thank God for that! Other verses show us how fleeting are our days on earth but the last verse says: 'Bless the Lord, all his works in all places of his dominion: Bless the Lord, O my soul.'

"To sum up, then. We desire the blessing described in the verse from Third John, verse two. The measure of our prosperity in the Lord, with the help of the Holy Spirit, is the same measure as our soul's prosperity. Only the Lord can make that happen, and our part is to allow Him to do it. If you're not sure how to allow Him, then pray that He will show you how. As you pray and seek His face He will teach you from His Word. After that you will be overwhelmed with the desire to praise Him. In turn, He will bless you, thereby brimming you full of the true prosperity, measured by a different standard."

Bruce closed his eyes and stood in silence for moments before concluding: "For a benediction I say: 'The Lord shall preserve thee from all evil. He shall preserve thy soul. The Lord shall preserve thy going out and thy coming in from this time forth. Even for ever more. Amen."

"Well, well, MacAlister! I never heard preachin' like that in all my born days." The carriage from Mannering Heights had come for Bruce as always, and after a few remarks about traveling in style, Barnie had subsided into a corner, his face covered with a brooding expression, as they journeyed into town. Now he sat up straight, throwing strangely vulnerable and wistful glances at Bruce.

The latter took up the challenge. "Have you heard that many sermons then?"

"Enough to recognize a good one when I hear it."

"A pity more folk won't think so. I'm afraid I've rubbed a few more sore spots raw this morning."

"How could the words you said be taken wrong?"

"You're a one to talk. You tell me your words are misunderstood all the time."

Barnie grinned sheepishly. "Not misunderstood. I mean it when I write insulting things. You never said a wrong word."

"I'm considered too soft on the sinner. Not enough fire and brimstone or quotations like, '. . . The wages of sin is death. . . .' "

"Yes, I noticed that, but I was glad of it."

"Some are glad enough, but the self-righteous get indignant. You see, by telling the folk not to fear and that the Lord is with them, I'm encouraging sloth and wasteful living. I should use terms like, 'no work, no eat,' and the like." The carriage pulled up at the manse close, and Bruce almost wished he had accepted the luncheon invitation given by Priscilla Mannering. In part he had refused because he suspected she and Reginald had been on yesterday's hunt. Barnie was still too close to the edge of his grief to risk stirring it up again.

"Mary Jean, what will we have for dinner? Oh, I know. The steak-and-kidney pie your Gran'speth baked and left in the cold larder. We'll pop it in the oven to warm. I'll peel some tatties and turnip and there's still plenty of shortbread in the tin. We'll do just fine."

His daughter had kept silent the whole way. Now she spoke very softly, "Yes, Daddy."

He gave her a surprised glance. "Are you all right, pet?"

"No, Daddy." Her whispered reply was so quiet he hardly heard it as they alighted from the carriage and sent it rattling on its return journey.

Barnie disappeared in the direction of the stable, calling over his shoulder that he had a book or two he wanted to show Bruce.

"What's wrong, pet?"

"Jeremy said that all the time."

"Said what, Mary Jean?"

"About the shepherd and the still waters and the valley of death."

"Come here, pet. If you remembered what I said, you'll know

that I didn't mention the 'valley of death' but the 'shadow of the valley of death.' That was for a reason. Our folks have had enough of shadows and death the now, and so have you. No, let me finish that part for you. 'I will fear no evil . . .', did Jeremy not say that, too?"

"Aye, he did. I forgot that bit. Gran'drew always said it to us when we went for the cows. Fear no evil but look after each other."

"Gran'drew knows that evil still lurks, but we're not to fear it, because God goes with us. Some evil thing separates us from Jeremy at the moment, but the Lord is with him and will restore him to us."

Mary Jean giggled, and he sighed with relief as she said, "I'm getting a kirk sermon all to myself the day."

He joined in the laugh. "You are that, pet, and it'll cost you a big hug and a kiss." He picked her up, and she squealed with joy just as Barnie returned, carrying a bundle of books.

"Did I not hear you mention a steak-and-kidney pie and some other comestables a while ago?"

Bruce eyed the books as he answered, "You did indeed, and it'll be ready in about an hour. I've an idea though. No more discussions today. After dinner we'll go for a walk to the falls, and then, that box of photographs you mentioned, Barnie, maybe you could show them to us—with appropriate captions, of course."

But their walk did not take them to the falls. Instead, Barnie requested that they go through the town, and then stroll past the burned-out mansion and the ruined works.

As they reached the outskirts Mary Jean said, "Can I go to see Dorrie and wee David John, please, Daddy?"

"Why not? We'll walk with you to the door."

He turned to Barnie with an explanation, but that man had a question. "More than half the houses have their blinds drawn, why's that?"

"Mourning for Sean O'Mulligan. The Irish Catholics have that tradition, you know. I believe they keep it up for a week. My, but a lot has transpired since last Sunday at this time!"

They had reached the Henderson house, and Mary Jean knocked on the door. Jake opened it and stood for a minute, blinking in the sudden brightness, before saying, "It's yersel', Reverend MacAlister. Come away in. Dorrie, here's Mary Jean to see you." Familiar noises floated out to them, including the cry of the newborn.

"You'll excuse us, Jake. Mary Jean wants to visit Dorrie and the new bairn. I'll not come in the day but will return for her in an hour."

The man was staring at Barnie, and suddenly Bruce had an idea. Why not? "Jake, this is my friend Barnie Hill. Barnie, meet Jake Henderson. We were on our way to see the ruins. Would you be wanting to come with us?"

The woebegone face lit up. "A wid that. I'll just tell the wife."

Jake proved to be a better tour guide than Bruce. He knew the history of the gunpowder works. By the time they reached the gates, Barnie had received a complete recital of the Galbraith factory, from its opening until its fatal ending last week.

Jake then turned to Bruce. "You were awa' to Glesca' I hear?"

"Yes, I—"

"Ye missed the funeral and the wee cafuffle we had then."

Bruce sighed. "What happened, Jake?"

" 'Twas a long funeral. A locum priest took it, as Father O'Mulligan is away in Ireland on a retreat."

Bruce digested this bit of information but refrained from asking why a family priest should be sent away and not allowed to attend his cousin's funeral. Bruce had been too involved in his own life's difficulties to pay much attention to Dennis O'Mulligan's lot.

Jake put a question: "Did ye not hear aboot that then?"

Not sure what he hadn't heard, Bruce knew he would find out soon enough. What Jake had to tell included the fact that so many strangers attended the funeral, among them a bunch of murmurers. The town council had been at the cemetery when the rabble rousers began their heckling. The more responsible citizens felt horrified that this should happen but everyone had listened avidly when the possibility of a new factory going up was mentioned. After the funeral, some townsfolk packed up and left, while others decided to wait a wee while to find out if the rumors might be true. Shamefully Bruce shuffled his feet, thinking of his neglect of the town in his pursuit of his own business.

Jake was still talking. "Naebuddy wis hurt, thank God, but a whean insults were flung aboot!"

"Who was throwing them, Jake?"

"Och, ane or twa o' the toffs turned up at the graveside. Miss Mannering and yon lawyer chap and the town clerk hissel'. I thocht it considerate o' them, but some o' the Irishmen didna' think so. Nae sooner was Sean settled in the grave then they hotheeds were at it, throwin' divots at the Protestants, beggin' you pardon, Reverend."

Bruce glanced round anxiously. "Maybe you shouldn't be seen with me, Jake. After all, I'm not only a Protestant, I'm a minister as well."

"Naw, naw! That'll be the day when I need permission to walk wi' who I like. I choose for massel'."

Barnie had been very quiet, but now he spoke: "There's a definite group of troublemakers, with a leader, then?"

"Aye. Sean O'Mulligan was that leader, but since he was shot and kilt, McCabe is doin' all the talkin'. He's a mean yin that. At least Sean was for fair play."

"*McCabe*, isn't he a tradesman?"

"Aye, a carpenter. In the works he did a' the odd jobs for Galbraith. It didna' seem to bother him then that the gaffer was a capitalist and a Protestant."

They had reached the scene of desolation, and as Bruce had not bothered to warn Barnie to say nothing about their plans yet, he wondered what might be forthcoming. He didn't have to wonder long.

"So this is it? The site of the latest Phoenix."

Bruce started. *Granny Mac's very expression.*

Jake narrowed his eyes at the stranger. "What do you mean, Mr. Hill?"

"Och, it's just a saying, I—"

Jake interrupted, "I ken the sayin' fine. It's aboot a great bird risin' up oot o' the ashes. Whit has that to do wi' all this?" He waved his hand toward the heaps of rubble while Barnie and Bruce stared at him in some astonishment. Catching a glimpse of their faces, he laughed. "Not such an ignoramus, am I?" He sobered at once and turned to Bruce. "Whit's to become of us—and Cairnglen—Reverend MacAlister?"

"I'm not sure yet, Jake, but it will be something good, I'm sure. I do know that much. Give me another few days and keep it to yourself for the now, but keep your spirits and your hopes up!"

"I kent ye wid hae something up your sleeve. I said to Kate just this mornin', 'Reverend MacAlister'll no' see us stuck.' "

"We'll have to wait and see, Jake. There are still some details to work through yet and a long way to go. Meanwhile I have some renovating to do at the manse. I could use your services and those of a mate or two, maybe even McCabe, as he's a carpenter."

Jake's mouth dropped open in amazement, then his face lit up for the second time within the hour. "Oh, I see! Aye, that's it then. I'll talk to McCabe, an' he'll likely be as glad o' the work as I am. Can I bring Jimmy?"

"Yes, bring Jimmy, too. I'll tell you when you come what I want done. I think Mary Jean will be about ready to go home now, and so am I. What about you, Barnie?"

"Aye, I'm coming."

"Daddy, fancy us nearly forgetting about school starting to-morrow!"

"Mercy! we did that. Now, if we hadn't visited Dorrie this afternoon, you might have been marked absent the first day."

Mary Jean thought this extremely funny. The men looked at each other as she developed a fit of giggling before deciding they might as well enjoy the joke, whatever it was. If Barnie's laugh sounded hollow, no one thought the worse of him for that.

-ᵒ⊰{ 21 }⊱ᵒ-

Sounds of a laden handcart, trundling over the paving stones and under the arch, woke the three manse inhabitants next morning at the crack of dawn. Jake and Jimmy were wasting no time in getting the project started, and the man McCabe, after a week or more of idling, was also glad to be at work.

Seeing them started on their first job of clearing everything out of the loft, Bruce came back to the kitchen and began to outline the rest of the day to Barnie and Mary Jean. "I'll walk Mary Jean to the school, and then I'll be at the kirk for a while. You usually get a half holiday on the first day, Mary Jean, so come to the kirk, and we'll come home together as well. That might be about two o'clock, Barnie."

"You mean to tell me you've other work to do after thon sermon on Sunday?" Bruce laughed at the other man. He had persuaded him to sleep in the house last night, and between them they had foraged a breakfast of sorts. Mary Jean hurried away to get her schoolbag ready. Missing Hamish, Bruce realized afresh how much he had taken him for granted throughout the years. He put the thoughts aside to deal with the now.

Not wishing to ask, but still curious, he had waited for Barnie to say what he would be doing this morning. Instead the man had voiced the ages-old myth about ministers only working one day in the week.

"Yes, Barnie, I've work to do. Sadly neglected this summer for one reason or another."

"So what is it you'll be doing the day?"

"Och, some administration jobs are waiting on my desk. Matters the beadle thinks he can't handle without me. Then I've a Wednesday-night session meeting to get ready for. Housekeeping details must go by the board this month, as the main topic will be the same one as the council's last week, the concerns mentioned after the service yesterday." Bruce knew he was speaking more than required, but he was a bit worried about leaving Barnie alone just yet.

"You mean, your good advice about not being anxious fell on deaf ears?"

"Not altogether, I pray, but there's always the practical application. Oh, there you are, Mary Jean." But he waited another minute, and at last Barnie said, "I'm going to dust off my camera. Maybe go up to thon falls and try for a photo or two. What about your workmen though?"

Mary Jean threw him a questioning glance. She had seen the camera in his hand when he told her he was going to bury Jude.

Her daddy was answering Barnie's query, "They'll do fine without any supervision for the day at least. Lock up when you go and leave the key—"

"Not under the welcome doormat, surely?"

"No, I'll show you the place. It's just about as obvious. A loose brick under the coach arch."

The day proceeded much as Bruce had described it, except that the schoolmaster had stopped him as he left Mary Jean at the school steps. He looked extremely anxious, and Bruce sighed inwardly. The man perpetually wore that worried frown, but today, as it turned out, he had good reason.

"How long will we be going on for, Reverend MacAlister?"

"As long as we can, Dominie. Have you had no directions or instructions?"

"Not yet, and I've not had my August stipend yet either."

Bruce threw him a keen glance. A trustworthy person, Rob Heriot, but certainly burdened down by the cares and responsibilities of this world. "Robbie, if you're in need, let me know. 'Twould be a personal, private matter between the two of us."

The man turned away quickly but did not refuse the offer. "Thank you, Reverend."

Suddenly Bruce recalled one of Gran'pa Bruce's wise sayings, "Dinna just talk—it's cheap enough—but do!" He called out, "Robbie, come to the kirk with Mary Jean, when you dismiss the school. I've something to tell you."

The dominie's countenance cleared at once. "I will that, Reverend!"

Barnie Hill had neglected to mention to Bruce that he dusted off more than his camera. One other item he slipped into the haversack before hoisting it on to his back and striding off up the path to the moor. Barnie liked his host. MacAlister was much more than a nice man or even a good minister; he was that rare being, one who cares. *I'm not deceiving him. He would be hard to deceive. No, he just would not understand what I must do now.*

The path ended and Barnie was once more on the open moor. This time he did not whistle or stride out in that blissfully unaware of danger attitude of the other morning. A wiser, sadder man today, he filled his mind with the things he had learned after yesterday's service. While Bruce and Mary Jean had greeted the worshipers, he had shamelessly pumped the garrulous Priscilla Mannering about the hunt. Learning that the so-called scouting party would be out again this morning, he had made his plans accordingly. Casually he had asked the lady about the hunt master and she had described the man in detail. Now all Barnie had to do was find a "hide" for himself and wait. Judging by the route taken two days ago, he searched for a spot facing the opposite direction but still within view.

Once he found what he was looking for, he settled down to wait. Carefully Barnie removed the outer lens from the second object in his pack. In effect he was not adding a telescope to his camera but was turning the telescope into a camera. He had learned the simple procedure many years ago and had used it on the battlefield.

Soon his efforts were rewarded as he heard and then saw the riders approach. Yes, this would do very well. His camera clicked once and then again before the hunters disappeared over the same hill, and Barnie made his way to his next stop. Setting up the camera once more, he tried to concentrate on taking pictures of the magnificent view. However, his mind was not on the art this morning, so he packed up again and tramped back to the manse.

Another handcart had joined the first outside the stables, also filled with a miscellany of builder's and carpenter's equipment. No sound of industry drifted out to him, and Barnie, his curiosity aroused, stepped through the stable door.

Two men, seated on either side of the empty manger, reacted each in his own way. The man he recognized as Jake Henderson stood up and tweaked his bonnet, while the other sat and glowered. "G'mornin', Mr. Hill."

"Good morning, Jake. I take it this is Mr. McCabe?"

"*Wattie*'ll do fine."

An awkward silence greeted this remark, but it was quickly broken by Jake. "We're no' sure yet what the reverend wants exactly. We hae some drawin's here." They had a bench set up between two trestles, and Jake called to the young lad who had just entered, "Bring another box for Mr. Hill, Jimmy."

It soon became evident to Barnie that McCabe knew his business. Given different circumstances, the man could and should have been an architect. As he warmed to the task of explaining to the others how he would do the job, if he had the chance, the Irishman's belligerence diminished. Bricks and mortar here, a wooden panel there, and the stairs should go up from the outside to meet just so.

Tiring of the detailed account, even if the place was to be his new abode, Barnie turned his attention to the boy. Thirteen or fourteen, he would guess, but then more likely older. Those children who started working at a young age often suffered retarded growth. This young fellow was not retarded in any other way though. Suddenly aware of the man's scrutiny, Jimmy turned and gave him look for look, obviously raised to the belief that he was anybody's equal. Barnie approved of that attitude, containing as it did no impertinence. He was the first to glance away, but he flashed the lad one of his rare smiles. The men were engrossed in an argument about the qualities of the new metal, aluminum, being used by some builders.

Barnie beckoned to Jimmy. "Do you like books, Jimmy?"

"Aye, I do, but I've only got the two."

"Is one about the Greek myths and such?"

"Aye, how did ye ken that?"

"Just a smart guess, I suppose." He waited a moment and then said, "I've some books you might like to look at."

The eager look disappeared as quickly as it had surfaced. "Ah havena time for readin'."

The voices of the planners had risen by a few degrees. "Bricks are too hard to get awa' oot here. We could get big stanes and rocks easier, I say."

"And I say that's no' ony easier. We'll need to consult the reverend. Who pays the piper ca's the tune, ye ken!" Jimmy placed himself beside his father, and Barnie moved out, leaving the workmen to their games.

Recovering the back-door key from its place, Barnie went straight to the room assigned to him. Ignoring the beauty of the furnishings, unheeding even of the lovely little escritoire, so obviously used by a lady of a bygone age, he scattered belongings and books and papers until he found the tome he wanted. Throwing himself across the bed, he soon became engrossed in *Photography, the Mirror of Modern Art.* The chapter absorbing his interest was entitled "The Camera, Quicker Than the Eye, Sees More."

Having spent the day with his books and photos and memories, Barnie Hill was more than ready for company when the town's jaunty cart rolled into the coach-house yard. Rushing to the door to welcome Bruce and Mary Jean, he stopped at the door. They were not alone. A man he recognized from Bruce's earlier descriptions as Ralph Smith was handing a lady down from the carriage.

Barnie's natural charm bubbled up and over. Thus, if Hamish's reaction to Barnabas Hill had been akin to hate, bringing with it the desire to be anywhere the despised person was not, Raju Singh displayed a completely opposite reaction.

❧ 22 ❧

Introductions were dealt with quickly and shortly. After that Barnie and Raju sat closeted together in the morning room. Bruce had gone to see what the men had accomplished in the stables, while Faye Felicity and Mary Jean had disappeared into the kitchen regions to explore the interesting boxes and bags brought by the travelers. The promise of gourmet delights lightened the atmosphere considerably, and the two photography enthusiasts settled down to some good talk.

"Am I understanding you correctly then, Mr. Hill? You are the photographic army correspondent who vanished with all those pictures of the Isandhawana slaughter in seventy-nine?"

Barnie held up a hand in protest. "Not *vanishing* so much as fleeing in the cause of self-preservation. Both sides were after my pictures and my reports, while caring not a whit for the photographer."

"You never destroyed them then?"

Barnie Hill shot a glance at the tall, handsome Indian. From his own travels and ability to judge men, he recognized high caste when he came in contact with it. This was a Brahmin if ever he saw one. Yet the earlier conversation confirmed him to be a practicing Christian of the same dimension as the MacAlister.

Barnie decided he could trust him. "I never destroyed them, but they're not a sight I'd want the women to see."

Raju nodded. Time enough later to mention his wife's firsthand knowledge of the results of famine in Lucknow or the photographs he himself had taken of the horrible scenes in some of India's teeming cities.

The other man was still talking. ". . . A scheme to make a fortune by writing the story, with graphic illustrations of course, but some of the pictures began to fade, along with my enthusiasm. I decided instead to start looking for better ways to perfect the art of photography. You're familiar with William Willes and his platinotype, I have no doubt?"

"I've heard of it but have not tried it. Wonders are there for the discovering, and the potential seems limitless. I've toyed a bit with superimposing myself."

He received another pointed glance from Barnie, who began to wonder if this discernment Christians spoke of so glibly could include mind reading. "Oh, aye? Have you done much of it? Superimposing, I mean."

"Not very much, no. I'm not keen on showing a distorted image, unless it's for a comic effect."

"Och, you mean a cartoon?"

Raju smiled. "Cartoons are fine, yes, but I would draw the line at lampooning. I find that offensive."

Puzzled, Barnie stared at Raju for a full minute before asking, "Offensive to whom?"

"First to myself. Then I believe we grieve the Holy Spirit when we distort parts of creation in that way."

Barnie had no reply. This was uncharted ground for him. He changed the subject. "Have you heard about my wee dog?"

"Only that you brought one and it met with an accident."

Barnie got up and walked to the window. He turned back and began to smash one clenched fist into his other hand. "Yon was no accident. The great white hunters shot him."

"I'm sorry to hear that Barnie, I didn't know—"

But the other man continued as if he hadn't heard, "Aye. Shot a wee, innocent pet, but I'm going to get them!"

Raju looked stunned. "You're not considering—"

Barnie's laugh was bitter. "Och, I'll not be shootin' wi' guns, man. I've a better notion. This morning, out on the moor, I took

some photos of the hunters as they set off. The Mortimer creature was in the lead of course. Then before I buried my wee
Jude, my spaniel, ye ken, I took a photo or two of him at
different angles. . . ."

Raju was beginning to understand, and he disliked the understanding, but he let his new friend finish.

"Then I wrote this caption. Ye'll not like it much, seein' ye're
for turnin' the other cheek, like the reverend, but like it or no',
ye'll have to admit it has . . . but listen: 'Bold and brave the
huntsman came. To shoot a stag was aye his aim. He couldny
fine one; just the same. He had to shoot at something! So, he
shot a wee bit spaniel. It's all in the sporting game. Now he'll
never find a stag, to put in his bag. . . . For they all died laughin'
when they heard his name. Englishman for shame, gang
hame."

There was silence in the room.

"It's not very good, it is, Raju?"

"Frankly, no! I think it demeans you and your talents. I have
some ideas on how they could be used more productively. Show
me. . . ."

When Mary Jean and Faye cautiously entered the room to
announce that food was ready, the two men were still deep in
discussion of the various methods of taking and developing
good, clear images, temporarily leaving behind the subject of
superimposing. Raju had learned that his new friend had attended a set of lectures in London, given by one Emerson, and
heartily agreed with some of the theories expounded there.

Catching his wife's almost pleading glance, Raju rose reluctantly. Barnie followed, and they proceeded to the dining al-
cove.

After the meal, Bruce joined their discussion, but knowing
next to nothing about photography, his interest lay mainly in
the new factory.

"I would like to have a more definite plan to present to the
council on Thursday. But for the now we can only put together
what we have. Barnie, what do you see?"

"I see some expertise, a wealth of enthusiasm, and very little else."

"Raju?"

"Much the same as Barnie. However, I think we have to have legal advice and set up a limited company."

"How do we do that?"

"The lawyer would tell us. You do have one?"

Bruce looked directly at Barnie. He was shaking his head emphatically. "Don't look at me like that. Two years in law school, and I skipped out of dull corporate law every chance I got. Did I not hear you say there was one on the council?"

"Yes, there's Reginald, of course."

"Reginald, does he ride to hounds?"

This time Bruce's glance at Barnie was sharp and penetrating. "He does. How did you know?"

"Talking to Miss Priscilla after kirk yesterday."

"I'll have a word with Reginald tomorrow. He may ride to hounds on Saturdays, but I know he's a most conscientious lawyer. Once a company is established, finding folk to invest should be easy enough." Barnie and Raju exchanged doubtful glances, and Bruce went on, "Not just any folk. I'd have to be sure they weren't in it for the profit alone."

Barnie's laugh was cynical. "There's no such creatures. Beggin' your pardon, Reverend. Except for yourselves here, I'll just say I've not met them."

"You're in for some surprises then. We know at least a dozen."

"A dozen with a few thousand pounds to invest should just about float the company."

Raju had a thoughtful look but made no further comments for a while.

Bruce broke the silence. "A company means a board of directors, each with a portfolio. Amounts invested would not need to be common knowledge among them, would it?"

Again Barnie laughed. "You're looking for Utopia, man. Money is power, power corrupts and—"

Bruce interrupted him again. "As I said before, some surprises will be coming your way, but for the now, could we stick to the facts we have and not project too far? A board of directors, eh, Raju? We'll include women. My mother, her mother, Mistress MacIntyre. The latter two will be absent members and silent, but my mother will have much to contribute. George Bennett and possibly Lady Mannering. Reginald, Ogilvie, the three of us here, that makes nine or ten. Eleven should suffice."

"My wife, although I haven't asked her, may—"

Barnie was openmouthed with astonishment. "Me, I couldna be on your board, man, I havena a penny to my name. Besides I don't know if I want to commit myself. I enjoy being a free agent. You said I was to be here in an advisory capacity, did you not?"

"Excuse me, Barnie, I got carried away. Maybe we've done enough for one day. I'm for a short stroll while it's still daylight. Anybody coming?" Raju declined. Faye had pleaded tiredness after the long train journey, broken only for one night in Glasgow, and her husband was feeling it, too. Mary Jean had spent an hour showing off her new schoolbooks to Faye Felicity before giving in and going off to her own bed.

Barnie rose. "I'll go with you as far as the woods." Understanding perfectly, Bruce merely nodded. This strong man was still in deep mourning for his wee pet dog, but it was all enclosed inside.

·─◦❈{ 23 }❈◦─·

So began the Phoenix Photography Factory. Later, their advertising slogan would read, WE DO EVERYTHING EXCEPT MAKE THAT FIRST CLICK! but for the time being, that *everything* added up to very little but talk.

When approached, Reginald, far from objecting, showed an enthusiasm that amazed Bruce and shocked all those who thought they knew the gangling lawyer. The town clerk, so relieved that he still might have a town to plan, watched and listened intently at the organizational meeting. Ogilvie, told at once that his part would be supervisory managerial, was inwardly jubilant, although he feared the business of photos was new to him. He would soon become Barnie's most apt pupil. But all that came later.

"The first job will be to design, then erect, the buildings themselves."

Reginald held up his pencil, some of his earlier enthusiasm evaporating. "I cannot agree, Reverend MacAlister, that that's the first job. We must be certain the funds are forthcoming. So far most of that is only paper promises."

"We do have enough to make a start though, do we not?"

"I see no point in beginning what we may not have the wherewithal to complete. We should delay—"

"Forgive me, Counselor, but there's to be no delay. We need to establish a work force at once, or the townsfolk will starve."

"I have every sympathy with the folk, Reverend, but—"

"No delays, I'm sorry." Three of those seated round the table agreed with Bruce and two with the lawyer. He made one more attempt.

"If you are willing to risk *your* investment on a construction crew, that's your business. . . . The rest of us . . . well!"

"No, it's my business, I'll grant you, but it's *your* business as well. We must pool all available resources. If you cannot, then you must forget the whole matter of coming in with us. It was my understanding that the legalities would get under way at once and you would be responsible for that."

"Yes, but let us not be foolhardy or hasty about it."

Both Ogilvie and Barnie Hill began to shuffle uncomfortably. Having no money to invest, they each felt they should have no say in this part of the proceedings.

Bruce thought otherwise. "Silent partners in this endeavor include only my grandmother, Mistress Munro of Edinburgh, along with my dead wife's grandmother, Mistress MacIntyre of Glasgow. Everyone else will speak his or her piece, regardless of monetary investment."

Raju, also silent to this point, cast his eyes round the table. Here indeed sat, not only a cross-representation of Cairnglen, but of society in general. His father-in-law's wedding gift of five thousand pounds would be available shortly for this venture. Without question he and his wife placed their trust completely in Bruce's judgment, positive the Lord was with the highlander on the whole matter.

Ogilvie raised his hand as Reginald subsided at last. "I can get a squad started in clearing up, even the day, if I get the word. The men'll be only too happy to be working and earning again. Yon's near two weeks, and nothing come in."

Reginald had another reservation to voice. "What about the Galbraith estate rights?"

The town clerk answered, "The property was leased to the Galbraith works by the town. The contract expired automatically when the fire stopped the works' operation."

"So the cleaning up is Cairnglen's responsibility?"

The clerk laughed outright. "Yes, until a new contract is made with another tenant."

"Could it be agreed, by this body, that the Phoenix Photographic Company be established here and now? We'll leave the paper business work to our codirector-shareholder Mr. Reginald Payne. Then the rest of us can get on with more urgent matters."

"I second that!" Raju's first words since the meeting began echoed strangely.

The town clerk took up his gavel of office and control. "Could you reword that into a motion, Reverend MacAlister?"

"I could. I move that we form the Phoenix Photographic Company as of this hour."

"I second that!" Raju repeated as the chairman said, "All those in favor say aye."

The ayes rang through the room, but Reginald did not vote until the chairman called, "Are ye opposed, then, Counselor?"

"Not opposed exactly, but it *is* all rather irregular!"

"We require the vote to be unanimous!"

"Aye!"

"Carried. Now the election of officers—" The administrator had slipped into his stride, and by the time Bruce, Raju, and Barnie left for the manse, each knew the dream of the company had become reality. Triumphant, Ogilvie could hardly wait to spread the word through the town.

Homeward bound, the trio from the manse met Henderson and McCabe, going in the opposite direction. The two workmen, looking pleased with themselves, stopped to describe their own productive day to Bruce.

I must make time to see their accomplishments, Bruce thought as he heartily bade the men good-night. Hurriedly catching up to his two friends, he decided to make an early night of it. He'd need a fresh start in the morning, if he wanted to accomplish all his plans for the day.

But Bruce's early night was not to be. When the men arrived at the manse door, an agitated Faye Felicity waited for them. Raju ran to her, with Bruce close behind.

"What is it, my love?"

"It's Mary Jean. She had a slight fever earlier, but I just thought it must be—" Already inside, Bruce raced toward his daughter's room, shouting back over his shoulder as he ran, "Fetch the doctor!"

Barnie and Raju stared blankly at each other and then at Faye. This normally sensible individual whom they knew as Reverend Bruce MacAlister had gone frantic before their eyes.

Raju grasped his wife's arm. "What are you thinking, Faye?"

Shuddering, she spoke the dreaded word in a whisper, as though afraid to confirm it, as indeed she was: "Diphtheria!"

24

"**D**iphtheria?" Two horror-filled echoes followed Faye's exclamation. Barnie's held a note of absolute terror.

Still whispering, Faye tried to soften her first announcement. "It might only be a bad throat infection."

"We darena' risk that. Diphtheria is deadly and a highly contagious disease. I should know. I watched my wee sister choke to death. . . . I'm immune myself. . . . Where will I find the doctor?"

"His house is on the same street as the school. I asked Mary Jean when I first felt her fever. Go back to the kirk, and then get the beadle to show you. That would be the best. Raju—?"

"I'll go with him. Faye, you must stay here."

"No, don't go. I'll need you here. I'm afraid for Bruce, and I'll need help to calm him down. You saw him just now. Mr. Hill?"

"Yes, I can find the way on my own."

An hour later a raving Bruce was bodily removed from his daughter's room, by Raju and Barnie, while Dr. Shaw and Faye worked on Mary Jean. Both were silent as the doctor made his examination.

The three men settled—if you could call it that—in the kitchen. Barnie sat near the door while Raju kept up with Bruce's pacing.

Bruce's voice was quieter now, but he spoke between clenched teeth. "How can we stay here, doing nothing, when my child could be dying?"

After exchanging glances with Raju, Barnie spoke. "She is not near death, man. The doctor doesn't even know if she has it or not."

Bruce stared at the speaker as if he had never before seen him. He sat down at the table and placed his head on his hands. A muffled question came to Raju, "Oh, Raju, what shall I do?"

"What you are doing now. Pray and pray and pray again. We've seen enough miracles."

Bruce ignored his friend's advice. "It's all my fault. I should have made sure she had enough fresh air and sound meals. Oh, I need Hamish."

At the sound of the doctor's footsteps on the stairs, the three men tensed, scarcely breathing. Dr. Shaw entered the kitchen and Bruce rushed toward him. "Well, Doctor?"

"I fear it *is* diphtheria, Reverend. But hold on there now—" Bruce made a compulsive movement toward the door leading to the stairway. "Mistress Smith is fumigatin' the rooms the now. I brought the necessary equipment along when I heard. Apart from that, there's not much more we can do but wait it out and, aye, I shouldna' need to tell you, pray."

"Of course I'll pray, but there must be something more tangible I can do! There has to be!"

Dr. Shaw was shaking his head, but Barnie spoke. "Have you heard of the new antitoxin being used to treat it, Doctor?"

The doctor bristled. "The best of medical science has not approved it for general use yet."

"But I've read reports of its wide use in countries like Germany and Sweden. I think—"

"Are you a medical man, sir?" The doctor's tone was icy.

"No, but I—"

"Then please mind your own business." Barnie backed away.

Bruce and Raju stood together in one corner, obviously praying. Dr. Shaw walked over to them, and Bruce raised tortured eyes. "Believe me, Reverend MacAlister, we will do all we can. Mistress Smith is an excellent nurse. You're very fortunate to have her. While you're at the praying, then, pray we'll not be having an epidemic in Cairnglen. I'll be back in the morning. I can do no more here the night."

The men listened without speaking until the sounds of his horse and buggy had faded into the night.

"Faye, my love, is there really nothing more we can do for Mary Jean?" Raju asked the question as he and his wife sat on in the kitchen. Bruce, having promised to be quiet, was seated by Mary Jean's bedside, and Barnie Hill was nowhere about.

Faye answered thoughtfully, "Don't say anything to Bruce yet, but I happen to know that Peter Blair was experimenting with that antitoxin your Mr. Hill mentioned. He achieved some success at his clinic. I'm trying to think of a way to make use of this." She sighed deeply before continuing, "The disease progresses, and then, even in a well-nourished child like Mary Jean, at the climax the chances are equal of eventual recovery or death."

"So we have nothing to lose by—"

"Raju, from what little I know of the antitoxin, it must be administered by the fourth day at the latest or—"

"There's no time to be lost then. How shall we do this? You must stay here with the child, so I must go to Peter!"

"I'll go!" Unseen by the couple, Barnie had slipped back into the kitchen, after one of his lone vigils to the dog's burial place.

Faye threw him an appraising glance. "Yes, that would be best. As the child's condition deteriorates further someone strong will need to handle Bruce. O dear Jesus!" Her last words formed a prayer. Raju looked at her sharply, but she quickly regained her composure.

"Here then is what we must do. I will write a letter to George Bennett and enclose a note for Agatha Rose and Peter. Raju, would you please compose a telegram for Aribaig? Hamish and Bruce's mother should both be here. You, Mr. Hill, can catch the early train—the milk train they call it—and when you get to Glasgow go straight to the Bennett residence. George will direct you from there. Bring the antitoxin back with instructions. Of course, should Peter—" Her strong spirit almost broke down again, but again she rallied.

Barnie's face held a shamefaced expression and Raju guessed the reason. "Here's money enough. Waste no time and spare nothing to gain your errand. Hire a private carriage everywhere you have to go. You may even be able to get back the same day." As Faye's eyes appealed to him he tempered that with, "At least early tomorrow."

An astonished Mistress Oliver opened Mr. Bennett's front door to this utter stranger. Seeing at once how determined he was to see the master, she showed him into the morning room with only a perfunctory, "A Mr. Hill to see you, sir. He says he has urgent news from Reverend Bruce."

With scarcely a lift of his bushy eyebrows, George Bennett read the letter quickly and noted the enclosures, while Barnie, at the gentle urging of the housekeeper, filled a plate with food. He gulped a cup of the delicious brewed coffee at the same time, choking it all down as his host said, "We'll go at once to Peter. Mistress Oliver, see that these letters are dispatched, order the carriage, and alert the prayer chain in the usual manner. It's for Bruce's daughter, but read the letter for yourself." He had been walking out the door as he spoke but stopped for a minute to consider his strange visitor. "Have you slept at all and—"

"Och, yes, I'm fine. The station has adequate facilities. Especially when one sports a first-class ticket!"

George raised his eyebrows again but said no more on the subject.

Moments later they were seated in the carriage, and George brought Barnie up-to-date. "Peter is greatly improved but has gone silent on us. By rights we should ask Dr. Grant if he can take this kind of pressure, but I'm trusting the Lord for all of that. Peter's father will be there, and the Lord again will guide us in what to do and say."

Barnie groaned inwardly. Another one of those expecting God to be in direct communication to clean up the human mess! He made no comment.

Agatha read her auntie Faye's note and hesitated for only a second. "Dr. Blair, Senior, is at the clinic, but my husband is in the parlor." Her eyes appealed to George, who only said, "You decide, my dear."

The shout that came from Peter, when he heard the news, would have gladdened the heart of those who knew him of old and who had watched his sad decline since the birth of his little girl. "That hielandman, can he no' take care o' his solitary ewe lamb? Of course I'll get the stuff, and I'll even go myself to make sure it's administered properly. Now Aggie, no arguments, I've made up my mind!"

Aggie was far from argument. Her tears of happy release flowed freely, and she cared not who would see her ravaged face.

Rushing from the schoolroom to find out what all the rumpus was about, the twins were in time to see their father throw off his dressing gown and run to his room to change. "What is it, Mother?" Douglas asked, while Stirling glared at the strange man standing in the hallway with Uncle George Bennett.

"I'll tell you after, boys. But Daddy is so much better, and he is going to Cairnglen." Recalling the critical reason for this, a fresh burst of tears sprang from Aggie's already puffed-up eyes.

Her keen-eyed son caught the drift of the drama. "Uncle Bruce? Mary Jean? What is it, Mother? Is it something bad?"

"Quite bad, Douglas, but Daddy will make it all right." She prayed as she added under her breath, "God being his helper."

Barnabas Hill felt as if he were wrapped in a snowball, rolling down a snowy hillside at an ever-increasing speed. When others had told him Dr. Peter Blair was morose, he had prepared himself for almost anything except what was now happening. A silent journey, at best, had been his imagining. But as they approached his own old hunting ground of the Gorbals Barnie discovered that this man, once started, could not stop talking.

First Peter gave a detailed account of his experiments with the antitoxin, relating to them how his one failure had occurred on the fifth day. "That bairn was starved, so she was, as well as having the rickets. Mary Jean will not be disadvantaged like that."

For the first time the doctor stared directly at Barnie Hill. "Do I not know you from somewhere, Mister—eh—Hill, is it?"

Barnie gazed out the window of their speeding vehicle. They

were crossing the Broomielaw bridge. He waited until they were over and the rattle was not so pronounced. "I'm Barnie Hill. You might have seen me hereabouts. Reverend MacAlister has hired me as a consultant in his new venture for Cairnglen."

A cloud passed over Peter's features, but cleared just as quickly. "Oh, I see. No matter, a friend of the MacAlisters is a friend of ours. Eh, George?"

Completely failing to hide his jubilation, George replied, " 'Tis so, Peter, lad, and praise the Lord for that!"

Dr. Blair, Senior, surrounded by the suffering dregs of the Gorbals who sought ease for their many complaints, responded less enthusiastically. A woman, hovering in the background, stepped forward to adjure him, "Father, don't be hasty now."

"Keep quiet, Deb, please. Peter, lad, I'm not sure I can sanction this gallivantin' away to the Trossachs after you bein' in your bed for two or three weeks. And this antitoxin! It's not been cleared or approved yet . . . I—"

George tapped his elbow. "Could I have a word in private, Doctor?"

Reluctantly Peter's father led the way into the small examining room.

Peter glanced round his humble dispensary as the woman stepped forward. "Oh, there you are, then, Deb! What—" A puzzled frown creased his forehead as he acknowledged his sister's presence; then he shrugged. One thing at a time. The cupboard holding his supplies was padlocked securely, and his father had the keys. Peter eyed the lock thoughtfully and turned back to Deb. But the man Hill and his sister were gazing at each other and paying him no attention. She spoke first. "My brother's lost his manners. I'm Deborah Blair."

Barnie gave himself an inward shake but kept his eyes on her. His thoughts had been chaotic, with one phrase uppermost. "Barnie Hill, but where have you been all my life?"

Deborah blushed but did not rebuke him. Her own thoughts had been running along similar lines.

Peter's determined move toward his cabinet brought them both out of their trance. Barnie was before him. "I wouldna' try it, Doctor. It seems to me, with all this talk of miracles, the worthy Mr. Bennett will persuade your father. A few more minutes'll not matter."

Conceding this, Peter sat back down on the bench where his patients usually waited. However, before Barnie could pursue his admiration of Deborah, Peter was up again and facing the other man. "Mary Jean was fine yesterday, you say?"

"To my knowledge, yes."

"So, if we go at once, I should have this stuff into her by the second day at the latest. How can we get there in a hurry?"

"I inquired at the trains, and there's one at three o'clock, but it's a shunter. The next express is not 'till the morning."

"I'm not waiting until the morning. Do we take the slow train or take my carriage or my flyer? Can you drive the horse? As my brilliant parent reminded me, I'm still convalescent and shouldna overdo it. I'll need all my strength for the battle."

"I can drive. What have ye in mind?" They talked transportation for a few more minutes, until Peter started to become agitated again.

"That's settled then, and curse it, Deb, see what's keeping Father."

At that moment the two elderly men reentered the dispensary. "I'm not altogether conveenced, ye ken that, George, but as you say—" The senior Blair gazed at his son, so recently trembling on the brink of destruction. Suddenly hope sprung up in that desolate place, and his lingering doubts dispersed. He had not seen that sparkle in Peter since before the wee lass Fessy was born. Without another word he handed his son the keys.

Barnie managed to steal another moment with Deborah. "Could I visit you sometime soon?"

She smiled and answered without coquetry, "I'll be here for a week or two yet."

He returned her smile. They had said all they needed to for the present.

25

There could only be one destination for the laddie on the bicycle. Hamish saw him first, from a long way off, and he called to his father, where he sat perched on the corn binder.

"Is that no' the polisman's lad? The one that delivers the telegraphs?" Confirming his own statement, Hamish threw down the sheaves of oats he had been setting in stooks and ran for the dyke. Leaping it, he yelled at the cyclist, "What have ye there, lad?"

"A telegraph for Mr. Cormack!"

"I'll tak it."

The boy looked doubtful. The Mr. Cormack he knew was the man on the corn binder.

"He's ma faither. Let me have it, lad." He read the few lines as Andrew plodded to join him.

"What is it, Hamish?"

"Mary Jean! She's taken badly. They want Elspeth and me to come."

Andrew stopped in amazement. "Did Bruce say that?"

"No. It just says 'R. & F. Smith.' That's the Indian man and his—"

"I ken who they are. My Lord, but Elspeth, and Gran'pa too'll be that vexed. Here they come now; they've seen us." Elspeth had been helping with the stooking, but she and Gran'pa made no pretense of keeping up with the binder or with Hamish. Her face blanched when she saw the all-too-familiar yellow envelope.

"Och, no, is it Bruce, Andrew?"

"Not Bruce, Elspeth, Mary Jean is badly. You and Hamish get ready to go to Cairnglen. Gran'pa, you harness up the other cairt. I'll bring Samson in the now. You'll catch McBrayne's omnibus to the fort and then the late train to Strathlarich."

Speechless with fright, Elspeth moved to obey, but suddenly all four of them stopped and looked at each other before turning to Gran'pa. He spoke for the first time. "We'll take a minute to pray!"

Word spread quickly through Cairnglen. Some, who knew of the implications of an epidemic, prepared themselves for the worst, while others wagged their heads knowingly.

"Three deaths. Always, they come in threes."

Not caring that his own auntie spoke the dreaded words, Jimmy Henderson turned and yelled, "Shut up, ye silly auld bisom! That's a daft auld wife's tale. Mary Jean couldna' be that bad. Yesterday she was at school, and she was fine then." A slap from his mother stopped the boy's words, but he rushed out of the house and down the street to the schoolhouse.

The dominie was frightened for his own children. Had he not been with the MacAlister girl, more than the others, yesterday? He knew what he had to do, however: fumigate the school and announce a three-day holiday until the fumes took hold. His own thoughts that fumigation now was like shutting the stable door after the horse had bolted didn't matter. It gave him something to do other than go home and listen to his wife's nagging.

Gloom clouded the manse. Bruce hardly left Mary Jean's bedside, and although Raju brought him food at intervals, it remained untouched. Faye worked diligently with her unprotesting patient, swabbing her throat and sponging down the small, wiry body. At first Mary Jean lay inert, then when a spasm racked her, she would clutch at her throat, emitting small gasps for air. Her face and neck had swollen alarmingly, out of all proportion to her body, and the jawline had almost disappeared.

Faye assured the distraught father that this was really a good sign. "The swelling is better to press outward than inward, Bruce. She's a little trooper, too!"

Bruce raised his eyes at the sound of his name and gave her a weak smile, but the frown had not left his brow since he first learned of this catastrophe.

Faye was encouraged to try again. "You need some rest, Bruce. Will you not go and lie down for an hour or two and take a bit of nourishment?" But he had retreated, and she sighed as she prayed. "Dear Jesus, let them come soon with the medicine!"

Raju paced the floor. He also prayed as Faye joined him after her fruitless attempt to get Bruce to eat or rest. He asked, "Not yet?"

"No, it's almost as if he's in a decline. Auntie Mac described the deep depression he went into when Jean died, and I'm afraid—" She shuddered, and her husband held her close.

"We must not be afraid, my love. Fear is the tool of the enemy. Just like the bacteria that is invading Mary Jean's body, fear creeps in to invade our minds and rob us of our peace."

Faye pulled out of his embrace. "We have to fight it, Raju. The disease I mean. I cannot, and will not, believe it is God's will for Mary Jean to succumb to this horror."

He drew her back. "Nor do I believe that. All I say is the battle is the Lord's, and we, as His soldiers merely have to obey. He will show us what to do. How is she now?"

"She's not complaining. I'm guessing she had early, scarcely detectable symptoms for a day before she told me. That would make it the third day. She may soon be completely comatose."

A disturbance at the door announced the arrival of Dr. Shaw, and Faye moved to meet him. The doctor spoke angrily. "There's a crowd of bairns outside in the lane. They'll not heed me, though I snapped my whip at them. Even when I said they could catch the smit from the very air!"

Raju went quickly to the window. Indeed a small group of people stood there, beside the arch, and he picked up his vinegar-soaked handkerchief before stepping to the door.

One slightly older youth, seemingly their spokesman, glared

at Raju belligerently. "We're stayin' 'till Mary Jean's better!" His tone implied that he would need to be moved bodily before changing his mind.

Raju smiled faintly. "What will you be doing then?"

The young fellow shuffled his feet in embarrassment. "We'll pray to Jesus, just like Mary Jean showed us one day, and Dorrie's wee cat got better."

The boy's words almost unmanned Raju, and he could not speak for a few moments. "Do you know you could catch it yourself?" he asked, finally.

Jimmy answered. "My mammy says we had the smit afore. Ma wee brither deed!"

Raju sighed, relieved at this news, but feeling a deep sense of sorrow at such a waste of life. Dr. Shaw had not mentioned any previous occurrence in the town. Raju glanced again at the dozen or so assorted faces gazing up at him—mostly young-sters of Mary Jean's own age—the most susceptible age group.

"Have you all had it then?" Unintelligible mutterings met this, and he decided to use schoolroom tactics and the local idiom. "Hands up, those who have not had this smit." Two pairs of hands shot up, and he said. "You go home, then; the rest of you just keep praying." Turning back to the ringleader, he asked, "You're Jimmy Henderson, are you not?" The lad nodded. "You might want to help me fill the coal bunkers and chop some firewood. We're using a lot."

So this scene greeted the travelers from north and south. First to arrive were Peter and Barnie, their lathered horses' heaving sides betraying the haste with which they had covered the fifty miles from Glasgow. As if it had been no more than a run from the town, Peter leaped down from the vehicle's running board, tightly clutching his physician's bag containing the precious serum. The youngsters, formed into a chain by Raju, stopped their labor of passing the buckets and logs to Jimmy, who was piling them neatly beside the kitchen door, to watch intently this latest development.

Barnie led the horses toward the stable. He unhitched them with an expert hand, rubbed them down with a swatch of hay, and left them munching contentedly as he stepped briskly through the back door. Raju welcomed him with a grim smile.

"How is she, Mr. Smith?"

"The pestilence progresses in its predictable way, Mr. Hill. Will you have some of this soup?"

"I will and thank you. I presume the fiery doctor is already with the patient?"

"He is, although he wisely took a moment to refresh and fortify."

Barnie looked long and hard at this man whom he already considered as a friend. The Oxford English, without trace of any other accent, and the cool aplomb showed confidence, yet without arrogance.

Eating the delicious soup, flavored with some aromatic herbs that Barnie had not tasted for many years and could not have named, he asked, "The urchins in the coach yard, did they appreciate the subtle flavors in your soup?"

Raju laughed. "Only that it was hot and filling, I'm afraid."

"They're here on some kind of watch, I take it?"

"More like a prayer vigil, displaying faith such as is seldom seen in the most upright of congregations."

Wiping his mouth, Barnie nodded. "From Bruce's parishioners?"

"Not altogether. I've discovered a few from each of Cairnglen's denominations, including one girl of the Jewish faith."

This time Barnie's glance held a glint of something closely resembling hostility. It was replaced at once by a defensive glare as he snapped, "Is that against the rules then?"

"Not to my knowledge, Barnie." The discussion ended as a rap sounded on the door. Raju called out, "Enter!" and Jimmy Henderson walked in.

"We've done the sticks, mister, and the coal bunker's fu'."

"Thank you, Jimmy. Away home now and come back in the morning. I'm sure your mothers will be worried."

"Aye!" But he made no attempt to move.

"Was there something else you wanted? I've explained that you cannot see Mary Jean for a day or two yet."

"Is she gettin' better then? We thought, when we prayed, she would get better."

"She'll be the better for your prayers, Jimmy, I'm sure of that. You saw the other doctor arriving a while ago?"

"Aye."

"He's brought a very powerful medicine. Sometimes God answers prayers through doctors and medicine, you know?"

For a moment Jimmy looked doubtful; then his brow cleared. "Och, aye. I see now. I'll tell the rest. We'll away then."

Jimmy's telling of the rest took place as they hurried along the lane toward their respective homes. On the way another carriage, the familiar one from Strathlarich, rushed past them. Two startled faces gazed out of the windows at the strange, rough delegation of youngsters.

"What do you think they could have been up to, Hamish?" Elspeth sat back in the coach for the last lap of the journey. "Not more uprisings, I pray!"

"Och, no. The one in front is Jimmy Henderson. His family's right enough. Likely speerin' after Mary Jean."

Reminded sharply of the purpose of her visit, Elspeth promptly forgot the delegation and began to prepare herself for whatever might be round the next bend in the road leading to the manse.

26

What awaited them was not good.

First, a distraught Bruce had been coerced away from Mary Jean's bedside, to allow Peter access with his treatment. Orders flew from the doctor, and Raju led Bruce back to the kitchen, supposedly to help him locate and prepare the materials requested. In his trouble, Bruce had scarcely acknowledged Peter's presence, having hardly slept for the two nights and days. He did notice his mother, though, and when she opened wide her arms, he went to her like a child. They disappeared together in the direction of the other wing. Hamish, after one belligerent glare at Hill, was the one to aid Raju.

Barnie wandered off, his usefulness apparently at a standstill for the time being. The place was becoming altogether too crowded. Hoping the rooms above the stable would be habitable by now, he walked toward it. No matter what, he would find a corner somewhere for this night at least.

In the sickroom Peter cataloged the progress of the illness to Faye Felicity. This information was something they both knew well enough, but relating it served to put both of them more at ease. While Faye gently held Mary Jean's chin, Peter just as gently probed her throat with a speculum.

"See here, the tonsils are very red and swollen, the soft palate is tender and also swollen. Sorry, pet, but I'm here to help you, and I'll be trying not to hurt you."

Unable to speak, Mary Jean stared up at Peter. Her expressive eyes held more than a trace of resentment as Peter kept up his dialogue. "Trust me, Mary Jean. I've brought medicine with me, and I'll just be giving you a wee jag. After that you'll start to get better."

The moment of consciousness left, and Faye rubbed the child's arm with refined spirits while Peter prepared the needle. Between them they administered the injection.

No sign came from Mary Jean, and Faye was tucking the clothes back when suddenly the small body began to heave and jerk as she went into convulsions. Peter and Faye knew exactly what to do, and as the doctor whipped into action the nurse did the same. In a moment the physician's smallest scalpel appeared in his hand, a hand solid and steady as a rock. Faye caught the fine rubber tube he threw at her and dipped it into the jar of spirits. Within moments the incision was made and the tube in place just at the base of the neck. Mary Jean's cheeks assumed their normal color as Faye held her upright. Life-giving air hissed through the tube and filled the chest cavity.

Doctor and nurse exchanged glances, while Peter whispered, "It's reached the larynx. We'll have to hurry." He had thrown the used scalpel into the basin, and Faye retrieved it as he reached into his bag again, this time for a handful of tiny clamps of the sort used in tonsil removal.

Faye raised her eyebrows. "Shall I give her the last drop of ether?"

"Aye, although she'll not be feeling any pain! The tissues are already—" he shook his head, reluctant to say the dreaded words. Faye bent to the task of helping him secure the clamps.

A short time later, as Peter rinsed his hands in another basin of disinfected water and Faye wrapped the diseased membrane, along with the other infected material that Peter had surgically removed from Mary Jean's throat cavity, for burning, he remarked, still in a whisper, "By God's grace, Faye, I think she might do! The lower parts are clean, and the odor is nothing compared to what it would be if we were too late. I'll give her another dose of antitoxin in an hour. Now to tell her father and the others. She doesn't look very bonny, I fear."

Faye nodded her agreement. The rubber tube still aided the

small patient's lungs to pull in and expel the air. Swollen glands on either side gave her a grotesque appearance, and of course her eyes, the feature that gave her the look of the blithe spirit she undoubtedly was, were closed.

"It would be better if we didn't have to let Bruce or the granny see her yet," Peter commented, "but I suppose—"

Raju and Hamish had padded in and out of the sickroom unobtrusively once or twice. After a single fearful glance, Hamish had kept his eyes averted from his niece's bed. Raju had reported that Bruce was with his mother, who would keep him away for a while yet. In fact she had sprinkled a mild soothing powder into his cup of tea, and he had fallen asleep.

At that moment the sounds of a carriage announced the arrival of Dr. Shaw on his afternoon visit. The two men looked at Peter. His would be the task of explaining his own presence.

Hearing about the intrusion of the city doctor and his use of the antitoxin, Cairnglen's doctor loudly and adamantly declared he washed his hands of the whole case. Feeling that he already had stretched his oath to the limit, visiting twice a day as he had, now, in Peter's hearing, he declared his disapproval. "I'll not be responsible for the results of these experiments, sir! In fact, I must warn you that I'll be reporting this to the BMS!"

Typically Peter responded, "Go then, and I detect some relief in your decision."

The short encounter between the medical men had included a fast résumé of each one's credentials. Peter ended his with, "Our oath states that our first obligation is to our patient. I concede the child was your patient, and I join her father in thanking you for the undoubted risks you took, but I have been called in for a second opinion and as a specialist. Also I've known the child since her birth." That was when Dr. Shaw had stamped off, brushing past Barnie Hill as he had returned in search of news and possibly some food.

As the doctor's carriage disappeared down the lane Barnie remarked to Raju. "An angry man, but a happier one, I believe!"

"Don't judge him too harshly. He is doing all in accordance with the light of his own experience."

Barnie's answering laugh held a touch of contempt, but he said no more.

Peter returned to the sickroom, and after assuring himself that Mary Jean was as well as she could be at this stage, he turned to Faye. "Off to bed with you, my girl. No arguments, if you please. I don't believe you've slept much yourself in the last forty-eight hours."

She gazed at her niece's husband for a long moment. "What about you, Dr. Peter Blair?"

"Stop worrying about me, Faye Felicity. I've been through the mill, but I've survived intact. It'll not happen again. As for sleeping, I've slept more this past week or so than I have for years . . . in fact since. . . . Well, anyway, when this crisis is over I'll be making it up to the highlandman. Go on now and send the granny in. Congratulations are in order, to you and your man, I understand, but that'll need to wait as well."

Faye stumbled out to where her husband waited. After she passed on her message, he swept her up in his arms and carried her away to their room.

Within minutes Elspeth tiptoed into the sickroom. Peter motioned to the chair at the end of the bed, while he settled on the other chair by his patient's head. They would share the night watch.

In the kitchen Hamish bustled about. He had something to say, but it was hard to begin. "Mr. Hill!"

Barnie glanced up from the rough drawing he had been studying. Elspeth had spread the table with good things, and his self-inflicted banishment had ended as he caught the smell of the cooking. He was making short work of the scones and pancakes, loaded with butter, that seemed to be this family's favorite nightcap. His eyes wordlessly questioned Hamish.

"I—er, eh—I've to ask ye to forgie me."

Barnie felt his face begin to burn with embarrassment. He waved a hand. "No need for that, man."

Hamish's face clouded. "There's need. The Lord says I must."

Barnie groaned inwardly. These folk again and their direct contact with the Almighty!

"If you must then, yes, all right, I accept your apology."

"Aye, but do ye forgie me?"

"Mr. Cormack, I'm not sure what I'm supposed to forgive you for!"

Hamish's embarrassment grew worse, but he went on bravely, "I judged ye and set mysel' up as the Lord's advo . . . advoc—"

"*Advocate?*"

"Aye. He doesna need me to do that."

"Shall we leave it there then? What more need be said or done?"

"Ye'll have to say it."

"I'll say it, but first could you tell me what changed your opinion?"

"You runnin' awa' tae Glesca to fetch the medicine and Dr. Peter for Mary Jean. Efter yer wee dug was killt an' a'!"

Barnie winced and could not speak for a few more minutes. Then, his voice a hoarse whisper, he said, "I forgive you, Hamish Cormack. Here's my hand on it!" The solemn handshake confirmed the pledge, and only then did Hamish start to ask about Barnie's comfort.

This was the midnight scene that Bruce stumbled into. Still too dazed to appreciate the significance, he said, "Hamish, tell me what's happening, and have you another cup of tea?"

Hamish quickly brought the tea as Bruce continued. "I've had a most blessed time of rest and with the Lord. He has assured me that Mary Jean has passed the crisis and will mend completely and soon."

This was just too much for Barnabas Hill. "I'll leave you then. Did I tell you that the workmen have finished the one room, and I sorted some of my stuff a while ago? The wall bed is fine and dandy. I found sheets and other necessary things in your press." The others merely nodded, and he beat a hasty retreat.

The brothers smiled at each other, in complete accord once again. Neither doubted that the Lord had made Himself real in the situations surrounding the family.

Hamish had only one remark to make, and that was about Barnie Hill: "Do you think he's comin' under conviction?"

"I certainly think he is seeking, and if so, we know he will find, or be found of the Holy Spirit."

"Aye! Will ye have some soup? I can warm it in a hurry. Here's a scone o' yer mother's bakin'."

"I will and be glad of it."

While he was eating, Hamish related the latest happenings. Smiling and nodding for most of it, Bruce frowned when Hamish reached the part about Dr. Shaw. "I'll have to make my peace with the good doctor. He was doing his best, according to his knowledge."

"Aye, nae doot, but his best wasna' helpin' Mary Jean."

Bruce shuddered at what might have been before saying, "With God all things are possible. We know that, Hamish. He is bringing good out of it all. Already you and Barnie, and well, there's Peter and me." Suddenly overwhelmed, the words caught in Bruce's throat, and he choked. The dam broke, and tears streamed down. Neither men noticed Elspeth as she came in search of a cup of tea for herself and Peter. She stood for a moment in the open doorway, watching, her own vision blurred, as Hamish roughly tried to comfort Bruce. Clearly this truly tender moment did not need her, but she had such good news to impart. She stepped back and reentered the kitchen. This time she approached noisily.

"The Fifer needs some sustenance, and I've to tell you the danger is past. The swelling is some less, and he's sure the thing's stopped growing!" Bruce rose to meet her, and Hamish went to fill the kettle again. Then, without further talk, the three fell on their knees.

Mere words were not required next morning, either, as Bruce and Peter confronted each other. Peter had just reported that the disease had arrested indeed and was beginning its declining stages.

"She'll need a lot of careful nursing, but I've no fears on that score. She shouldna' talk at all for a while, and then only a wee bit at a time. Her own strength will guide you. Liquids only, for a day or two, then gruel." Feeling Bruce's eyes boring into him, he stopped speaking at last. Bruce took one step in his direction, and then they were enfolding each other in a manly embrace.

Hamish stepped out to meet Barnie in the hallway. "They'll not be needin' us for a wee while. Show me the new loft."

Mary Jean slowly opened her eyes. She had been having such a terrible dream. Somebody or something awful had been trying to choke her, and a lot of folk had been coming out and in her dream. Daddy and Auntie Faye, fighting with the black thing tearing at her throat. After that it went away for a wee while. Then Gran'speth and Uncle Hamie, too, had tried to get the thing off her. By now she felt she was choking to death, but—and this was the funniest bit of the dream—Uncle Peter, the old Uncle Peter she remembered from before, had come in roaring at the thing. He had been wearing a helmet and a suit of armor as well as a long sword. Uncle Peter had killed it! She struggled to move. Daddy would laugh when she told him the dream.

Her father's voice, his real voice, spoke then, and it was in its sternest mood, "Lie still, pet, and don't try to talk!"

She focused her vision, clear for the first time in ten days, did she but know it, and gazed up at her beloved daddy. He placed his hand on her brow and began to explain.

27

Peter's flyer was returning to Glasgow at a much more leisurely pace. His passengers included Elspeth, as far as Strathlarich, where she would board the train for the fort and go home. Raju sat in the dickey seat for that part of the journey. The point of discussion pivoted, not surprisingly, round the person of Mary Jean MacAlister.

"She'll do just fine now. Good beef tea and Hamish's fine cooking, along with giant doses of love at all intervals, will see to that."

Elspeth nodded. She had no worries about Mary Jean now, or Bruce either, for that matter.

"What about yourself, Peter?"

"I'm fine, too, Elspeth. It's funny how things have cleared in my mind. Many's the time Bruce tried to help me face up to Fessy, but I was so . . . well, stubborn. Then there was young Jeremy. In my heart I knew I was being unfair, but I just couldn't seem to help myself."

"I understand, Peter, and I'm glad you feel differently now. What will you do?"

He rubbed his eyes in a vulnerable gesture, and Elspeth's heart went out to him as she waited for his answer.

"I'll get back to the clinic at once. The pater has covered up for me long enough. My wife and children have not had a right husband or father for a while. I'll make it up to them, especially Agatha Rose. Douglas will be understanding, I know; for his age he's a canny lad. Stirling will be harder to convince, but there's good stuff in him, too. As for wee Felicity, she'll always be my pet, my baby. But instead of putting her back on the trophy shelf I'll be treating her differently—protecting in a more realistic way. About thon Jeremy, how am I to make up for him?"

Elspeth's eyes filled. Compassion for the man beside her she certainly had, but her whole being ached for the other one, her adopted lad, Jeremy. How could any of them make up to Jeremy, if they didn't know where he was or even if he still lived?

"We have heard something, you know. Raju has contacts in Glasgow who are trying to find out more."

He still looked anxious, and she touched his arm. "Peter, you did what you, as a father, thought you had to do in a time of great stress. Stop blaming yourself and join us in praying for results to be confirmed. None of us knows how that will come about, but we have faith. God is greater than any bad thing that might happen."

"My wife talks like that, but we'll see." He gazed at the passing landscape without seeing it for a moment before saying, "I wonder if that Dr. Shaw has sent his letter to the British Medical Society yet?"

"Likely not. He's been so busy, even if no epidemic came after all."

"I've a feeling our hielandman will have a word with him."

After making sure Elspeth had her ticket and that her small valise was safely in the guard's van, Peter and Raju continued on their journey to Glasgow. Raju's errands would include finding and bringing back to Cairnglen all available writings on the subject of photography. Peter had invited him to stay at his house, but both Bruce and Faye thought he should go to Granny Mac's. She would want firsthand information about everything. Peter would give her the medical viewpoint, which was that although Mary Jean was now allowed up for a short while every day, she still required a lot of nursing, and Faye Felicity was on hand to provide that.

Waving to Raju, Peter proceeded on the last lap of his journey. His own family would be so pleased. He patted his pocket. Letters rested there, one for Aggie, from Faye; one for each of the twins, from Mary Jean, dictated to her father in faint whispers; and last, but not least, a tightly sealed missive for his sister Deborah from Mr. Barnabas Hill. In their brief time together Barnie had confessed to Peter how he was a new man altogether now, Deborah being just one of the reasons for the change. Along with that, the confidence the hielandman was showing in him and a growing desire to find out more about this personal God, Jesus, were also changing Barnie Hill, according to his own assessment, beyond recognition.

The Phoenix Photographic Company's planning meeting was well under way. Bruce had invited the board of directors to come to the manse for it, as he still didn't want to be away from Mary Jean for too long. Watching Barnie Hill, deep in conversation with Reginald, he remembered the strange actions and even stranger remarks made by Barnie at the time of Jude's death. The man's pain seemed to be easing, and Hamish had been teaching the newspaperman about the healing power of the Lord's forgiveness. No need for further concern here.

On Sunday, Bruce had been surprised when, following the morning service, Dr. Shaw had approached him with a request to be included as a shareholder in the new company. He had told the doctor it would have to be a group decision. He had taken the opportunity to ask, "By the way, Dr. Shaw, did you receive word from the BMS regarding my daughter's cure?"

"Och, I got too busy to write to them, and then she got better and, well, I suppose no harm has been done. I hear, too, that they're trying the stuff, with a modicum of success, on selected human subjects in Sweden now."

Bruce had only said, "I'm thankful to God for it, anyway."

"To be sure! To be sure!" the doctor replied.

Dr. Shaw was accepted as a shareholder upon Bruce's motion.

·--·{ 28 }·--·

The family was gathered round the manse table. It was teatime, and Mary Jean's very first visitor, Dorrie Henderson, sat beside her. Dorrie was bringing the news from the town.

"The dominie was that excitit aboot the 'miracle cure,' ye ken? Oor Jimmy had tellt it aboot the town, how their prayers had made Mary Jean get better. Naebuddy laughed or tried to deny it. Maist folk in Cairnglen are that thankful for the new works."

Bruce was thanking the Lord, too, for all that had happened, including the provision of bread and meat for the town's tables. The ground was cleared and ready for the time Raju, Mr. Ralph Smith, as he would be known in Cairnglen, returned from Glasgow, hopefully with his bag full of books on the subject of photographic processing. The board of directors and most of the townsfolk had already viewed the site and approved its condition. Cairnglen was set to be better than ever before.

"So you see, Andrew and Gran'pa, Cairnglen will be better than ever now, it's just—"

The two men looked at each other with the same question on both their minds. "Jeremy?"

"Aye, him, too, but I'm thinking Bruce will now be considering another move. I sensed his restlessness!"

"Tuts, woman, you're imaginin' things again."

"Maybe, we'll see. I'll put the kettle on the hob before Taylor comes."

But Gran'pa Bruce was holding up a restraining hand. "First, I would read a bit from the Word of the Lord."

Andrew nodded and Elspeth stopped on her way to the hearth as the old man picked up his Bible. "It's from Jeremiah thirty-one, and I'll start the readin' in the middle of verse nine. It's for us the day: ' . . . I will cause them to walk by the rivers of waters in a straight way, wherein they shall not stumble: for I am a father to Israel, and Ephraim is my firstborn. Hear the word of the Lord, O ye nations, and declare it in the isles afar off, and say, he that scattereth Israel will gather him, and keep him, as a shepherd doth his flock. . . .' Andrew!"

"What is it Gran'pa?"

"Will you read the next two verses? I'm a bit out o' breath. . . . No, don't worry, lass, just listen." Elspeth had turned her gaze to her father-in-law in some concern. He never admitted to being out of breath.

Andrew had done as requested, but she had only heard snatches of the reading. "For the Lord hath redeemed Jacob, and ransomed him from the hand of him that was stronger than he. . . . they shall come and sing . . . and shall flow together to the goodness of the Lord, for wheat, and for wine and for oil, and for the young of the flock and of the herd: and their soul shall be as a watered garden; and they shall not sorrow any more at all."

Elspeth had returned to her seat at the table, and they sat in silence for a full minute before she asked, "Jeremy? Bruce?"

"Both of them, Elspeth, lass, and we'll not have much longer to wait. Do ye hear Melly shouting at Taylor? I wonder what he'll bring us the day?"

Taylor the Post placed his bicycle carefully beside the gable end. Unlike his predecessor, he did not always try to guess at the contents of the letters he delivered here, but this day was different. The big envelope with the funny stamps and what he knew to be his own friend Jeremy's writing would herald a great day for them at the Mains. Waving it triumphantly, he ran across the steading, an excited troop of dogs yapping at his heels.